Castle in the Rock

By the same author:

Lord Rivington's Lady
Autumn Lace

Castle in the Rock

Eileen Jackson

WALKER AND COMPANY
New York

First published in the United States of America
in 1979 by the Walker Publishing Company, Inc.

Published simultaneously in Canada by Beaverbooks,
Limited, Pickering, Ontario.

ISBN: 0-8027-0623-1

Library of Congress Catalog Card Number: 78-73361

Printed in the United States of America

10 9 8 7 6 5 4 3 2 1

Chapter 1

RHONWEN MORGAN SAW the sea for the first time on her eighteenth birthday, and on that day her life altered completely. Her mother's only close friend, Ida Blake, arrived at their two-room lodging in Shoreditch, beaming her pleasurable anticipation of a voyage on the Thames in mellow autumn weather, and, easing her bulk into an upholstered chair, she opened her large bag she produced something from it with a flourish.

"There you are, Rhonwen, a card to mark the day."

As Rhonwen took the card she saw the quick mischief in Ida's face and knew that the gesture had been made partly out of kindness but sprang also from a wish to tease her mother.

Ida laughed when Beatrice said testily, "New-fangled rubbish! I gave her cotton thread to fashion herself a new collar and cuffs. Fancy wasting your money like that! Well, it is lucky you are to have it to throw away when most folk want all they have for their necessities."

"It is lucky you are," taunted Ida, grinning. "You and your Welsh expressions. You people never lose the lingo, do you; nor I've never yet met one who didn't have a fine singing voice like yours, Bea."

Rhonwen had begun to open the flat package, but she looked up anxiously. The compliment might please her unpredictable mother, or it might serve to remind her that almost the only times she sang were those when she and Ida drank too freely of gin. These lapses in correct conduct were followed by a morning headache and intense irritability as Beatrice struggled with her memories of a strict Methodist upbringing, which had nurtured a Puritan abomination of yielding to self-indulgence.

Rhonwen stared at the first card of her life and smoothed the silk flowers and the birds with real feathers for tails. The inscription read: "To Rhonwen, with affection, from Ida Blake, September 3rd, 1878." In an unprecedented gesture, she kissed Mrs. Blake, then stood back, her face flaming at her presumption; but Ida tutted in a pleased way as she peered into the chimney breast mirror to secure her dislodged hat with long, jet-tipped pins.

Moved to sudden perversity Beatrice said, "I don't think we have time to go on the trip, Ida. I've had an order for lace handkerchiefs which have to be hemmed for a trousseau."

An acrimonious argument developed between the two women. Rhonwen felt her usual embarrassment at the frank insults, then marvelled again at their enduring friendship as the quarrel died down as suddenly as it had erupted, and Ida accepted Beatrice's offer of the loan of a coveted tortoise-shell comb. A temporary sharing of their few treasures was their accustomed way of making peace, and as Ida thrust the comb into her bun, she good-humoredly ignored Beatrice's mutterings about work that would need to be finished far into the night.

Later that day Rhonwen sailed down the Thames in the steamboat *The Princess Alice* as far as Sheerness where she saw the beauty of the restless sea, and, on the return voyage, sat opposite her mother and Ida Blake beneath a bright harvest moon.

Beatrice's mellowness was evaporating with the day and she snorted, "Stop staring at Ida and me! I bring you on a boat trip and all you can do is gawp at us."

"Leave her be," begged Ida. "You meant no rudeness, did you, ducks?"

Rhonwen shook her head.

"Cat got your tongue?" snapped Beatrice. "Is that the way Miss Reeves teaches you to behave? I don't know why I bothered to raise you in a ladylike way. Most have to earn their bread practically from the cradle."

"You can't blame her for the way you reared her," said Ida.

"She'd do more if you let her. I'm not the only one who thinks you've made her unfit for her life. You'd do more, if you could, wouldn't you, Rhon?"

"Don't call her that!" cried Beatrice. "Her name's Rhonwen and I'll thank you, Ida Blake—"

Rhonwen's nerves tautened at the prospect of another quarrel, but Ida delved into her bag and showed them a brief glimpse of a bottle. "Here we are, then. I reckoned we'd need a drop of gin to perk us up about now. Come on, Bea; let's go to the front end of this tub and watch where we're heading."

Beatrice fought a losing battle with her conscience, staring at Rhonwen, her fingers caressing the gilt cross and bright red stones of her best brooch.

"I'll come," she accepted ungraciously, "but don't think I'll ever give way over what I think is proper."

Ida gave Rhonwen a surreptitious wink as she followed the grumbling Beatrice, and they walked away, their wide hips in rigid corsets and black silk gowns swaying with the motion of the boat. They were of similar height and build. Ida was a cook for a merchant, and Beatrice took in sewing and went on cooking jobs when a spare pair of hands was needed. They often chuckled at the quantity of food they consumed at their employers' expense—for who could deny a cook's right to taste her products—and sometimes Beatrice brought Rhonwen a treat. Perhaps a bit of French game pie or a sweetmeat dripping with rum syrup.

The deck lurched and they clutched their enormous hats, heavily laden with artificial fruits and flowers, and Beatrice reprimanded a small boy who had jostled her. The boat carried many passengers, including a large number of children supervised by their Sunday School teachers. The boy stuck out his tongue at Beatrice's back and ran grubby hands through his tousled hair. He looked as if he had been swimming, and Rhonwen felt a pang of envy. When she was nine, before the advent of Miss Reeves, her mother had obtained a post which kept her long hours from home. While she was gone, Rhonwen had daily crept out of their rooms to nearby Victoria Park lake with a group of local children, where she achieved the exhilaration of a dozen swimming strokes before her mother discovered what she was doing. She had beaten Rhonwen severely and, in her temper, torn to pieces the cotton drawers and chemise Rhonwen had used for a bathing dress. It was the only time Rhonwen had mixed freely with other children and, although her mother had shown her usual grudging remorse at her outburst of fury, she had never relaxed her rule of isolation.

Rhonwen sat among the other passengers, alone as usual, but able from long practised discipline to extract full value from any rare pleasure. Her foot tapped as the band struck up the lively chorus of *Nancy Lee,* and Rhonwen decided that even a gas holder could seem attractive in the blue-white light of the moon. The luxury of pleasure so cocooned her that moments passed before her senses told her that the atmosphere had altered. A significant murmuring had taken the place of fading laughter as the voices of parents called anxiously for their children.

A stab of apprehension pierced her as she turned sharply to see an enormous dark shape outlined against the sky. Another, very much larger vessel was approaching the *Princess Alice* and looked frighteningly near. A steam whistle sounded from the smaller boat, and a voice of authority shouted from the bridge: "Where are you coming to?"

There was no response and no apparent sign of life on the other vessel. The *Princess Alice* shuddered as the helmsman made a desperate attempt to turn her. The Voices grew louder and began to explode in shrieks of terror and warning. Then the massive shape was directly above their heads. There was a splintering of wood, and the prow of the enormous iron vessel drove straight into the starboard side of the pleasure steamer.

Rhonwen grabbed the ship's rail and hung on as, rigid with horror, she saw the steamboat's back break in two and the foredeck, with its cargo of human freight, slide beneath the swift-flowing waters of the Thames. The afterdeck began to tilt and grew impossibly steep. Those without a handhold were catapulted into the water as if down an open shaft. A sailor scrambled in to a small boat and, in panic, slashed at the retaining ropes so that it fell empty into the river. Still Rhonwen clung to the only part of the stern remaining above water until the voices about her weeping and praying were silenced as they submerged.

She struggled and fought against the water that filled her

nostrils, but with the memory of her swimming lessons she drew a deep breath before she went under and held it until splinters of light jagged through her brain. Her long skirts wrapped around her legs like waterweed as she kicked downwards; then she sensed air and exhaled and gasped as she attempted to swim. The *Princess Alice* had disappeared, and the iron ship that had destroyed her sprang too late into life as her sailors threw out anything that might help those in the river below. Just Rhonwen felt her strength failing a wooden bench supporting several figures floated by. Someone heard her gasp for help; a hand was thrust out; she grasped it and was carried downstream.

A woman opposite her cried repeatedly for her child, and an old man gave a groan before he lost his grip and sank. The man who had pulled her to the bench moaned, "Dear God, but many have died this day."

The cold began to penetrate Rhonwen until she felt sure she must let go when she heard the splash of oars and strong arms lifted her into a boat, where she lay helpless while the rowers went on with their search. One other person was hauled aboard, and a dripping shawl was drawn up on the end of a drag hook, wrung out and preserved.

"This might identify some poor soul," said an oarsman. "I shouldn't think we stand much chance of picking up anyone else, Mr. Trewby. There's lots more boats now and no one crying for rescue."

The man addressed agreed sadly, and Rhonwen and the others were taken to his house by the Beckton Gas Works where, Mr. Trewby explained, he was the manager. She sat wrapped in blankets near a roaring fire and was given hot drinks. A woman crouching on the fireside rug sobbed frantically, and a maid whispered, "She's lost all her family. A husband and four young'uns. Was you by yourself, miss?"

Tears spilled suddenly down Rhonwen's face. "My mother must be drowned. She and her friend were on the foredeck and I saw it sink like a stone."

There was a fresh outburst of sobs from the woman and the maid went to her. Rhonwen sat, shivering, unable to control her weeping, until Mrs. Trewby led her to her own bedroom where she helped her change into dry garments. "Can we contact your family?" she asked, as Rhonwen huddled in a knitted shawl.

"I. . . . I have no family, that is, I know of none. My mother was all I had and she has perished."

"My poor child! Your friends, then; there must be someone to whom you can turn."

"N. . . . not really, unless I could ask Mr. Baker and Miss Reeves. They have been my teachers."

"Your governess," declared Mrs. Trewby in tones of such obvious relief that Rhonwen could not argue, especially as the room held several other distraught women whom maids were assisting into dry clothes. Mrs. Trewby was clearly a generous woman, but Rhonwen could not presume on her further by arguing that Mr. Baker and Miss Reeves were only fellow lodgers who had given her tuition in return for services from Beatrice as a cleaner.

"I shall call a hansom cab," said Mrs. Trewby, "and you shall go to your Miss Reeves."

Rhonwen's protests that she had no money were waved aside by Mr. Trewby, who paid the cab driver. Soon afterwards Rhonwen was outside the tall, terraced house in the seedy district that was the only home she had known.

Her landlady met her in the hall and took in her appearance with sharp glances of her small green eyes.

"You've lost your hat! And your hair's all mussed up. Wait till I tell your ma what a state you came home in."

Rhonwen was overtaken by intense weariness as she described the accident. Mrs. Mason was incredulous.

"I never heard the like! Poor Mrs. Morgan and Mrs. Blake. Well! Things like that happen at sea, but not on the Thames! Come along with me, deary, and I'll make you a nice cup of tea while you tell me all about it."

Rhonwen longed above all things to escape to her own rooms, but she felt despairingly that she was no match for Mrs. Mason. She was relieved to hear the calm tones of Miss Reeves from the stairs.

"Rhonwen should go to bed. Come, my child, I could not help hearing. What a dreadful calamity!"

Mrs. Mason's bosom quivered.

"Well! I'm perfectly capable, thank you, of looking after Rhonwen, ain't I, dear?"

But Rhonwen allowed herself to be rescued by Miss Reeves while the landlady's indignant mutterings followed them upstairs as she stumped back into her room and slammed the door.

At the door of the interconnecting rooms she shared with her mother, Rhonwen stopped.

"I have no key! It must be at the bottom of the river."

Again the tears fell and Miss Reeves led her to her own small room, where Rhonwen obediently drank hot soup while the teacher fetched a spare key from Mrs. Mason.

"And Mr. Baker has gone to try to discover news of any possible survivors, Rhonwen. Will you not stay with me tonight?"

Rhonwen begged to be allowed to go to her own lodgings. She felt in a nebulous way that if she waited for her mother in their own home, it might bring Beatrice back.

The first thing that caught her eye was the bright birthday card propped on the mantleshelf; then she knelt and put a match to the paper and sticks in the grate. All her movements were automatic, and she had to curb an impulse to begin hemming the handkerchiefs. She walked about restlessly, staring at the familiar furnishings: the neat double bed and white counterpane, the marble washstand with its ewer and basin and covered slop bucket beneath, and the box. It was in its usual place on the tallboy. She touched it, her fingers wandering over the heavy carved oak designs of flowers and fruit, the convolutions of ivy about the cross on the lid with its centre piece of a deephearted wooden rose. Beatrice had explained that the box was very old and since childhood Rhonwen had watched her mother lift it from the tallboy and carry it to the sitting room, closing the door between them. Then there would come the sound of clinking metal, the rustle of paper, and sometimes a quickly muffled sob. Always after her examination of her box Beatrice would be troubled by dreams, and Rhonwen heard strange names, some more frequently than others. Cristin and Bryn, Edwina, and most often, in tones of anguish, Meredith. Once Beatrice had moaned, "The babe—the babe—it lies so still. God help me," before she had lapsed into her own Welsh language, which was unintelligible to Rhonwen though the names sounded the same.

Rhonwen tore the wrapping paper from her sodden clothes and wrinkled her nose at the strong river stench. She threw them into a covered pail, too weary to cope with them, before she heated water and gave herself a sponge bath. Then she put on her nightgown and pulled on her white cotton stockings slowly, still held by the notion that to follow all Beatrice's strictures might in some way placate the gods. It had been a long time since she had asked her mother why she must always keep her feet covered. "The good Lord saw fit to make you slightly imperfect, Rhonwen, but it's not for you to go flaunting His small mistakes before others."

Being born with her two small toes missing did not seem important to Rhonwen, but her mother had made so much of wearing her stockings that she had kept them on even when swimming, ignoring the jeers of the other children, and had walked home with her feet slopping in her shoes.

She climbed into bed, hoping that exhaustion would grant her instant sleep; but sudden fear kept her wakeful. She would have given anything to see her mother's plump form bustling through the door, though Beatrice's first act would most likely be to rant at her for wasting precious fuel by lighting a fire late at night.

She was still sleepless when she heard Mr. Baker return and got up and opened the door, wearing Mrs. Trewby's borrowed coat. Miss Reeves brought the retired schoolmaster in. He sank into a chair and as he drank hot milk, a little colour crept back into the parchment skin stretched over his cheekbones.

"Rhonwen, I fear I do not bring good news. It is terrible. I have been to the Woolwich office of the London Steamboat Company, and it is besieged by despairing people. Some are themselves survivors, their clothing still dripping with river slime, looking for their families and friends. It is the same at all the company offices. But don't give way to pessimism, my dear; tomorrow I will try again. People have been rescued by many different agencies."

Finally Rhonwen slept, and this time she dreamt her own particular nightmare. It always began in the same way. She was in a large house where the ceilings were high, and she ran up a wide stairway. She raced along passages and reached a narrower stair that she climbed, her legs feeling like leaden weights, until she arrived at a closed door. Fear was so strong in her that the memory of it could keep sleep at bay; and even stronger than fear was an unendurable grief that made her cry out in anguish. Sometimes the door would not open and she knew she would be overtaken by the terror behind her. At other times she entered the room; but even then she could not be sure of the end of fear as she scuttled around, gasping and choking, until awakened by a disgruntled Beatrice. But occasionally she experienced the lifting of panic and misery in the room, and a peace and trust so great that she awoke with tears of joy on her cheeks. She knew that the removal of horror was bound up with someone whose only substance in her dream was two loving arms that held her close.

Tonight in her dream the door remained sealed. and her despair lasted interminably as she banged and rattled the handle until she awoke at dawn with one of the headaches that gave her such excruciating pain she was forced to lie still until it passed.

Miss Reeves watched over her, and late in the afternoon, Rhonwen rose and sat hemming the handkerchiefs, feeling better. She knew it to be useless labour since she had no means of discovering for whom they were intended, but it kept her busy.

When Miss Reeves next came to her she seemed disturbed.

"Rhonwen, Mr. Baker has returned and must speak with you."

The retired schoolmaster looked stricken as he said, "My child, I bring you no good news. Worse—I have to ask you to accompany me to Woolwich Dockyard. There are many poor victims there. They must be identified."

Rhonwen felt sick.

"I cannot! Surely it is not necessary. Cannot you, dear Mr. Baker, or Miss Reeves . . ." She stopped, choked with horror, aware that she must go.

Miss Reeves put a kind hand on her shoulder.

"The . . . bodies have all been brought to one spot and the coroner cannot allow them to be interred until relatives have seen them. It has to be gone through."

In the long open shed of the dockyard, Rhonwen strove for calm as she followed an official carrying a lamp against the gathering dusk from one still form to another, hearing the sobs of anguish of someone whose recognition of a loved one had driven out hope; but always she shook her head. At last they came to corpses apart from the others, and the official gave her a worried look.

"We have had to cover the faces of these, miss. Being in the river, you see, among the passing ships and grappling irons . . . well, to put it short, they are not recognisable. We are hoping that their garments, some bit of jewellery, perhaps . . ."

He stopped as Rhonwen gave a cry and bent over one of the faceless ones. Her hands were bloated and the black silk dress was ripped to shreds, but still pinned to the bosom was Beatrice's treasured brooch. Someone had cleaned off the river muck and the red stones gleamed incongruously.

"She is my mother!"

The official nodded and marked his list before beckoning to Miss Reeves.

"Please take her over yonder. There's piles of things we salvaged."

"I don't want anything," cried Rhonwen, hysteria mounting; but the man insisted, and when Rhonwen discovered her mother's bag, he solemnly made another mark on his paper and yet another when she found Ida Blake's bag.

"Sign here, please, miss, for your ma's things and here's the brooch."

Back in the lodging house Rhonwen opened the bag and removed the soaking contents, including a purse containing ten shillings in silver and two keys. That night Miss Reeves insisted on sharing Rhonwen's bed, holding the shocked girl's hand until she drifted into sleep.

The next day, as Rhonwen was bundling Mrs. Trewby's garments and her own for the local washerwoman, Mrs. Mason entered, a hand pressed theatrically to her bosom.

"You poor dear. It's definite then that your ma's departed this vale of tears. Well, there's a lot gone with her. And Ida Blake, as well. They say no one in the fore part of the boat survived. I can't tell you how grieved I am, but life has to go on and with all the worrying I reckon you've forgot my money. I'll take it now, please."

Rhonwen stared at her. "Money?"

"Bless you, the rent, of course. Six shillings and sixpence a week. Dearer than some places, but you have to pay for being in a clean, respectable house—and I never keep a lodger who don't pay regular though, lor' save you, I know that won't apply to you."

Mingled alarm at her ignorance of her financial position and disgust at Mrs. Mason's heartlessness made Rhonwen cringe inwardly, but from deep within came a flame of pride and she said coldly, "I will come to you later with the money. Pray have the goodness to leave me now."

Mrs. Mason's eyes narrowed. "Fine words to be sure. Your ma raised you to think you better than you are, but you'll find it was a mistake soon enough." And she stalked out.

Rhonwen's courage died, leaving her shaken. The money from her mother's bag would take care of her this week, but she must have some for the future—and there would be the funeral. She could not endure the idea of allowing Beatrice to be buried in one of the communal graves being dug for the victims of the disaster. A search brought only fifteen shillings more, and Rhonwen stood in the bedroom, gnawing her knuckles, recognising her complete dependence on her mother and wishing the latter had not been so reticent.

As her eyes roamed the room, searching for possible hiding places, they lit on the box. The repeated shocks, allied with her mother's dictum that she must never handle it, had blotted it from her mind. Now she lifted it from the tallboy and carried it to the sitting-room table. The larger of the two keys rescued from the river fitted the lodging door, so she tried the smaller, delicately wrought one and in a moment was raising the carved lid.

The box was lined in midnight blue velvet and the contents seemed disappointingly few. First she took out a slim leather case containing a locket on a chain. She thought it gilt until she found a gold hallmark. Where had her mother come by such an expensive ornament? She eased a fingernail into the locket and it opened to reveal a coil of brown hair and one of black. Perhaps one had belonged to her father. She knew nothing of him except that he had died. Beatrice refused to discuss him, leaving Rhonwen with the impression that he must have been bad. A small linen bag clinked as she moved it, and when she shook it, ten gold sovereigns fell, winking in the candlelight. It was a fortune, and she sighed with relief that for the moment her money worries were shelved. Next she unwrapped a twist of tissue paper. Gold again, this time in the form of a heavy ring with a deep cut design.

It was too large for any of her fingers and had probably belonged to a man. At the bottom of the box lay an envelope which she opened with a prayer in her heart that it might contain a clue to a family she surely must possess. She was torn by disappointment to find two drawings in childish scrawls of different hands. For a moment she sat still, realising that the box had meant far more to her than she had known. It had held mystery and magic, perhaps the key to her existence; but there seemed nothing here to help her.

She picked up one of the drawings. It was of a village surrounded by high mountains, and when she turned it over, she felt a prickle of excitement. There were words on the back. "Glyn Dedwydd!" She peered more closely at the picture and saw, cunningly hidden in the tangle of bushes in the foreground, the name, "Bryn." It was one that Beatrice had said in her sleep. Quickly she examined the other drawing. It was more skilful and was of a stone castle done from an angle above it. A straight horizon in the distance suggested water. This time the name was hidden among the slate roofs. "Cristin"—another of the names from her mother's past—and the legend on the back said, "Castell Craig, 1859."

She hurried to show her finds to Miss Reeves and Mr. Baker, who advanced the opinion that the names were all Welsh.

"I have a friend who was born there. I will ask his opinion," said Mr. Baker.

He and Miss Reeves supported Rhonwen through the ordeal of the funeral conducted in the local Methodist chapel. Miss Reeves also dealt with Mrs. Mason, who was scathing.

"Some funeral," she scorned. "Not even a bit of ham afterwards."

But she had her rent money and she stumped back into her own quarters.

Then the three discussed Rhonwen's future.

"You have a well-informed mind," stated Miss Reeves, "but not enough accomplishments to become a governess in a rich house, though you might manage a more humble post." She sighed. "But I wonder if it would suit your temperament. It did not mine, I assure you. If my small legacy had not enabled me to retire here, I would have fared ill. And you are so pretty," she finished, in what seemed to Rhonwen an inconsequential conclusion.

"Is that bad?"

Miss Reeves failed to return her smile.

"It might be. Women are often reluctant to employ young and pretty girls, especially in a small house where they easily meet husbands and brothers. They think of the possible temptation to them. Girls in a living-in position are dreadfully at the mercy of the males of the household, who often regard them as what they would term 'fair game'."

She kissed Rhonwen unexpectedly.

"Take off that worried frown. Between us we will think of something. Mr. Baker and I are determined to see you well settled."

But she, too, was frowning, and Rhonwen sensed her uncertainty and was disturbed. She had no claim on the two good people who had helped her so generously.

Mr. Baker's friend confirmed the origin of the names and said he believed Glyn Dedwydd to be a small village somewhere in the hills near Harlech and that Castell Craig was an ancient Welsh dwelling owned by a family employing much labour in different ventures.

Rhonwen thought about her future. She could not stay on in these lodgings, which were far too expensive; and when she contemplated the local employment, and recalled the endless toil and young-old faces of the women who existed in the city, her prospects seemed bleak.

Although she had smiled at Miss Reeves's anxiety over her looks, she was under no illusions as to the fate of many young girls who were used by those who battened on the beauty of women. She would never be such a fool as to fall for illicit blandishments.

But her next uninvited and unwelcome visitors forced her to face stark reality and revealed a decision her unconscious mind had already made.

Chapter 2

THEY ARRIVED in the early evening and took advantage of Rhonwen's speechless surprise and indignation to enter, filling the small sitting room with the odours of cheap scent and cosmetics.

Rhonwen and Jacenta Lane stared at one another, and an insolent grin stretched Jacenta's painted mouth as she gestured towards her companion.

"This is Miss Tana Peach, Miss Morgan. Pretty, ain't she? Aren't you going to ask us to sit down? I've come to offer my condolences and give you some help."

Without waiting for Rhonwen's reply Jacenta settled herself in Beatrice's chair and Tana perched on the edge of the sofa. Beatrice had always warned Rhonwen never to speak to Jacenta Lane or any of her women, and now the notorious creature sat in her mother's place, where she leaned back comfortably, laughing from slanting brown eyes and patting her improbably black hair.

Rhonwen's anger simmered as she sought for words that would dismiss them without provoking an unpleasant scene.

"Miss . . . Mrs . . . Lane . . . I am sure you mean well. It is kind of you to come to me with sympathy . . ."

As she faltered beneath the madam's knowing grin, Rhonwen saw that one of her yellowing teeth was broken—most likely in a fight—and she lowered her eyes, only to be confronted by Jacenta's bright yellow, low-cut gown, which all but revealed her nipples and did nothing to conceal signs of advancing age in her wrinkled cleavage.

All amusement was wiped from Jacenta's face.

"Don't you dare look at me as if I was dirt," she rasped. "Tana and me came to offer help. Tana lost her ma not long ago and she never knew her pa, either, just like you, Rhonwen Morgan. I know all about you, and I could say things about your ma except that I won't speak ill of the dead."

Rhonwen's head jerked up. "I need nothing from you, Mrs. Lane. I shall obtain employment."

Jacenta looked at Tana. "Just you tell her how you was when I found you."

Tana spoke with direct simplicity, smoothing a crease from her pink satin gown.

"My ma was took by a lung fever, though it was all the work and starving that really killed her. I was with other women sewing sacks round a lamp post at night—we didn't have no candles—and Mrs. Lane passed by in her carriage and saw me. She took me home and gave me a lovely new name, and I'm never cold nor hungry now, and I don't have to do much for it. Well, nothing to signify, anyhow."

Rhonwen considered that Tana was not much above fourteen and shivered. Then she was taken by surprise as Jacenta moved swiftly to her and, with a practised movement, tugged out the comb that secured her hair in the severe style ordered by her mother. Hair pins fell with sharp little taps to the oil-cloth covered floor as a red-gold curtain of shimmering silk floated round Rhonwen's shoulders in natural waves and curls.

Tana gave an involuntary gasp of admiration as Jacenta said triumphantly, "There, Tana, what did I tell you? Didn't I always say that Miss Morgan was a beauty and wasted here?"

Rhonwen's efforts to prevent herself being dragged before the mirror were futile against the strength of a woman skilled in handling undisciplined girls and troublesome men, and she was forced to stare at the reflection of her disordered hair, her creamy skin pink with humiliation, her stormy grey-blue eyes.

"God, you'll be a sensation," breathed Jacenta, almost reverently, "but you need someone to show you the ropes. We don't want a lovely armful like you gettin' into the wrong company, do we?"

Rhonwen jerked back violently and Jacenta let her go. "Mrs. Lane, I neither want your help nor do I need it."

"Stow it, ducky! What'll you do? Sell flowers in the street? Make hats for the gentry? Starve? You've got no kinfolk. Where will you go?"

Rhonwen's voice seemed to speak almost without her will. "I shall go to my people in Wales."

Her reply was as startling to herself as to Jacenta, who jeered, "You haven't got anyone. I told you—I know about you."

"Well, you don't know everything, so oblige me by leaving!"

Jacenta stalked to the door, her half-train scattering hair pins; then she turned.

"You think you're better than the rest of us, don't you? Your ma was a fool. Just don't come crawling to me when you're in the gutter, that's all. Come on, Tana, we ain't got all day."

Rhonwen threw open the window to allow the sickly smells to disperse and raised her head to look above the London chimneys at the sky glowing smokily pink in the setting sun.

"I shall go to Wales." The decision had been made for her somewhere in an unexplored recess of her mind, but she did not question it.

Miss Reeves did not oppose her idea, and Mr. Baker was quite enthusiastic as he sat in his easy chair, his legs covered by a rug.

"Who knows, Rhonwen, you may find an aunt or cousins with whom you can live."

"And even if you do not," declared Miss Reeves, "I daresay there will be some kind of respectable employment in the countryside. And you must promise that you will write to us for assistance should you need any."

A week later Rhonwen stood in Paddington Station and said goodbye to her two teachers. She kissed them both.

"Write to me, please," she begged, "as soon as I can send an address. Take care of yourselves. Do not neglect to take your dyspepsia medicine, Mr. Baker. I shall be thinking of you both."

She leaned out the window of the train and, in spite of her alarm at the gathering speed, waved until the figures became lost in a haze of distance and tears; then she settled herself into her seat and was suddenly struck by the reality of her situation.

She was going to an unknown land to seek out relatives who might not even exist, and as the train rattled and swayed, she had to fight down her apprehension. All her material possessions were in a shabby carpetbag and, after settling her debts, she had a one-way rail ticket, a few shillings in her purse and seven gold sovereigns sewn into an inner skirt pocket. Mr. Baker's friend had said that Glyn Dedwydd, translated, meant "The Happy Valley," and she could only hope that it might prove so for her.

She was grateful for a short stroll when the train stopped at Chester and glad of the amenities of the ladies third-class waiting room, sketchy though they were, before she resumed her seat. Then the beauty of rolling farmland, hills and estuaries, rivers and meadows filled her with a glow of appreciation, and after changing trains at Barmouth she felt a quiver of excited anticipation at the imminent end of her journey. Yet when the train stopped and she stepped down at the tiny halt that served Llanbedr, and looked about her at the fields and hedges, she wondered where the village could be.

The only activity was centred round the guard's van where a man was talking to the guard. It was already half past seven in the evening and, in her mounting anxiety, Rhonwen became bold as she hurried to the two strangers.

"Pray, excuse me, but I need to get to Llanbedr as soon as possible to bespeak accommodation. I had thought to find myself in the village when I left the train. Please—can you help me?"

The guard's face went pink with indignation at this interruption from a poorly clad girl who had travelled in the cheapest class, and he snapped, "Can't you see I'm talking to this gentleman? The village lies but a mile along the lane."

He turned back to the man with an apologetic smile.

"I trust the family is all well, sir, and that your aunt finds what she needs in the parcel."

He handed a package to the young man who took it absently, his eyes on Rhonwen. As the guard blew his whistle and waved a green flag and the train chuffed away, Rhonwen endeavoured to return the man's stare with equal intensity, but before his penetrating gaze she was forced to lower her lids.

"You are bound for Llanbedr!"

The words were rapped out more like a command than a question, and Rhonwen's head went up. She was extremely weary and still suffering from the shocks of the past few days.

"What is it to you, sir? I have my direction from the guard. I need nothing more, I think."

The man grinned, showing strong white teeth, and, in spite of her repudiation, Rhonwen felt drawn by his powerful magnetism. Angered further by her own weakness, she tried again to stare him down and again he won the subtle battle and she flushed as she looked down at his highly polished riding boots. Then, with an air of dismissal, she returned to pick up her carpetbag and resolutely walked towards the small exit gate. The man stayed still, watching her as she hurried past him, before he called, "The walk to the village is not so long, but if your bag is heavy, I could assist you."

Rhonwen faltered in her stride. She almost marched on, but there had been a tinge of sympathy in his voice and she was very weary. In the same instant it occurred to her that his accent was cultured and that he could probably guide her to a decent lodging. Slowly she turned and gave him a more thoughtful appraisal.

He was almost six feet tall with a thin, tanned face, dark eyes and brown hair with a slight wave. His strong chin, heavy black brows and highbridged prominent nose destroyed any pretensions to handsome looks. He exuded an air of rough strength and masculine vitality that made Rhonwen wary.

"Well, do I pass muster?"

The colour deepened in her cheeks. "I beg your pardon, sir, I did not mean to stare, but I . . . I . . . "

"A girl cannot be too careful, eh?"

Rhonwen tried to ignore the humourous mockery of his tone and answered, "I believe you mentioned help."

She had meant to keep her voice even, but her attempt to conceal her attack of nerves made her remark sound snappy.

He grinned again. "The pretty kitten has claws."

Before she could obey a further impulse to chance her fortune alone he smiled properly. All the teasing left his face, she saw that his mobile mouth was well-shaped and that his smile transformed his face to friendship.

"I am tired, sir; I would be most grateful for some form of transport."

He laughed as he picked up her carpetbag.

"Transport you shall have, my lady," and he led the way to the lane.

She looked about her for a carriage, but the man went to a powerful horse tethered to a rail, which was leading a pack animal loaded with sacks.

"I always prefer to ride," said the man. "You were fortunate that I met the train today. I was visiting a friend in the village and was made messenger for the entire household. Here you behold flour, dried peas and lentils, and if I shift them so . . ." he heaved the heavy sacks as if they had been feather pillows and slung them further back on the patient animal.

"Then if I put this so . . ." He removed his cord jacket, revealing rolled up shirt sleeves and muscular arms, and placed it on the pack animal's back.

"Sir, I had no idea you meant this form of transport. I have never been on a horse in my life."

He raised his eyebrows.

"Have you not? Well, have no fear, madam; I do assure you that our pack horses are picked for their even natures as well as for their endurance. We do not run the risk of having expensive items damaged on their way to the mountains."

Rhonwen took a step back, but he behaved as if she had not moved, simply strapping her bag to the pack horse before turning to her expectantly. Further protest could only make her appear silly, so, gritting her teeth, she walked towards him. The man reached forward and in a single movement placed strong hands about her slender waist and sat her on his jacket with little more ceremony than he had moved the sacks. He looked down at her feet in their button boots as they swung ineffectively against the pony's belly and laughed.

"We shall travel slowly and you must cling to his mane. You will not hurt him and you will feel more secure."

He swung lithely onto his own mount and they set off down the lane. As Rhonwen became accustomed to the slight rocking motion she looked about her, studying the high hedges guarding wild flowers, the trees that stood like sentinels at intervals in the hedgerows, showing the end of summer in the golds and red of their foliage, enjoying the scents of autumn.

They reached a river where the horses hooves squelched in muddy pools along the low bank before the man guided them across an ancient bridge and Rhonwen saw the cluster of grey stone houses which must be Llanbedr.

"This is where we part company, madam."

He swung himself down and lifted her to the dusty road. Her calm drained away and she shivered a little.

"Are you cold? Surely not on so warm an evening."

"No, thank you. If you will be so kind as to pass me my bag I will find where I may sleep tonight."

The man's heavy brows drew together in a frown.

"Ah, I recall that you asked about accommodation. Has no one written to secure a bed for you?"

Abruptly he directed upon her the most searching glance she had ever encountered.

"What are you doing here? Why have your people permitted you to travel unaccompanied without proper arrangements?"

The devastating look encompassed her clothes and worn boots.

"You wear the garb of a poor woman, yet your voice tells a different story. Are you running away? You are, perhaps, a schoolgirl who fancies herself hard done by! Have you no consideration for those who will be frantic about you?"

How dare he address her in such a fashion! But she bit back furious words and said as mildly as she could, "I have run from nowhere, sir. I have no family and my friends do know where I am. I would be most grateful if you could direct me to a respectable lodging."

It was galling to plead for his help, but the evening shadows had begun to stretch long fingers across the village street.

He stared at her thoughtfully.

"The houses which take paying guests during the holiday season are most likely all occupied. In any event the folk around here are conservative in their outlook and would prove even more suspicious than I if you turned up wearing those idiotic clothes and spoke in cultured tones. I had better take you to the inn."

Rhonwen's eyes widened. "I thought no respectable woman would stay alone at an inn."

His brows rose. "You have perhaps a better notion."
Rhonwen shook her head.

"Then you had best obey me and stop arguing."

He tethered the horses outside the long, low inn that was situated on the river's edge and offered Rhonwen his arm. She placed her fingertips upon it. He laughed down at her.

"They teach you pretty manners at this ephemeral school to which you do not go."

Goaded, Rhonwen replied, "I am telling the truth. I have always had teachers at home."

This was a mistake. The man whistled through his teeth and subjected her to another questioning look.

"Teachers at home? And do you still maintain that you are not escaping disguised as—what?"

As she obstinately refused to be drawn he sighed.

"Well, it is no affair of mine, and I know you will be safe here."

At his shout a woman entered the hall wiping floury hands on a snowy cloth. She curtseyed to the man, but her woman's eye took in all the details of Rhonwen's appearance at a single, practised glance.

"Will you be wanting refreshment, sir. You and the—young lady?"

"For her, food and lodging for the night, please, Mrs. Jones. She is a poor, benighted traveller whose arrangements appear to have gone awry. I know that our good innkeeper's lady will not turn away a damsel in distress."

Mrs. Jones would need to have a very hard nature to resist the subtle flattery in the man's voice, and she bestowed a friendly smile on Rhonwen.

"Stranded, is it you are? Don't worry yourself any further. Megan Jones will look after you. And you, sir, will you be taking a drink before you go?"

"No, thank you. I am expected home for dinner and my cousin is impatient to see if the particular shade of green silk she ordered matches up properly. I understand she will need to unpick her sewing and begin again if it does not. Please convey my regards to your husband."

"That I will! And you please give my best respects to Miss Edwina."

The man bowed to Rhonwen, and she felt that if he had been wearing a hat he would have removed it with a flourish.

"Good night to you, madam. I trust your visit to Llanbedr will prove a happy one."

Moments later horses' hooves clattered along a lane at the side of the inn, but Rhonwen was scarcely aware of the sound, so engrossed was she in the fact that "Edwina" had been one of the names so often cried by her mother in her troubled sleep. The innkeeper's wife had to raise her voice to obtain a response. Then Rhonwen allowed herself to be led to a small back parlour where she was able to appease some of the pangs of hunger with a slice of spicy bread, thickly spread with butter, and a glass of milk.

Mrs. Jones seemed in no hurry to resume her baking.

"Are you here on holiday, miss?"

"I am taking a short rest," replied Rhonwen. "I felt I needed one."

The landlady's face was a mask of suspicion.

"You're young to be needing a rest. Have you been ill?"

"I have recently suffered a bereavement. My mother . . ."

The memory of the disaster fused with her weariness and confusion brought tears to her eyes, and Mrs. Jones was contrite.

"Oh, I am sorry, miss. I didn't mean to upset you. Do go on eating your Bara Brith. You seem to like it."

Welcoming the change of subject Rhonwen praised her baking, and Mrs. Jones said, "I make most of the food we serve here, but I hope I'm honest enough to admit that there's one who makes better Bara Brith than I do and she baked this. She's the wife of the blacksmith in Glyn Dedwydd."

Rhonwen managed to keep her voice steady.

"Is that near here?"

"A matter of an hour or so's walk. Lots of folk come from England to tramp the hills. Is that what you are going to do?"

Rhonwen nodded and asked casually, "Does the man who helped me from the station live in Glyn Dedwydd?"

"Him! Indeed he does not! Mr. Bryn's home is Castell Craig, and his family own most of the land round here. Fancy taking Mr. Bryn for a village man!"

She laughed at length, giving Rhonwen time to assimilate the news that she had almost certainly met the originator of one of the childish drawings that lay in the box at the bottom of her carpetbag and that he lived in the castle depicted in the other.

She longed to pour out questions but caution held her tongue fast. She still had no idea why her mother had left Wales to hide herself and her child in London, or why she had steadfastly refused to discuss her past or family. It was possible that Rhonwen had been born out of wedlock, and she had no wish to despoil her mother's memory. No, nor to proclaim herself illegitimate, remembering the harsh judgement pronounced on such unfortunates. A sense of depression hit her as she began to question her wisdom in travelling so far, perhaps only to uncover secrets best left buried; yet she felt an increasingly compelling need to matter to someone.

After Mrs. Jones had gone she leaned her head on the hard settle back and closed her eyes. She had had time to think on the long journey to her mother's beautiful homeland, and she was beginning to struggle with a sense of deprivation. Great though her grief was at the loss of her mother, she felt bitter regret, which was even more profound. Beatrice had permitted no one, not even her daughter, to draw close to her, and Rhonwen had been forced to smother most of the emotion that welled within her.

Yet, in spite of the hard seat and her dejection of spirit, her tired body took its toll and she dozed. Suddenly she was in the dream, back on the familiar stairway, running—running—

A hand shook her shoulder and she jerked awake to see the sympathetic face of the landlady.

"Poor lamb, you're worn out. You were moaning in your sleep. Come and eat a bite of supper, then you can go to bed."

"Thank you, Mrs. Jones." She hesitated, then said, "I . . . I am not affluent. Can you give me a modest room?"

Mrs. Jones looked her up and down before answering dryly, "I had not thought you rich, miss, and I've ordered an attic to be made ready. It's small, but clean and comfy enough."

After a satisfying meal of Welsh mutton with rowanberry sauce, Rhonwen was taken to her room and lay that night in an iron bed with scrollwork ends, beneath a sloping whitewashed ceiling, while over her head hung a framed plaque inviting her to "Rejoice in the Lord." The mattress was of feathers, the sheets smelled of sweet herbs and she was lulled into a refreshing sleep from which she was awakened by a maid in print dress and cap drawing back the curtains.

"Good morning, miss. The sun's shining. Are you going walking? Would you like these cleaned?"

Rhonwen stared at the boots held by the maid and wished they did not look so shabby. For years now she had cleaned her own and her mother's footwear, and she felt shy as she answered, "If you please, and I . . . I was wondering if I could borrow a smoothing iron. My gowns have become sadly creased."

"Bless you, miss, I will iron for you."

She threw open the wardrobe door.

"Three is it you have? Well, I daresay that's enough to carry. Some ladies travel with clothes enough to last me forever. Which would you like first?"

"The blue serge. It is a good, all-purpose garment."

The maid's expression left Rhonwen in no doubt as to what she thought of her dull attire, but she smiled pleasantly as she left.

"People are judged by what they wear!" Rhonwen fancied she could hear Beatrice's voice. "A man thinks he can take liberties with a girl who dresses in flashy finery, especially when her only protector is a weak woman." But her mother had not been weak. She had been tough and uncompromising.

As Rhonwen pulled on her rough cotton underwear, she was surprised by a sudden longing for the feel of satin or silk upon her skin, and she felt afraid. Had Beatrice formed her rigid lines of conduct because she suspected her daughter might be frivolous at heart, someone who could fall easily into wanton ways? Her sharp tongue had hinted of it at times. From whom could she have inherited such possible weaknesses? From Beatrice? From her father—that fugitive figure of whom she had not even seen a likeness?

The maid returned with the gown. "Here you are, Miss Morgan. It's a Welsh name you've got, isn't it? Is it Welsh you are? Is your family living hereabouts?"

"Not that I know of," replied Rhonwen unguardedly.

The maid was wide-eyed. "Don't you know then? I thought everyone knew where their folks were! Were you born in Wales?"

"I was born in London," said Rhonwen shortly. "Pray send up my boots. I have no other footwear with me."

The maid scowled. "The boy is doing them now. And missus wants to know if you'll be needing sandwiches to take out, and do you want ginger beer, though you'll likely be able to buy milk somewhere, she says."

Rhonwen ordered the food. She had no time to waste. When her money ran out she must be in a position to earn more. She pulled on her gown, taking a mild pleasure in the knowledge that other hands than hers had smoothed out the creases. She fastened the long line of tiny buttons reaching to the top of her high-necked collar and drew on a pair of fresh white cuffs. A tousle-haired urchin came in with her boots polished to shiny blackness, and she went down to a substantial breakfast.

Mrs. Jones brought her picnic lunch in a webbing bag.

"My children used it to carry their food on outings. Are you thinking of any particular route? Can I direct you?"

"You mentioned Glyn Dedwydd," said Rhonwen. "Is it a pretty walk there?"

Mrs. Jones looked enquiringly at her.

"Glyn Dedwydd, is it? Take the road which runs by the inn and follow the River Artro. It's a fair old climb and if a mist should come down from the hills you had best turn back. The mountains are lovely, so they are, but they've taken many a life."

At Rhonwen's look of alarm she smiled.

"You'll be all right if you stay on the well-trodden roads, Miss Morgan, and if you reach the village you could call on Mary Evans. She's the one who makes my Bara Brith. Tell her I sent you. She'll give you a rest and a drink should you want them."

A few minutes later Rhonwen, wearing her black jacket, the webbing bag slung over her shoulder, was swinging up the hill with easy grace, breathing appreciatively of the mingled scents. The odour of damp beechwoods wreathed among the perfume of late roses in a cottage garden and a faint but delectable peaty smell rose from the tumbling river. Rhonwen's contentment seemed to seep from the earth through the soles of her feet. She felt at home. Surely here she must find her roots and settle in her people's land.

The road grew steeper, and the river fell away to a gorge to her right. Hills rose steeply on her left and small oaks clung to the sparse soil, their branches intertwining, their roots twisted and clinging to boulders, each preserving the other from tumbling to the valley.

A woman in a small holding gave her further directions and insisted on her drinking a glass of buttermilk, and Rhonwen's sense of well being expanded in the human warmth as she walked on, in and out of patches of sunlight, where men had cleared ground for their animals to graze.

As noon was approaching she rounded a bend and came upon a turning to the right. A group of stone dwellings clustered about a wide track that led directly to the river. "This must be Glyn Dedwydd," she thought, and she walked the length of the road while children stopped their play to stare and women came to their doorways to watch her. She was about to ask her way to the forge when the sounds of hammering and the whinny of a horse guided her to a large cottage set back from the others. Standing apart from it was the forge. Through the wide doorway she could see men and a beautiful grey horse tethered to an iron wall ring. A youth stood at its head and murmured soothingly to it while a man bent over a hind hoof, which he held between his knees upon his leather apron. A rancid smell of burnt horn wafted on the smoke as he completed the fitting and began to hammer at the shoe with rythmic motions of his heavily muscled arm, using nails he took deftly from his mouth.

Rhonwen encompassed all this at a glance before she became aware of another figure standing in the dimness of the forge. The figure took a step forward, and she found herself looking at a man in expertly tailored corduroy breeches and jacket, highly polished top boots and a hard felt hat. His face remained shadowed, yet she knew that he had fixed her with a hard stare. She felt uneasy, as if she sensed a quality of something menacing flowing towards her. Then the figure moved out of the forge and she decided that her overwrought nerves must have been playing tricks as the man lifted his hat and tendered a small bow. He was tall, slim and lithe. Dark brown hair waved softly over a well-formed head. His lips were thin beneath a golden brown moustache, but the smile that curved them was friendly.

"How do you do?" he said in cultured tones. "Are you looking for someone? Can I help you?"

Rhonwen's feelings were a mixture of pleasure and surprise. Nothing in her garb could impress a man so obviously well placed. He could have ignored her presence, yet he was going out of his way to be courteous.

She curtseyed in the way she had been taught by Miss Reeves.

"Thank you, sir, but I am merely walking for pleasure and came upon this delightful village."

The movement of his brows were almost imperceptible, and she sensed his surprise at her voice as his glance swept over her. She knew instinctively that here was a man who understood female fashion.

He smiled again. "You are well garbed for our rough mountains. So many ladies wear foolish fripperies and wonder why their gowns become torn and their feet grow blistered."

He was going out of his way to excuse clothes that he must know no woman worthy of his consideration would give her maid, and she felt an appreciation of his tact but a certain wariness at a curious abrasive quality in his tone.

Before she could frame a reply the blacksmith straightened. He was bigger than he had seemed and his voice came deep and powerful from a barrel chest.

"He'll do now, Mr. Cristin."

Rhonwen was thankful that the stranger had turned to the blacksmith or he must have seen her shock, which betrayed more than a passing interest in him. Here was another of the names that had haunted her mother.

The blacksmith continued to hold his attention.

"I reckon you'll be wanting the frost nails for the horses soon. The weather can turn to ice at this time of year."

"My brother will attend to it," replied the man carelessly, looking back towards Rhonwen who was struggling to control her mounting excitement. Once more she had met someone who, until now, had been to her an image in another's dream, a word on a childish drawing. He must be connected with her mother's past life and perhaps with her own present.

Chapter 3

"WILL YOU TAKE refreshment, Mr. Cristin?"

The owner of the voice was a small woman with a round, healthy face who had come from the cottage. Her broad smile showed the loss of one or two teeth, her soft, dark hair was streaked with grey and flour floated from her apron to whiten the slate path. She looked with surprise at Rhonwen.

"Is it a young lady you have with you then? Why did you not step into my house, miss? Mr. Cristin knows you would be welcome."

Rhonwen was embarrassed at this coupling of her name with the stranger, but he answered with easy familiarity. "The young lady is, alas, not my companion, though if she will do me the honour of partaking of a glass of your excellent Birch beer with me—and if you have been baking . . ." He looked at Rhonwen. "Let us hope that she has made a batch of Bara Sinsir—Welsh Gingerbread, ma'am. Until you have tasted Mary Evan's gingerbread you cannot claim to have lived."

Mary laughed. "Pay him no mind, miss. He has always been the one for teasing. You are making her blush, sir."

"I came to see you, Mrs. Evans," said Rhonwen. "The land-lady at "The George" recommended it. She has provided me with food, though."

"And good food must not go to waste, eh. It's plain to see you've been properly taught. But still you can wash it down with a glass or two of my beer, and you can have a small taste of Bara Sinsir."

She led the way into a big kitchen floored with heavy slate slabs. A shiny black cooking range occupied almost all one wall and a huge fire glowed red in the grate. Hams and bacon flitches were slung on hooks on the walls and near the smoke. An appetising smell made Rhonwen feel suddenly giddy with hunger. She took a chair near the window and began to eat her sandwiches.

The man they called "Cristin" flung himself into an elbow chair near the range and stretched his long legs. "There is no place more beautiful than a true Welsh kitchen, Mary Evans. And what is that bubbling in your stove pot?"

The blacksmith's wife chuckled as she reached for a big ladle suspended from the chimney piece, lifted the pot lid, dipped and stirred, releasing a rich aroma. "What should it be on a working day but good Cawl Cymreig? Will you take some, sir? I've only to add the leeks so it'll be ready in five minutes."

"And why should you suppose I timed my visit at this hour? Perhaps the young lady would care to sample some. Can you find room for a little of the best stew in Wales, Miss . . . ?"

"Morgan," supplied Rhonwen. "My name is Rhonwen Morgan."

It seemed to her that for an instant the man stopped all movement, even breathing, and that his brown eyes bored so deeply into hers that he must read the secrets of her mind. She felt an impulse of alarm before he smiled, and again she inwardly chided herself for allowing her over-charged emotions to distort the normal.

"A Welsh name," he mused. "Yet your accents are not at all Welsh."

"As yours are not, sir."

Mary Evans laughed. "She has you there! Why should you think yourself the only person to go to an English school!"

"Is that what you did, Miss Morgan?" asked Cristin.

"In a way," replied Rhonwen coolly. She felt he was pushing with his questions and he irritated her. He would not have been so familiar had she been escorted—or even better gowned.

Perhaps she allowed her annoyance to show, for he said, "I beg your pardon. My interest in you leads me to curiosity."

They began to talk of her walk and her appreciation of the country until Rhonwen, after tasting the bowl of stew, which she couldn't resist, said, "This is more delicious by far than anything I ate from a rich London house."

Mary looked gratified, but Cristin's eyes were immediately alert.

"You are familiar with such houses?"

Again his manner sought to dominate her, and Rhonwen felt a surge of anger. She would not pretend to be anything she was not. "My mother went out as a cook and brought back delicacies for me to taste," she said.

"I see." He looked as if he wanted to say much more, but he remained silent, though he continued to direct watchful glances at her.

Mrs. Evans laid the scrubbed wooden table in the centre of the room, covered it with a blue checked cloth and set out blue and white bowls and spoons. She added platters of homemade bread and dishes of yellow butter, and moments later the kitchen seemed to shrink in size beneath the presence of too many people for Rhonwen to comprehend at once. They gave her shy smiles, and the blacksmith murmured a welcome, though he was bashful in the presence of a stranger.

As the family ate, Rhonwen was able to study them. Besides Mary and her husband there were seven others, ranging from a tall youth resembling his father, through girls and boys, to a sturdy boy of about six. There was also a man who was bigger than the blacksmith. He had greying dark hair and strange, opaque black eyes. He still wore the leather apron of the forge. The family treated him as if he were a child, and it was easy to see that his brawn far outstripped his brain. He smiled many times at Rhonwen, a foolish but singularly sweet smile.

"Eat your good dinner, Tomos, and don't stare," commanded Mary, and he obeyed without question.

"Tomos is our assistant," Mary explained to Rhonwen, "and this tall fellow here is our eldest son, Hugh, who is an apprentice to the trade and will take over the forge as his father before him and as the Evans men have done for hundreds of years. One day my Owen will need to rest his old bones."

Her husband grinned at her. "Hold your peace, woman. That day is long ahead."

Rhonwen sensed the loving fellowship that flowed round the family and felt envious.

"How is your young man, Megan?" asked Cristin, and the eldest of the three girls blushed to the roots of her curly brown hair.

Her mother answered for her. "I shall be losing my girl sooner than I expected, Mr. Cristin. Howell's poor mother took a chill and died within a week. A month ago it happened, and Mr. Pugh and Howell need my Megan badly to cook and clean for them. Megan will be sixteen in four weeks and we shall bring the wedding forward to the day." She sighed. "I shall miss her, so I shall, but I am trusting Marged to take her place. She is thirteen, and little Rose is promising finely."

Marged pushed her stew around her dish. "Rose is better now than I shall ever be. She *likes* housework."

"You will be keeping a civil tongue in your head towards your mother," said Mr. Evans.

Marged flushed and Mary tutted, but Cristin laughed easily. "You must look for a rich husband who will supply you with servants."

Owen Evans looked round and said slowly, "That is a wrong notion to be putting into a young girl's head, Mr. Cristin. She knows her station and will stick to it."

Cristin was unabashed. "Is that so, Marged?"

"I don't want to stay on this old mountain all my life," she grumbled. "I would like to see something exciting. Go to . . . to London maybe."

"Oh, no!" exclaimed Rhonwen. She stopped as everyone stared at her. "I beg your pardon. It is not for me to say."

The blacksmith looked hard at her. "I would like you to explain, please."

She received complete attention as she tried to tell them something of the people among whom she had lived, of the garment makers, the little crossing sweepers and match girls, and, managing to keep her meaning delicate enough to penetrate only the comprehension of the older ones, of the possible fate lying in wait for inexperienced girls as pretty as Marged.

Marged tried to maintain her defiant air but she looked troubled, and Cristin applauded softly. "Well said, Miss Morgan. I confess I should like to hear more of the London you know. Perhaps I could accompany you part of the way home. I should deem it a favour."

He was smiling at her, his handsome face alight with exaggerated entreaty, and she felt the strength of his charm. Yet she had the curious idea that deep within him lurked a being who stood apart and watched her with speculation.

Mary said, "Mr. Cristin has to go part of your way to reach his own home. You must not leave it too late. Darkness comes down the mountain fast now summer is ended."

Rhonwen yielded but begged a few private words with Mary before she and Cristin left, he leading his horse.

"Women's secrets," he quizzed her as they left the village.

Rhonwen looked enquiringly at him. "Do you refer to my talk with Mrs. Evans?"

She paced a few steps before answering his question. "I asked her if she could give me lodging for a while and she says she can. I am much taken with this lovely part of Wales."

"I see. And I daresay you will look at a couple of mountains, sigh over a stream or two, clasp your hands in enchantment at a waterfall, then return to London."

"Does it annoy you, sir, that tourists come to Wales?"

"No, indeed, why should it? But I find it difficult to retain patience with folk who tell me how much they envy me my beautiful home before they dash back to the pleasures and amenities of the city. Tell me more of your life, Miss Morgan. I confess it fascinates me since I know only the portals of the rich."

"And I do not need to dwell upon the miseries of the poor. Not that I know the worst of them at firsthand, for my mother was able to keep us in a respectable way of life."

"Respectability is much valued by a certain class of person, is it not? Yet here you are, on a mountain with a complete stranger and no mother to keep you—respectable."

"My mother—is dead, sir."

He was immediately contrite. "I beg your pardon. Is your bereavement recent?"

"My mother was one of the unfortunates who drowned in the *Princess Alice* disaster."

"That was terrible! Please accept my condolences and say you forgive me my levity."

They walked on between the darkening woods, listening to the sounds of river and birdsong and to the horse clip-clopping on the road, and Rhonwen asked, "Do you have a brother named Bryn?"

"Why do you ask?" His tone was sharp enough to make her hesitate before answering. "I . . . I am simply interested, that is all. A man called Bryn was kind enough to help me when I arrived."

"I do have a brother of that name, but he does not resemble me, save that we both have the Caradog nose. Were you perceptive enough to detect a likeness, Miss Morgan?"

She had the feeling that there was purpose behind every question, and they walked on for a moment while she stared down a steep, rocky gully to the river. "Wales is so beautiful," she said, "but she could be a little frightening to a townbred person."

Cristin did not answer and she said, "I cannot tell you why I associated you with Bryn. Perhaps I heard your names linked in the inn."

"Perhaps you did, Miss Morgan. Have you a more serious reason than a vacation for coming to Wales? Are you visiting your mother's birthplace?"

Rhonwen turned startled eyes to him. "Why do you ask?"

He shrugged. "Why should I not? It seems to me a perfectly natural question. I am assuming that if you knew of relatives you would not be seeking a lodging."

"I do not know where my mother was born. I know only that she was Welsh."

"Yet presumably something brought you to *this* part of Wales rather than another. Have you no clue?"

"My mother was . . . reticent about her past life, yet I have reason to think she might once have been in Glyn Dedwydd."

"How fortunate that she left you sufficient funds to travel. I would not have thought a cook able to earn much."

Rhonwen was angry. "My financial state—my purpose in coming here—are my own affairs, sir."

Immediately she regretted her loss of control. Already she had met Bryn Caradog and made nothing of her opportunity, and now she was on the verge of a quarrel with his brother. She must try to make amends. Before she could speak he slowed down so that the horse's hooves slid on the road, and his face was full of winning charm.

"I am led into impertinence. Pray, do not blame me for allowing my sympathy to make me curious. I lost both my parents in an accident and know how you must feel. Their coach overturned quite near here. Papa died instantly and Mama a few hours later."

"That was dreadful. Did it happen recently?"

"Oh, no. I was only six and my brother aged four. We were here on a visit, but Edwina kept us and was a mother to us. As she is to her cousin's child, Idris, whose mother died. When his father remarried and took his wife to Australia, we all recognized Idris's right to remain here.

"Our home is Castell Craig. There have always been Caradogs there. If a Caradog woman changes her name in marriage her eldest child reverts to the family name. No one questions it. It has always been so."

Rhonwen was relieved that the gloom hid her eyes, which she felt must blaze with excitement at having found the one family of which Beatrice had kept records. Yet she would be cautious. Her mother had not hidden herself and her child for nothing.

"It must be wonderful to know your whole family history," she exclaimed. She had spoken without thought, driven by an almost obsessive desire to belong to someone.

But Cristin accepted her declaration without question, and she felt the intense pride that her remark generated. "Wonderful? Yes, it could be called that. I have always known my ancestry. I have a sense of security, of continuity, which I value. I can trace my family back far in time and always we have been connected with Castell Craig. There were Caradogs on this land long before the castle was built and that is centuries old. My home means more to me than ever you could imagine, Miss Morgan, and one day it will all be mine in truth."

"That must make you very happy," said Rhonwen.

It was doubtful if he noticed her reply. He seemed to have forgotten her except as someone to whom to direct his spoken thoughts. "Castell Craig will be mine. Always it has been willed to the eldest child of the family. There is no entail. It has never been needed. No one would break with tradition—no one! I know everything about my family. There was Gwenfrewi, daughter of Ynyr, who, hearing that her father and brothers were killed fighting the English, led her men into battle. She met and loved Gwgan, who was also slain, and she bore him a child out of wedlock but she did not lose her pride, and her son became master of Castell Craig."

Cristin seemed to recollect himself with a start. "I beg your pardon, Miss Morgan. Illegitimacy is scarcely a conventional subject for a young lady's ears."

"It is of no consequence," replied Rhonwen. She felt apprehensive. That baby born long ago to a warrior woman might be a source of pride to the Caradogs, but nowadays people followed the patterns of behaviour set by the virtuous Queen Victoria, and she did not doubt that they viewed the birth of a child outside of marriage with abhorrence. She had best continue to keep her enquiries into her birth a secret from everyone.

Almost as if he sensed her fears Cristin said, "Will you dig and delve until you discover your origins? That is an occupation that does not always pay dividends. What if you should find something undesirable? You would be better off not knowing if your mother had escaped from some unpleasantness."

Rhonwen looked sharply at him. He kept his eyes ahead, and she saw that the jutting Caradog nose did indeed give him a resemblance to Bryn. "Perhaps you know something of my mother," she said bluntly.

He smiled pleasantly at her. "No, I do not, though I would help you if I was able. It is only that I have heard of people who have discovered things about their heritage they would sooner have left uncovered. My advice is to think well before you continue your search."

They had reached an old stone bridge spanning the river. The forest was changing character, the stunted oaks giving place to tall beeches, which tossed down golden leaves in the sighing wind. It was quiet and growing dark and Rhonwen gave a small shiver. "You sound very solemn, sir! Are you positive you have not heard of my mother? Her name was Beatrice Morgan."

She could not see Cristin's face clearly, but after a moment he gave her the smile that curved his narrow lips and relieved the severity of his classically handsome features. "The name of

Morgan is common in Wales, but I will enquire of the servants. Someone may have knowledge of her."

He removed his hat and bowed. "It seems unlikely that we shall meet again, but I will send a message to the forge if necessary. I take it that you will spend a few days there."

He swung himself on his horse, dug his heels into its sides and almost immediately drew rein. "Wait a moment! I have remembered a path on the other bank that will get you back more swiftly. If you cross the bridge you will arrive at the inn before dark. Goodbye, Miss Morgan."

She watched him go, the sound of hooves drowned in the rush of water over mossy stones, then looked about her at the gloom of the woods and across the Artro where open meadows still retained the red and gold of late sunlight. Again she shivered and wished she had brought her shawl; then, with sudden decision, she walked over the bridge and took a well-defined path.

She crossed the meadows, gritting her teeth as she passed a herd of cows. She had not realised that they were so big, but they showed only a passing interest in her before they returned to tug at the lush grass. Following the path along the river she began to pick her way between scattered bushes and reedy grass, her town-bred senses failing to warn her that such vegetation concealed shallow swamps. She was startled when she squelched into spongy ground, her boots sometimes sinking so deep that the water seeped through. As she struggled on she wondered how long it was since Cristin Caradog had walked this path. With relief she left the wet ground and trod warily over tangled roots until she found herself in thick forest, where her sodden feet could find little purchase on the carpet of slippery leaves. A sudden movement from a small furry animal made her cry out as she slipped and sat heavily in a muddy patch. Fuming, she rose and pushed on, feeling that she must by now be nearer the inn than the bridge and wondering why she had been directed to a path that was like an obstacle course. At last she came upon open ground beyond which she saw the lights of the inn in a welcoming yellow glow.

Figures moved in the rooms, and she decided that somehow she must contrive to reach her room before she was seen in such a sorry mess. She scraped mud from her shoes in the grass,

entered the door of the inn and was halfway across the hall
when a burst of male laughter made her pause. She raised her
soaking skirts and fled towards the stairs as a door opened and
a man, still looking behind him and laughing, came out and
collided with her.

She almost fell and he grabbed her, apologising anxiously.
"Forgive me, please, ma'am. I am exceedingly sorry . . . I was
not looking . . ."

Red with embarrassment, Rhonwen put up a hand to tuck
strands of hair under her hat and saw too late that she must have
left streaks of mud on her face. She looked at the man and could
have wept with mortification. Bryn Caradog! It was beginning
to seem as if any meeting with a member of this family could
end only in trouble.

"Well, if it isn't my mysterious lady from the train." His dark
eyes swept over her. "What have you been up to now? Kittens
do not generally care for water and certainly not for mud."

"Take your hands from me, pray, and I will go to my room.
I had a slight accident."

He allowed his hands to fall to his sides as he asked, "Did
not Mrs. Jones warn you before you left? You should not have
ventured to leave the road. Clearly you have done so."

His voice was grave but his eyes sparkled with mischief, and
Rhonwen's anger overcame discretion. "I would not have, sir,
had your own brother not suggested it."

All mirth was wiped from his face. "My brother? What has
he done to you?"

"He pointed out a short cut. I suppose he meant to be help-
ful, but never have I known such a path. When next you see
him, you might tell him to think before he gives his advice in
future."

Bryn stared at her. "I hadn't realised how very pretty you
are, even with mud on your nose."

"I would much prefer you to keep your opinion of me to
yourself." But her tone lacked conviction. He and his brother
seemed subject to bewildering changes of mood, and now
Rhonwen was caught by the admiration in his eyes. In a feminine gesture, her hand went to her head and he grinned.

"Have you the courage to look in that mirror while I watch?"

She paused, then walked firmly across the hall and stared at herself. Immediately she wished she had not accepted his challenge. Her hair had escaped from its severe bun and hung in damp tails from beneath her hat. Her face was dirty, and as she tore a handkerchief from her pocket, she saw a scratch on the back of her hand. She looked down at herself, then back in the mirror, to find Bryn beside her so that their eyes met in their reflected images. His were filled with amusement, and she was abruptly overtaken by an awareness of her ludicrous appearance. Laughter gurgled in her throat and became overpowering, and together they gave way to helpless mirth. Then the weeks of worry and strain began to take their toll and hysteria threatened until she leaned against the man beside her while tears coursed down her cheeks, making rivulets in the grime.

With surprising gentleness Bryn took out his own large handkerchief and wiped her eyes. "Poor little lost girl," he said, softly. "Go to your room and wash and change, and I will wait here for you. Perhaps you will do me the honour of dining with me. After all, I think we may consider ourselves introduced."

Chapter 4

RHONWEN STOOD in her petticoat and stared at her two remaining gowns before reaching for the grey poplin, regretting that she had nothing pretty to wear on her first engagement with a man. She was so nervous that her hands shook as she fastened the row of tiny pearl buttons that continued into the high collar. Then she sat before the mirror and brushed her hair until it gleamed like fire in the candlelight. She wished she had experience in dressing hair as she pulled it back and wound it into coils at the nape of her neck, for once allowing two errant curls to remain loose about her ears. She toyed with the idea of wearing the gold locket from her mother's box but decided against it. Until she knew more about her legacy she had best keep it a secret.

Bryn rose to greet her.

"My congratulations, madam. You have made me wait an astonishingly short time—and how pretty you look."

He pulled out her chair from the table laid for two, and she seated herself as if used to such attentions all her life. Bryn sat opposite her.

"I have asked Mrs. Jones to serve our meal here in the parlour as I felt sure you would not wish to brave the stares of the folk in the public rooms. Everyone is speculating as to whom you might be, Miss Morgan. You see, I have learned your name. You must be of Welsh descent. I wonder if I know your people."

"I shouldn't think so," declared Rhonwen, "but I have learned that you are a member of an old established family from a very large house in the hills. I asked your brother if he knew of my mother and he said he did not."

"I suppose that settles it then. Of course, the name of Morgan is not exactly uncommon in Wales."

He was laughing at her, but she did not mind. She felt at ease with him as she might have with a brother or cousin.

The meal was ordered, and they sipped creamy sherry as they waited.

"Tell me," said Bryn, moving his glass so that the wine spun in amber gleams, "did my brother give you a warning before you left the road today?"

"A warning?" She was startled, remembering Cristin's curious air of watchfulness. "Of what should he warn me?"

"Of the inconveniences of the path. What else?"

"Oh! No, he did not. He told me I should arrive back at the inn quicker."

"My brother often means well. I daresay he might not have walked that track since he was in knickerbockers. If ever he rides it he would not notice its imperfections. We must give him the benefit of the doubt, Miss Morgan."

"What doubt? Why should he have sent me that way with any ulterior motive?"

"I cannot answer that! I should advise him not to recommend the path to any other female on foot, but he would not listen. My brother, Cristin, is a man who takes advice from no one."

Rhonwen sipped her wine and felt it trickle down her throat to warm her stomach. It was delicious, and she wondered why Beatrice had so often railed against the evils of drink. Clearly there was no harm in a glass of wine. Or even two or three, she decided, as the meal progressed. The wine was changed with each course, and Rhonwen enjoyed every morsel of mutton chops with thyme, apple pie with sweet crumbly pastry, and cheese. She drank hock and madeira and even a glass of port. Bryn talked to her of Castell Craig, and she sensed that his love for his home held a different quality from Cristin's. It seemed to stem from his belief that the land was held in trust for all those who worked it and not from the power of possession. Yet, in spite of the wine, she retained her grip on her resolve to keep the secret of the box until she judged the time ready for confidences.

It was not until she rose at the end of the meal that she realised with horror that her legs seemed to have no muscles and she had to put a hand on the table to steady herself as the room dipped and swayed. She looked at Bryn, who was grinning wickedly.

"How many times have you had wine?"

"N . . . never before," she confessed.

At that he laughed aloud and she giggled before putting a hand over her mouth to stem such an unladylike sound.

"You little idiot, you should have told me you were unused to alcohol."

But he still smiled as he put a strong hand beneath her arm and led her to a fireside chair where a cheerful glow kept away the autumn damp.

"Sit still, Miss Morgan, while I order quantities of coffee. I shall remain here until I know you will not disgrace yourself before Mrs. Jones."

He turned at the door.

"You are not safe to be let out alone, you know. Has no one warned you of what could happen to runaway girls who fall into the clutches of men who ply them with strong drink?"

His chuckle lingered in the air and Rhonwen smiled, feeling instinctively that with Bryn Caradog she was safe. She wondered fleetingly how Cristin might have behaved in similar circumstances.

That night she made a vow to take wine with caution, and the following morning found her endorsing it heartily as she sat up in bed and held a hand over her eyes. Strong tea did much to restore her, and after breakfast she took a seat in the dog cart sent by Mary Evans and driven by her second son, a slim four-teen-year-old who introduced himself as David.

He seemed as bashful as his father and answered Rhonwen's attempts at conversation with such brevity that she lapsed into silence and sat back to enjoy the journey. Her mind wandered to memories of the previous evening. Bryn had ordered her to drink her coffee black and laughed at her grimace of dislike.

"Next time I should be more circumspect where wine is concerned," he advised.

"There is to be a next time, is there?" asked Rhonwen, then flushed as she realised how horribly flirtatious she sounded.

But Bryn seemed to understand that she had lost her hold on her inhibitions and he merely bowed and said, "I should be honoured, of course, though, when you have had your fill of the Rhinogs, I daresay you will move on—or maybe return to your home. You should, you know."

Rhonwen chose to ignore his last remark.

"The Rhinogs, Mr. Caradog? What are they?"

"Rhinog Fawr and Rhinog Fach, which tower over the mountains like guardian giants. My ancestors chose to build their home between the two peaks, the foundations rising from the living rock. Castell Craig grows from the very body of the mountains."

Rhonwen looked at him enviously. When he and his brother spoke of their home, she sensed their passionate pride. It made her lonely and very conscious of being excluded from an experience she had no way of comprehending. Bryn recollected her presence and begged her pardon for allowing his enthusiasm to outstrip his manners.

"I fear I wax lyrical when I talk of Castell Craig. It is the one thing I have in common with Cristin . . ."

He stopped abruptly and looked at his watch. "Are you feeling better now? The hour grows late, and I must not keep you longer from your bed. I daresay you retire far earlier than this in the normal way."

Perhaps the wine had loosened his tongue, too, for he startled her by demanding, "Just how old are you?"

"I am eighteen, sir, and where I lived that was considered entirely adult. Most of the girls around me earned their living much younger."

Bryn's brows had risen. "You persist in your assertion that you spring from humble origins. You know, Miss Morgan, if you are set upon a life of independence you must not underestimate the people you meet. Everything about you, save your clothes, points to a delicate upbringing. Will you not confide in me and allow me to contact your family, who must be exceedingly worried about you?"

"You are mistaken, Mr. Caradog. There is no one."

"I see. Well, have it your own way."

She knew he was disappointed in her, and she felt disproportionately sad. She had an urge to reveal the contents of her mother's box and ask his advice, but innate caution kept her silent. Bryn, who had been watching her face intently, made a small grimace.

"Well, I cannot force you to speak. Off to bed then. Young ladies like their beauty sleep though, to be sure, you have no need of such a commodity."

The conversation had taken a frivolous turn, which she regretted.

"I am speaking the truth, you know. I wish I had a place of which I could be proud. You are very fortunate."

If only he would invite her to his home. She had a powerful inner conviction that someone there must be able to help her discover her origins, else why should her mother have preserved a childish drawing for so many years? It crossed her mind briefly that she could try to inveigle him into issuing an invitation; then she felt shame at her boldness and simply thanked him politely for the meal and retired.

Now, as she was drawn up the hills by the sturdy mountain cob, she considered the possibility of obtaining a post as a domestic in the castle. At the same time she recognised how few skills she had. Women's lives were so restricted. A picture of Tana Peach came to her mind and she yearned for her mother, who had been such a stalwart shield.

David pulled on the reins and gave a command in Welsh to the pony, and they turned into the village and stopped outside the blacksmith's cottage where Mary Evans was waiting. She greeted Rhonwen with a welcoming smile and showed her to a tiny bedroom with a sloping ceiling. The room contained a window giving a view of the river and the woods beyond stretching up the mountainside.

"You'll be cosy here, won't you? I thought you'd prefer a little place and bed on your own rather than share with one of the girls."

"How thoughtful you are," exclaimed Rhonwen, and Mrs. Evans looked pleased.

"I'll leave you then to get settled in. Here's David with your bag."

Left alone, Rhonwen looked about her. The room was too

small to contain much furniture, but the oak bed was covered with a blue quilt, and the blue and white curtains blowing in the soft, sweet smelling breeze matched the china on the white marble washstand. A bamboo table stood beside the bed, and someone had filled a vase with sprays of scarlet-berried twigs and glossy, dark green leaves. Rhonwen sank into the basket-work easy chair, plumping up the cushion at her back, and exhaled her breath in a long sigh as contentment washed over her. Mary Evans was clearly a woman who considered the well-being of those about her. Rhonwen felt she could have stayed forever, relaxing in the bright room, until the memory of the Caradog brothers and the growing conviction that somehow they could be connected with her mother's past made her stir uneasily.

She washed her hands and face in the soft Welsh water and descended to the kitchen where Mary greeted her with a smile. The sounds of hammering came from the forge, and the kitchen was filled with baking smells.

"There you are then, Miss Morgan. Will you be wanting me to make you up a packet of food?"

She chuckled at Rhonwen's look of surprise.

"You have come to walk in the hills, haven't you?"

Rhonwen perched on the edge of the settle and looked at Mrs. Evans, who was giving her a searching stare.

"In a way, I suppose; but I think you have guessed that I have another reason for wanting to be here."

Mary slid her hands into the flour and fat in the earthenware bowl and began to crumble the mix in experienced fingers.

"Let us just say that I find you an unusual sort of holiday-maker. You speak ever so nicely and your manners are an example for us all, but your clothes and boots are as plain as can be and both have repairs and patches, if you'll pardon my plain speaking. I daresay you are not above nineteen or so, and it's only human nature to wonder what you are about on our wild Welsh mountains."

Rhonwen watched as Mary lifted the dough to a floured board and began to roll it with a water-filled glass rolling pin. It would be such a relief to confide in someone, at least partially. She said cautiously, "I am here for a definite purpose, Mrs. Evans."

Keeping her voice as even as possible she explained how her mother had died, and Mary stopped work as she expressed her sympathy.

"Poor lamb! I should not badger you with questions. Don't go on, if you'd rather not."

But, having begun, Rhonwen found the relief of talking more than she could resist. She told Mary, without going into detail, that she had found papers among her mother's belongings that had led her to Glyn Dedwydd and Castell Craig.

"So you see," she finished, "it's all very simple really. I just want to belong somewhere—to someone."

"And very natural, too," agreed Mary. "If we can help in any way, please tell us."

She put her pastry into a deep dish and began to peel and slice apples.

"You say you've had no training for work." She tutted. "I wonder your mam kept you so ignorant, knowing you would have to earn a living. But maybe the poor soul had a notion of telling you of your folk and was called by the Lord before she had time. It never does to put things off. Not one of us knows the day of our passing."

She spooned sugar over the apples and covered them with dough, and glanced at Rhonwen's intent face. "You seem very interested in what I'm doing."

"I've never seen anyone bake a pie before."

Mary stopped work to stare in astonishment. "And your mam was a cook!"

"Well, we had only the fire to simmer our soup or boil a kettle. If we wanted meat we took it to the local baker's oven. Poor folk do that in London. And we bought his pastries or Mother brought some from her place of work."

"Well, I never! There's a lot you need to learn. I've been wondering—my Megan is going away and I'll miss her sadly. Would you like to stay in her place and I'll teach you about housekeeping? Marged admires you, and if she saw you working about the house she might be more biddable, and if you prove apt you could find work in a kitchen. Perhaps at Castell Craig. They employ dozens of servants up there. Of course I wouldn't be taking rent from you if you helped me."

Rhonwen felt tears sting the backs of her eyes at the Welsh

woman's generosity, but since she knew she would be of little use at first, she insisted on paying towards her board and reluctantly Mary agreed.

"To be sure I like your spirit. Now when my man comes in from the forge we'll ask him if he's heard of your mother. I wasn't reared in these parts. I met Owen in Barmouth when we were both sixteen. I was a nursery maid on holiday with the children, and he had come to the local fair with his father, who was there to pull teeth." Mary laughed. "You look amazed. It's a regular thing for the smith to cure the toothache. Da-in-law took out the two from this gap here."

When Mary asked Owen about Beatrice, he finished drying his hands at the sink then rubbed his chin.

"I do seem to recall something about a female servant who disappeared suddenly from the big house. It was a year or so before we were married. There was a mystery about it at the time, but I was a heedless lad and took no thought of what my elders talked of."

At Rhonwen's disappointed look he frowned in an effort to think. "I've got an idea. There's old Mervyn Parry—he is still head gardener at the big house." He grinned. "He's a terrible trial to the young gardeners, so I've heard, making them do everything just as it's always been and never changing the garden one bit. Miss Edwina doesn't want change, he says. And there's his wife, Sophy—now she might be best to ask, for she was head housemaid until her rheumatics got so bad she couldn't work."

"She sound ideal," said Rhonwen excitedly. "Where might I find her?"

"That's not so easy. She lives with Mervyn in a cottage on the Caradog Estate right up in the hills. Miss Caradog looks after her well and sends servants every day to clean the cottage and make Sophy comfortable. Aye, and she pays the doctor's bills. A good woman is Edwina Caradog."

At Rhonwen's crestfallen look Mary said, "All the more reason for you to learn some housewifely skills and maybe you'll get taken on as a maid."

She explained briefly to her husband, who nodded slowly. "Very glad to have you, Miss Morgan. Marged will likely pester you with questions about London, but I have no doubts you will answer her in a fitting way."

Rhonwen slipped easily into the life in the blacksmith's cottage and was soon treated as a member of the family. She learned to make pastry light enough to fool the others into believing it came from Mary's delicate touch. She made the oatcakes that Owen liked to eat with his morning bacon, and Teisen Fel, the honey cake, golden brown with points of meringue. She mixed good furniture polish and enjoyed using it on the solid oak furniture until it shone like glass; she blended lavender and herbs into sachets for the linen cupboards. The busy days among the loving family soothed her sorrow and gave her dreamless nights, and she would have known absolute contentment if it were not for the nagging need to continue her quest for her beginnings.

September yielded to October. The heather made purple splashes of colour among the bracken, which was turning brown in the autumn sun. The date of Megan's marriage was growing near, and she and her mother spent hours with their heads bent over sewing machine and needle as they added to the growing pile of underwear and bridal clothes and put finishing touches to sheets, pillow slips and tablecloths.

Owen laughed at them indulgently.

"There must be linen enough in the Pugh house. Why do you need so much more?"

Mary said, tossing her head indignantly, "Our girl will not be going to her wedding in a state that will give the neighbours talk. When all the gifts and linen are laid out in the parlour, our Megan will have cause for pride."

Rhonwen was able now to relieve Mary of many tasks, and one day when Megan and her mother were upstairs fitting the wedding gown, she stood at the wide kitchen table, her slender form enveloped in one of Mary's aprons, and plunged her hands into floury bread dough and began to knead.

A sound made her glance up and she saw Bryn Caradog. He was leaning against the open door, the sun striking blue gleams from his black hair, his teeth white in his tanned face as he grinned at her.

"Do you always cover your nose with whatever you happen to be near, Miss Morgan? Last time we met it was mud. I confess I care more for flour."

Rhonwen felt a flash of irritation.

"I do not think it gentlemanly of you to watch me without making your presence known, Mr. Caradog. I would have thought you had been taught better manners."

He was unabashed.

"Oh, I was very well taught; but one has more amusement if manners are sometimes set aside. Do not you agree?"

She did not answer and continued to knead with increased vigour so that Bryn laughed softly.

"Is it my head you imagine you have under your hands?"

"I have more to do than worry about you, sir. Megan will be wed a week from now."

"I thought you were here on a little holiday. Did you dispense with the plan?"

Rhonwen pulled the edges of the dough to the middle and continued her kneading before she said, "I do not recall telling you I was on holiday."

Bryn threw up his hand.

"*Touché!* You did not. I was trying to extract information. You must admit that it piques the curiosity when a gently reared girl appears in a remote corner of Wales and settles into a life of servitude in a family that for all their goodness, must be inferior to her own."

"I wish you would rid yourself of the notion that I am a runaway from—"

"From what?"

"From nothing, sir."

The entrance of Marged brought the conversation to a close. Her respectful curtsey and immediate offer to bring refreshment suddenly emphasised the gulf between Rhonwen and the Evans family. Beatrice had reared her in a way that made her proudly different, and she felt desolate as she recognised that there could be no place in which she felt entirely at home. Her loneliness must have shown in her face, for Bryn's mocking tones were gone as he said, "Forgive me for teasing you. People who know me would tell you that I am exceedingly polite with those I do not like."

Marged came from the pantry with ginger beer so cold that mist formed on the glass. As Bryn drank with relish, she fetched her mother, who hurried in, her print gown stuck with a whole row of pins and a threaded needle in her hand.

"Good day to you, Mr. Bryn. Marged has given you a drink? As you see, we are very busy. Megan . . ."

". . . is soon to be wed," he finished. "That is one reason I am here. Cousin Edwina has sent a gift and best wishes for the future happiness of the bride and groom."

He went out and returned with a box into which Megan came and delved. She lifted out a brass oil lamp with a delicate green glass shade at which the women exclaimed in admiration.

"There's something else," cried Marged as she rustled through the quantities of tissue paper and produced a dressing table set of black *papier-mâché,* the tray and boxes inlaid with delicate shells and semiprecious stones and exquisitely painted in shades of red and gold.

Megan looked close to tears as Marged said with satisfaction, "There's nothing so fine in all Harlech, I'll be bound. Megan, you'll be the envy of everyone."

Mary tutted at her daughter's boastful speech, but she couldn't give much of a reproof when her own pride was written plain on her face. Rhonwen saw how Bryn could look unreservedly happy at the delight of others before he caught her glance and his dark eyes grew watchful and teasing.

The wedding day dawned in a light mist that gave promise of the sun to follow. A large and spirited party of family and guests saw Megan walk up the aisle of the local Methodist chapel attended by her sister. Owen Evans looked unfamiliar and ill at ease in a suit of black worsted and a stiff white wing collar, which threatened to burst as the muscles in his throat flexed with nervous swallows. After a short but moving ceremony, Megan and Howell Pugh left the chapel as man and wife, and the strains of the small organ followed them as they led the company to the smith's cottage where trestles had been set out under the trees.

Small boys employed to swish away insects now reaped their reward as they shared in hams and tomatoes, many kinds of bread piled beside the rich butter and cheeses, buttered parsnips, cold roast beef, bowls of apples and nectarines, and got their ears cuffed good humouredly as they tried to take surreptitious swigs at the ale.

The health of the newly wed pair was drunk, and Megan,

looking flushed and pretty in a gown of white and a hat adorned with cherries and ribbons, was driven away by a bashful, grinning groom in the gig that was the gift of the bride's parents to her new home above the draper's shop in Harlech.

The atmosphere grew flat as the gig disappeared from the village street. Many guests drifted indoors to have a second look at the array of gifts. Rhonwen sank into a chair beneath a beech tree and closed her eyes for a moment. When she opened them, she found Bryn Caradog watching her. She sat up hastily, smoothing the folds of her grey poplin and straightening her unfashionable grey felt bonnet that she had enlivened with clusters of lilac taffeta ribbon.

"So you are still here."

"As you perceive and correctly point out, I am still here," countered Rhonwen shortly.

"You must find the Evan's menage very inviting. And, of course, it is a good place to hide. Who would think of searching for a young lady in the cottage of a mountain blacksmith?"

"I am not trying to hide," said Rhonwen a little wearily, for the hard work of the past days was beginning to take its toll.

"You are tired! Are they working you too hard? I daresay you are unused to manual toil."

She did not vouchsafe an answer, and as a fiddler struck up a lively tune, Bryn smiled.

"I came only to wish Godspeed to the happy couple, but I have a mind to stay for the dancing—that is, if you will do me the honour."

She ignored his outstretched arm.

"Do not let me detain you, sir. As it happens dancing was not one of the accomplishments Mother saw fit to have me learn."

Bryn looked exaggeratedly amazed.

"Well, Miss Morgan, that does give me fodder for thought. I believed that all young ladies must know how to dance."

"This one does not."

"Nevertheless, I beg you to take the floor—or rather the grass—with me!"

The musician was well away, his arm and fingers flying, and most of the young people and some of the older were whirling among the remnants of dead leaves left behind when the grass was swept by birch brooms. Rhonwen's feet were twitching in time to the music, but she made a last reluctant protest.

"I'll make a fool of myself out there."

"Impossible! They'll dance the waltz and the polka, and all you need remember is three steps for one and four for the other."

She took his arm and they joined the dancers. Rhonwen forgot she was tired as she discovered a talent for rythmic, graceful movement, and she and Bryn danced until the last couple left the grassy patch and the musician took his well-earned payment and began his walk to Llanbedr.

Owen, his shirt sleeves rolled up and his collar unfastened, began to take in the lamps while Tomos picked up and folded the heavy trestles as if they had been toys and stacked them ready to return to the chapel hall. Mary and her friends bustled about carrying dishes to the was house where David was stoking the fire and ladling gallons of steaming water into copper tubs for the washing up. Marged, her eyes still shining, her daffodil-yellow gown wilting a little, helped carry the remaining food to the pantry; children ran about, shrieking their appreciation at still being up and about long after bedtime.

As the youngsters were collected and carried protestingly away, Bryn and Rhonwen stood beneath the beech tree and watched the half-bare branches swaying against the rising moon. Rhonwen said dreamily, " 'When it is evening, ye say, it will be fair weather: for the sky is red'."

"That sounds quite biblical, Miss Morgan."

"It should, for it is."

"You do not strike me as being particularly religious."

"Indeed! And how does my behaviour lead you to such a conclusion?"

Rhonwen saw the flash of Bryn's teeth in the moonlight that was beginning to flood the earth with blue light.

"You have a most disconcerting way of picking up the things I say and demanding explanations. Young ladies should have a supply of flirtatious chatter with which to beguile a man."

Rhonwen disregarded his invitation to flirt and said, "Mother had a fund of quotes from what she termed the Good Book, though she did not attend chapel."

She forgot her surroundings and saw Beatrice as she attempted to instil a sense of an all-powerful God into her daughter. Yet after the episode of the swimming in the park Beatrice had withdrawn her from the Sunday School. She had been an enigma—at one moment embracing a code of conduct as rigid as it was extreme, at another capitulating to an over-indulgence in drink and laughing at Ida Blake's irreverent jests in a way that was entirely at odds with her expressed ideals of good conduct. Rhonwen felt a sudden despair that now she never could come closer to her mother and perhaps discover the loving woman she had dimly sensed, and her eyes and throat ached with distress.

Bryn looked into her face and said gently, "I am sorry, my dear girl. It was not my intention to seem to be critical of you or your mother. Say you pardon me."

"There is nothing to pardon. I am tired, that is all."

Bryn took a step nearer and grasped her hand, and Rhonwen took comfort from his compassion. He said very quietly, "So we are friends, are we not? I should like to think so."

"Indeed we are."

"And to seal the bargain will you come to my home to dinner one night? You will like my Cousin Edwina, I feel sure, and she could not but help taking to you."

Rhonwen barely suppressed the impulse to clutch at Bryn's hand in her surprised gratification. An invitation to Castell Craig was more than she had hoped for. She withdrew her hand, ostensibly to smooth her hair, for she had thrown aside her bonnet an hour ago. She felt that if she allowed Bryn to continue to touch her he must sense her inner elation.

"I am happy to accept, sir."

"Good! Then that is settled, and one week from today I shall come down and fetch you."

Rhonwen waited while Bryn took his leave of Owen and Mary and watched as he mounted his horse and trotted through the village. He gave her a last wave then was lost to view as he turned into the road that led him home.

Chapter 5

MARY REFUSED any help from Rhonwen that night.

"Away with you," she ordered. "You look tired out. I daresay you are not yet over the shocks of the past weeks."

Other women, aprons over their best dresses, arms deep in soapsuds or carefully wiping the china and glass that had come from every village cupboard for Megan's wedding, smiled sympathetically and nodded agreement.

Rhonwen felt suddenly unbearably weary as she climbed to her small room. She leaned for a moment at the window, her head on the white wall, allowing the cool breeze to waft over her hot face, before she shivered and, undressing quickly, made her way to bed.

It must have been the excessive excitement of the day combined with fatigue that brought the dream, for she had not experienced it since arriving at Glyn Dedwydd. She awoke with the familiar feeling of terror, her heart pounding in her throat, and reached automatically for her mother before remembering that Beatrice was dead. She lay drawing deep breaths to regain calm, the muted light from the dawning autumn sun slanting across her bed. The small, but insistent, doubt she had as to the wisdom of an unmarried girl accepting the invitation of a bachelor without a card from the senior woman of his family was drowned in her need to unravel the mystery that gripped at her in such unreasoning urgency.

Mary Evans had no such doubts.

"You don't mean to tell me you said you'd go! Well, I heard

that you'd dined with Mr. Bryn in the village . . ." She stopped, a flood of colour deepening the pink of her cheeks. "I'm sorry, bach; that sounds as if I've been gossiping. But nothing happens in these parts without everyone knowing, and I was sure the moment I set eyes on you that you were a good girl. But you don't even know if Miss Caradog will be at her home."

"Don't be angry with me, Mary. If I wait to hear from Miss Caradog I shall wait forever, for she knows nothing of me, and I must get to the castle. Please understand."

Marged entered, carrying a pile of freshly laundered table linen. "Where are the lavender bags, Mam?" She stopped, eyeing them suspiciously. "You are not quarrelling, are you?"

"Indeed we are not," declared her mother. "We have a little difference of opinion, that is all."

Rhonwen bit her lip. She knew that Mary must be thinking of the improvement in Marged since her arrival. She had seen that a young lady like Miss Morgan had embraced housekeeping with zeal and decided that it was not, after all, such a boring occupation. For Rhonwen to go against Mary's opinion might upset Marged, and after the Evans family's generosity she could not put their daughter's new-found contentment in jeopardy.

"Don't worry, Marged. You mother was giving me good advice, which I shall take."

Mary's look of gratitude almost compensated her for her sacrifice, and she was even happier that she had submitted when, later in the day, a groom came bearing a card from Miss Caradog requesting the company of Miss Morgan at dinner. She thought Mary would be as relieved as herself and was surprised when the Welsh woman still appeared doubtful.

"Rhonwen, have you considered that if you go as a guest to the castle you will scarcely be able to apply for a post as a maid later on?"

"I expect you're right," agreed Rhonwen, "but I have no guarantee that I would be taken on. This could be my only opportunity to speak with Sophy Parry."

Mary shook her head. "I don't see how you'll get a chance to visit Sophy. What excuse could you give for wanting to leave the dinner party?"

At Rhonwen's despairing look she continued, "I have an idea that might work. Sophy has a weakness for my Teisen Lap—

that's a fruity plate cake—and an even bigger one for my Cowslip wine. You shall take some of each to the castle, and it may get you into her cottage."

"Miss Edwina is a good soul. She never leaves the castle grounds nowadays, but she remembers the village folk. I saw her once, long ago, at the funeral of the old rector, and she had such a sadness in her eyes, the kind that lives in people's hearts. I daresay she knows of your recent bereavement and thinks the invitation a kindly gesture on Mr. Bryn's part."

Marged's eyes opened wide when she saw the card. "What will you wear?" she asked simply.

Mary tutted at her daughter's preoccupation with such material considerations, but she was feminine enough to admit that Rhonwen had no suitable gown. So the following morning found Rhonwen and Mary sitting side by side in the rear of the dog cart, their backs to Tomos, who handled the reins with skill and who was full of smiles as he caught the excitment of two ladies about to spend time poring over fashion. His black eyes had lingered on Rhonwen as he helped her mount the step, and his smile had grown sweeter. Mary said beneath the covering sound of the wheels as they rumbled over the rough tracks, "He's taken a regular liking to you. You'll not be nervous of him, will you? He's more child than man, and he's never harmed a living creature."

She chuckled. "My mother-in-law used to laugh as she told of the day my Owen's father went to the orphan asylum to fetch home a sturdy lad to help him in the forge and arrived back with as skinny and pale a ten-year-old as she'd ever seen because he felt sorry for him. She gave her husband the length of her tongue, but she grumbled even more when the poor man offered to return him to the asylum. She couldn't help giving love to the skinny little waif and, after being fed good victuals, he turned out as strong as an ox and a loyal servant."

Rhonwen enjoyed the journey over the mountain roads, drinking in the beauty of rugged crags, heather and grassland, streams and waterfalls, and as they approached Harlech, she exclaimed at the glimpses of the sea, glinting blue and white as it rolled towards the flatlands and dunes that had pushed it back from the old castle, whose walls had once been sea-girt.

Megan was delighted to see them in the shop. She showed

her happiness and pride in her new status as she dispensed tea and tiny home-baked cakes in the parlour as they studied the fashion magazines before going into the front to choose material. Rhonwen decided on a pattern of a simple sheath gown and bought slate-grey velveteen, grey brocade for pleats at the hem, and pale, dove-coloured lace for trimming.

"Such ordinary colours," mourned Marged," and a V-shaped neck that is almost high, and *long* sleeves. When I am allowed a party frock I shall buy emerald-green satin and have a gown like no one has ever seen before."

Mary's eyes met Rhonwen's in amusement.

"Rhonwen needs something she can use again, young lady. Invitations to Castell Craig are unlikely to come again for her, and for you, never."

Each evening until the dinner party Mary, Rhonwen and Marged stitched busily, and Rhonwen was very conscious of the kindness of her new friends. Megan had even insisted that she borrow her white satin wedding boots, refusing to listen to Rhonwen's protests.

"You cannot go to the castle in your old black ones, now can you, love?" she said. "And you said yourself you can't afford to spend money on anything but strong footwear."

When Rhonwen was dressed and waiting for Bryn, all three were delighted by the results of their work. Marged clasped her hands.

"It's beautiful you look, Rhonwen. I never supposed that plain colours could make up so well. When you move, the velveteen shines like . . . like the rain on the roof, and it makes your head look more gold than red."

Mary produced a necklace of tiny lavender-coloured beads she had entwined with purple anemones, and Rhonwen sat while the little Welsh woman brushed her hair before she drew it back into shining coils secured by the homemade ornament.

"If only your mother could see you," exclaimed Marged, then blushed fiery red. "Oh, I'm so sorry. I could cut out my clumsy tongue."

"It is perfectly all right," comforted Rhonwen. "I wish she were alive to see me."

'But if she had not died I would not be here,' she thought, assailed suddenly by the welter of sensations that memory of her mother released. Her childish embraces had often been repulsed, yet sometimes Beatrice had held her so close she could hardly breathe, smoothing her hair, kissing her face, murmuring in Welsh and looking so distraught that Rhonwen was afraid.

When Bryn arrived he looked very different from the casually dressed man she knew. His open, calf-length ulster revealed that his muscular shoulders were clothed in immaculate black superfine, beneath which he wore a plain white waistcoat topped with a white wing collar and black bow tie. He raised his hat to Rhonwen with a flourish and bowed.

"Your coach awaits you, ma'am. Well, figuratively speaking. As my ancestors chose to build in such a high place, consideration for our horses impels us to drive only light vehicles. I trust you will not find a hooded gig below your dignity."

He led the way to where David held the head of a spirited looking pony and assisted her into the gig. His dark eyes swept over her and lingered for a moment on her uncovered head and softly flushed face.

She smoothed the skirts of her velveteen dress to avoid creases before she sat, and as Bryn swung himself up beside her and signalled David to release the horse's bit, she said, "I should not find any form of private transport beneath me, sir, when I have been used to travel on omnibuses."

Bryn drove the gig along the village street, skilfully avoiding the worst of the ruts.

"Ah, yes, I keep forgetting. The privately educated lady springs from poverty."

Rhonwen decided to ignore this remark. She stared ahead as she said, "It was kind of Miss Caradog to send an invitation."

"Would you have come without one from her?"

She was glad the growing darkness hid her embarrassment but he spared her the necessity of replying.

"Mary Evans would have been scandalised, would she not, had you kept a dinner engagement with a young bacherlor in his home?"

Rhonwen kept her tone cool. "The question is irrelevant since your cousin did send me a card."

She heard his soft chuckle in the darkness. "I am willing to bet that Mrs. Evans referred to our dinner together in the village inn! I was thoughtless that night. I should have remembered that tongues would wag. You cannot sneeze in these parts without word going round that you have caught a deathly chill."

"It is of no consequence, sir. I have received nothing but kindness from Mrs. Evans and the village women."

Bryn was silent as he guided horse and gig over the stone bridge spanning the Artro.

"Let us not spar, Miss Morgan, I beg of you. That evening at the inn remains one of my happier memories. I have few good friends, but I should like to think of you as one. Shall we call a truce?"

"Gladly, Mr. Caradog."

They sat in companionable silence. Both man and horse knew the way so well that, in spite of the dark, which was little relieved by carriage lamps, they made good progress. The track grew rougher as they reached the end of the forest and began a steep ascent between boulders, which became bigger until they were driving between walls of rock. A turn in the road brought them to a sight that made Rhonwen gasp. Roofs and towers were outlined against the sky almost, it seemed, directly above their heads.

"My home," stated Bryn. "Does it look grim to you at the moment? Against a blue sky it is beautiful. Well, to me it is, anyway."

Rhonwen could not reply as her breathing became faster and her heart bumped against her ribs. Nervousness of her first invitation to a grand house was coupled with a hope that tonight she might discover part of the jigsaw of her life.

At Bryn's shout tall iron gates were opened by a lodge keeper, and they were driven between stone pillars topped by shining copper and steel lanterns. Before they reached the end of the curving driveway, a glow of light made Rhonwen lean forward, and the final bend brought her face to face with Castell Craig. After the gloom of the drive the brilliance of light streaming from mullioned windows was enhanced, and she marvelled at the lawns and flowerbeds, their perfection obvious in the glow.

She sighed, "How enchanting it is. I had not realised it would be possible to create such a garden so high in the mountains."

"My family, Miss Morgan, does not know the word impossible. They want a garden; so therefore, soil is carried up regularly from the rich lowlands and an army of gardeners tend it. It has always been so."

There was nothing boastful in his tone. He was simply stating facts, and Rhonwen became more vitally aware of the gulf between these people and a girl from one of the sleazier London districts.

Grooms came running to take the horse and gig. Bryn handed Rhonwen down and led her to the front door, which was opened by a footman, and they entered a large hall.

"Take Madam's jacket," commanded the butler unnecessarily as the footman moved to her side. Rhonwen tried to ignore its shabbiness so clearly revealed in the brightness from enough candles to last a poor family for years. She looked about her. There was too much to encompass in detail, but she saw the tessellated floor in ancient designs, the wide stairway curving gracefully to an upper gallery, the tables with vases of hot-house blooms, bric-a-brac, which she recognised instinctively as being costly as well as beautiful, and pictures, statues, velvet brocade and drapes. For miserable seconds she wished herself back in Mary and Owen's cottage; then Bryn held out his arm and she placed fingertips upon it and walked inevitably with him towards closed double doors. Perhaps he sensed her nervousness, for he paused and glanced down with a small reassuring smile before a servant threw open the doors. They were entered a room that seemed to her as unbelievably luxurious as the hall, containing a greater number of people than she had expected.

Bryn led her straight to a woman who sat in an easy chair by a bright fire.

"Here she is, Cousin Edwina. Please permit me to present Miss Rhonwen Morgan. Miss Morgan, my dear cousin."

Rhonwen took the hand held out to her.

"Welcome to Castell Craig. Bryn has told me of your late grievous loss. You have all my sympathy."

Rhonwen saw at once what Mary had meant by the sadness in Edwina Caradog's eyes. They were deep-set, brown and soft as pansies, but the welcoming smile on her pale lips did little to relieve their innate melancholy.

"Thank you for your invitation, Miss Caradog," she murmured shyly.

"It is always a pleasure to have young people about me. Bryn, introduce her to the others. Bryn's brother, Cristin, will be here soon, Miss Morgan. He has been away on business for a few days, but his train will have reached the Halt half an hour ago. You will not mind waiting a little longer for your dinner? Bryn shall give you a glass of sauterne. Such a pleasant, refreshing way to wait for a meal, I think."

Bryn's quizzical glance at Rhonwen told her that he recalled her reaction to her first experience with wine and caused her to reply to Edwina with an incoherent murmur; but the older woman smiled again, bent her head over her embroidery frame and resumed sewing with hands that looked unexpectedly strong and capable.

"Am I never to have an introduction, Bryn?"

The cool question came from a woman who reclined on a sofa near a window draped in crimson. She could not have chosen a better backdrop, and as soon as Rhonwen saw her, she knew that all her efforts at fashion had been belittled. The woman's ivory satin gown flowed about her slender figure like shining water. Her deep brown hair had been dressed in the latest style and curls graced a high white forehead. Her complexion was as clear as a child's, and the rose of her cheeks was mirrored to perfection by the pink of her pearl necklace and drop earrings.

Rhonwen needed no one to tell her that the jewels were real and costly, and the woman's dark eyes left her in no doubt that her own apparel had been priced to the last detail of the inexpensive cotton lace.

Bryn bowed. "Good evening, Frances. Allow me to introduce to you, Miss Rhonwen Morgan. Miss Morgan—Miss Frances Kendrick. Frances, Cristin and I have been playmates from our nursery days."

Frances smiled lazily. "We are too advanced in years for such a a description now, my dear Bryn. Playmates no longer, Miss Morgan."

Rhonwen gained an impression that Miss Kendrick would like to say much more. Her eyes seemed to flash a message—almost a warning. What kind of threat could she possibly be to this self-assured, obviously rich and lovely creature? Was she jealous of her relationship with Bryn? Rhonwen wished there was a way to tell her that they were simply friends.

Frances was regarding her over the rim of her glass of pale gold wine in amused contempt as she allowed her glance deliberately to sweep over Rhonwen from head to toe. For an irrational moment Rhonwen was thankful that Megan's white satin slippers peeped from beneath the hem of grey brocade before she felt a surge of irritation at Miss Kendrick's ill-mannered conduct.

Bryn next led her to a woman who was as colourless and nervous as Miss Kendrick was beautiful and self-confident. Rhonwen gathered that she was Miss Watkins, a distant relative and Frances's chaperon. Rhonwen sat on a small gilt chair and was surprised when she realised that the room contained only herself and four others, until it dawned on her that any room that held Miss Kendrick must seem overpoweringly full to a shy stranger.

There was desultory talk for a while before Bryn looked at his watch. "Are you positive Cristin is returning? I am famished."

"Patience never was one of your virtues," admonished Frances, but her smile made the rebuke sound like praise.

"I have never thought that patience in every circumstance was to be striven for," returned Bryn. "If one wants something one should go after it."

"You always were the same, even as a child," said Edwina in her gentle way. "Cristin, Miss Morgan, is very different. He prefers to bide his time and let events shape themselves. He seldom tries to intervene."

"And is certainly more ruthless than I when he has need," observed Bryn.

Sounds from the hall turned their heads towards the doors and seconds later they were flung open and Cristin entered wearing a tweed suit, bringing with him an aura of cold air. Something made Rhonwen glance at Frances, and for an instant she surprised an expression in the dark eyes that told her that there were turbulent emotions beneath the cool exterior as she looked at Cristin. The moment passed before Rhonwen could define whether they were of attraction or dislike, and Frances was laughing as she held out a hand to Cristin.

"At last! We were debating if we should begin dinner without you. Your brother is clearly of the opinion that if you cannot arrive on time you should be punished by being ignored."

Rhonwen stared at Frances who, in one skilfully composed sentence, had managed to insinuate an antagonistic tone to the conversation that had preceded Cristin's entrance. It seemed as if she wanted to keep any rivalry between the brothers at simmering level.

Cristin turned, but whatever he might have answered was lost as he caught sight of Rhonwen. His face was not clearly visible to the others, and only she perceived the fleeting expression that passed across it before he walked to her, bowed over her hand and said coolly, "What a pleasant surprise, Miss Morgan. I had no idea you and Cousin Edwina had met."

"We had not," smiled Edwina, "but when your brother told me that a young lady of quality who had suffered a bereavement was holidaying in the village, I had no hesitation in inviting her to join us for dinner."

Cristin's brows rose a mere fraction at Edwina's description of Rhonwen. Then he took Edwina's hand and raised it to his lips. "You never fail to be charitable, cousin. I am all praise for her, Miss Morgan."

"I fear your praise is misplaced," said Edwina as she laid her embroidery frame on a small table beside her chair, "for it was your brother who discovered Miss Morgan's presence in Glyn Dedwydd and was thoughtful enough to ask if she might dine."

"Why, Bryn, I had no idea you could be so full of the milk of human kindness," mocked Frances.

"Nor I," agreed Cristin. "In general, Miss Morgan, my brother busies himself so much in the affairs of our estates he has no time for the softer preoccupations of life."

Rhonwen wished momentarily that she had not come. She felt in an odd way that she was being used as a source of further contention between the brothers, and she was not helped by dark looks from Frances as she followed the interchange of words.

If Edwina sensed the atmosphere she gave no sign. Perhaps

she was so used to the polite bickering she found it simpler to ignore it. After excusing Cristin from changing to evening dress she rose.

"We are more ladies than gentlemen, Miss Morgan, but perhaps you will not mind since we are a small party. Bryn, give me your arm, and you, Miss Watkins, must take his other side. Cristin, be so good as to lead in Frances and Miss Morgan."

It may have been a family occasion to the others, but to Rhonwen the dining room was formidably spacious and formal. Yet Frances leaned across Cristin and said, "I adore this room, Miss Morgan. It is so much more intimate than the large apartments. Do you not find it cosy?"

Her tone seemed to hold more than good-humoured banter, and Rhonwen felt again that for some undefinable reason Frances Kendrick regarded her as a worrying interloper and was determined to make her as uncomfortable as she could.

Pride kept her steady, and she walked with a firm step and seated herself in a chair held out by a footman and would not allow herself to study the tapestry curtains, the carved and painted fireplace, the marble-topped side tables, but contented herself with looking appreciatively at the elegant appointments of the table where candlelight danced on silver and crystal.

Frances had no such inhibitions and offered compliments with the gracious ease that spoke of years of intimacy.

"How well the table looks, Edwina. I envy your gardener. Do you not dote on Miss Caradog's flower arrangements, Miss Morgan?"

Rhonwen looked at the pair of porcelain swans whose hollow backs were filled with pastel-coloured flowers and delicate greenery and murmured her admiration. As the servants carried round soup Frances said, "You must know, Miss Morgan, that the head gardener here is so old I think he has forgotten the year of his birth, but he rules the undergardeners with an iron hand. The Caradog hothouses are quite famed for their fruit and blooms. More than one person has tried to tempt old Parry away, but he remains loyal to this house."

"He and his wife, poor soul," said Edwina, breaking her bread and taking a mouthful of soup.

"She still lives!"

The diffident remark from Miss Watkins was more statement

than question, but Frances said swiftly, "Of course she does! If she had died I would have been informed. Nothing happens here that I do not know, does it, Edwina?"

"That is very true," laughed Cristin. "We would not dare to make any move without consulting you, Frances."

Rhonwen was busy wondering how she could turn the conversation towards her own needs, but she caught the look between Frances and Cristin. On his side it was one of possessive fondness, but for an instant Frances lowered her guard and Rhonwen saw that she desired Cristin with passionate intensity.

Their emotions were not her concern, however, and she swallowed before saying, "Mrs. Evans spoke to me of Sophy Parry. She told me she has severe rheumatism. I am sorry for anyone so afflicted. I have seen folk in London bent double by it."

Edwina gave her a warm look. "Sophy worked well here even after she should have rested. When finally she had to yield to her illness we made her as comfortable as we could. She has no children to care for her."

"I was told she has a cottage in the grounds of Castell Craig," pursued Rhonwen. "Is it near the castle?"

"Such an interest in old family retainers!" Frances's tone was faintly mocking. "Perhaps you would care to visit Sophy after dinner."

"Stop teasing!" ordered Cristin. "What an absurd suggestion! Of course Rhonwen does not wish to do anything of the sort!"

"Cristin, are you never going to carve?" demanded Bryn. "We have had to wait long enough for our meal."

Cristin lifted his tall-stemmed wine glass and lazily toasted his brother.

"You do it, there's a good fellow. London tires one so. I cannot conceive how anyone could live there all year round."

As Bryn carved thin slices of beef Frances said, "Miss Morgan, Bryn told us you have come from London. Is your principal residence there? Where is your country seat? Is it in Wales? You have a Welsh name. Many of my friends have purchased homes near the capital, but I do not recall meeting anyone of your family."

Rhonwen kept her eyes on the dish of buttered carrots a

servant was holding in front of her. She was becoming increasingly sure that Frances had summed her up correctly and was aware of her humble circumstances. She came to a quick decision. Why should she try to hide her poverty? It was not shameful. She would tell them exactly how she had lived and put an end to Frances's tormenting. She would not be asked here again as a guest, but it would not prevent her from applying to the housekeeper or cook for a job. She thought that a servant might work for years in Castell Craig and never meet an employer.

Frances's dark eyes were sparkling with malicious enjoyment, and even Edwina and Miss Watkins were beginning to look at Rhonwen enquiringly. She had opened her mouth to reply when Cristin preceded her.

"Do stop plying Miss Morgan with questions, Fran. You should talk to me. You have asked me nothing about my visit to London. I am feeling neglected."

Frances narrowed her eyes and her smile died.

"If you do not desire me to speak to Miss Morgan then I will refrain. Dear Cristin, do please tell me of your London trip."

Cristin chose to disregard the implied boredom in her studiedly courteous tones and spoke of mutual acquaintances and amusing encounters until he coaxed a smile from her.

Rhonwen sat silent. Cristin had intervened to prevent her revealing her origins, and she wondered why. It was clear that he had not mentioned their previous meeting at the forge, and he had not done so now when it would have been logical.

And she remembered his look when he had returned to find her unexpectedly in Castell Craig and had regarded her for a fleeting instant with hastily controlled fury.

Chapter 6

BY THE TIME dessert was served Rhonwen felt drained in her efforts to keep up a part in the conversation and, at the same time, cope with the many sets of cutlery, dishes and wine glasses that appeared necessary for even an informal meal. Once, when she hesitated over a choice of knife, she sensed eyes upon her and looked up to see Frances watching her with a look of scorn that she transformed swiftly to a polite smile.

Silver baskets of nectarines, peaches and apples, tall, graceful stands of grapes with vine leaves, nuts and raisins were put on the table while the butler poured Madeira or claret. Rhonwen would have loved to try one of the perfect, velvety peaches, but the idea of managing the juice, even with the help of finger bowls of warm water and sliced lemon that the servants were laying by each plate, led her to pick up an apple. She peeled it with a small silver knife and put a piece in her mouth. She discovered Frances watching her again. She, too, chose an apple and placed each dainty morsel in her mouth with yet another fork, and Rhonwen was vexed to feel herself flushing with mortification.

Even as she felt impressed by the luxury, she had a sudden hysterical impulse to cry, "You are so nice in your notions of polite behaviour, yet not so far away children are starving in city gutters." Then she allowed the apple to brown in her plate as she struggled with the frustration of her distorted sensations.

At Edwina's signal the ladies left the men to their port and retired to an oak-panelled drawing room. Rhonwen's feet sank into the deep carpet pile, and she marvelled at the gloss of the wood, which was so highly polished that the elegant lines of the furniture were repeated in reflections. She wondered how many aching knees and elbows had gone into such a task, then bit her lip as she realised that even her thoughts would never attain equality with Frances Kendrick, who sat in an easy chair watching Edwina pour coffee and hand it to be served round by a footman.

All Edwina's actions were practised and precise. She looked about forty years of age, though her skin was almost unlined and she was still pretty. Her brown hair, lightly streaked with grey, was dressed in a simple style beneath a wisp of a lace cap. The room contained cushion covers, antimacassars and fire screens all embroidered, Rhonwen was sure, by her hostess whose sewing frame was being carried to her by a maid. Rhonwen wondered why a woman who must have been a beauty, and was rich and charming, should have remained unwed and decided that it must be by Edwina's choice. Had no man ever stirred her? Had she always been so exact in her movements, so tranquil in behaviour? Her inbred courtesy had built a barrier around her more impregnable than ice. Who would dare to tamper with such isolation?

"You are interested in embroidery, Miss Morgan?"

Frances's tones were smooth, and Rhonwen realised she had been staring at Edwina for longer than could be considered polite. "I . . . I find Miss Caradog's sewing fascinating," she stammered. "She is so sure in her stitching. When Mother and I hemmed handkerchiefs I must confess I became impatient."

Edwina looked up. "Did you, my dear? Well, that is not surprising. Making handkerchiefs is tedious work. Always white—even the monograms needing to be in white silk."

"I wonder, Miss Morgan, that you were not allowed to do something more satisfying," said Frances. "Mama realised very early that I cared nothing for the boredom of plain sewing, and I made watch cases for Papa and things of that nature. I never sew now, thank heavens. Paris and London are full of women only too glad to make my clothes. Do you not dote upon the London mantua makers?"

Rhonwen said quietly, "I have had no experience with them. We were not rich. We made our own clothes."

"Really! How clever you must be! Did you make the gown you are wearing?"

"With the help of Mrs. Evans, yes."

"Mrs. Evans? Oh, the village woman with whom you are staying." Frances concealed a small yawn behind a white hand. "Thank goodness dear Mama and Papa bequeathed me enough to enable me to eschew such mundane tasks. Edwina, what can the men be talking about? I do think it unfair the way we ladies have to wait for their company."

Edwina smiled at Rhonwen, a warm smile that lit her brown eyes momentarily. "I do not think it so bad a custom, do you, Miss Morgan? Ladies can be cosy together and discuss matters that bore the gentlemen."

Her words asked for no reply and her tone suggested a mild rebuke for Frances, who shrugged and examined her nails.

Rhonwen made a quick decision and said before she lost her courage, "Miss Caradog, Mrs. Evans wondered—I wondered, if you would mind my bringing some small gifts to Sophy Parry. It seems she has a particular weakness for . . ."

". . . Mary Evans's cooking and wine-making skill. Yes, I do know and, of course, I do not mind. Anything that would cheer Sophy is welcome." She reached for the bell pull. "A servant shall take your little offering at once."

"Oh, no!" said Rhonwen with such emphasis that Edwina stayed her hand and Frances looked at her with narrowed eyes. "I beg your pardon, Miss Caradog. How rude you must think me! It is only that . . . that when one brings a gift, it seems a little . . ."

"Churlish not to deliver it oneself," said Edwina, again finishing Rhonwen's sentence. "How right you are, my dear, and how thoughtful. Would you like to go at once? A footman will conduct you."

Five minutes later, stifling her guilty feeling of having been less than honest with Miss Caradog, Rhonwen, swathed in the soft folds of a borrowed shawl, was walking beside a young footman who carried her basket. He held an oil lamp, and the light swung over formal flower beds, paved walks and the leaves of small shrubs and trees. They arrived at a wooden gate leading into a short path, through a tiny patch of garden and finally at the door of the Parry's grey stone cottage.

The door opened at the footman's rapping and an old man peered out.

"Who's making that din at this hour? My wife and me are on our way to our rest."

"We've brought a gift for Sophy," said the footman.

"Is that you, young Tudur? I'll thank you to be civil. My wife is 'Mrs. Parry' to you. Who's that with you? A young lady, is it?"

"A guest of Miss Edwina's. She brought Mrs. Parry something."

"Come in, please, miss. You can wait outside, Tudur. It'll do you good to cool your heels."

He closed the door behind Rhonwen muttering, "Saucy young jackanapes. In my day we knew our place where our elders and betters were concerned. Young servants nowadays—! Mrs. Parry's in here, miss. But how do you come to know her?"

Rhonwen explained and he nodded. "Mary Evans is one of the best. Please to wait a minute. The maids have been to settle my Sophy, but she's only taken her sleeping draught a minute or two gone and it won't have worked yet. Miss Edwina always sees to it that Sophy has something to ease her pain. My poor wife has much to bear."

He disappeared through an inner door, and Rhonwen heard the murmur of voices as she looked about her. The living room was small and contained little furniture, but the wood was highly polished, the grate gleamed with black lead and copper pans threw back the fire's red-and-orange lights. The remains of Mervyn Parry's supper of bread, cheese and ale were on the scrubbed table.

"She's ready for you," he announced from the door, and Rhonwen went to meet the woman who might hold a key to the puzzle of her birth.

Sophy was propped up in a box bed. Her face was heavily wrinkled beneath her nightcap and her hands, twisted with rheumatism, lay on the white quilt. She looked small and helpless as she stared at Rhonwen with blurred, dark eyes.

"I hope I am not keeping you awake," said Rhonwen feeling awkward beneath the intense gaze. "I have brought gifts from Mrs. Evans."

Sophy motioned her to place the basket on the bed, but when Rhonwen tried to unwrap the contents, she snapped in a thin voice, "Let me be. I can manage."

"Pay no heed to her," whispered Mervyn. "She doesn't mean to sound crotchety. It's the pain, you see, and she likes to do as much as she can for herself."

"I can hear you whispering," accused Sophy. "If you've something to say, speak up so I can join in."

She struggled with the paper, her hands pulling almost ineffectively, and Rhonwen had to clench her fists to stop herself from trying to help; but at last Sophy drew out the cake with a grunt of pleasure. "Plate cake, is it? I hoped for that. And Cowslip wine, too. Pour me a drop, Mervyn."

"Ah, no, the doctor said you were not to take drink at bed time with the sleeping draught."

"Hush up, man, will you! What can it matter if I take too much of anything? My life's a burden to me, so it is."

Mervyn shook his head and tutted, but obeyed, and Sophy smacked her lips as she sipped the wine. "Who might you be?" she demanded, so abruptly that Rhonwen started.

"I am . . . I am . . ."

"Well, don't you know who you are, girl?"

Rhonwen took a deep breath. "N . . . not really. In fact, I am hoping you can help me."

Sophy sipped again and her face was impassive as she said, "I've heard of you. You're the English girl with the Welsh name, and you've been staying with the Evans's, and your speech and dress don't match. There's a mystery about you, they say."

"Who says?"

"Never you mind. I've got my ways of knowing what goes on around these parts."

Sophy grinned, showing few teeth in sunken gums, and Rhonwen felt annoyance both at the idea of strangers discussing her and the obvious glee of this old woman. "Have you ever heard of Beatrice Morgan?" she asked quickly, but Sophy was not easily taken by surprise.

She sipped again and her eyes roamed over Rhonwen. "I might have—and then again I might not. It depends on why you want to know."

"She was my mother."

Something flickered in Sophy's eyes. "I heard you had lost your mam in an accident. Mervyn, leave us and brew up your hot drink!"

Mervyn went and for a full minute Sophy stared at Rhonwen. "Beatrice Morgan's girl, are you? And where is your father?"

"He—died—I think. Mother never wanted to talk of him."

"How old are you? When were you born?"

"I've not long passed my eighteenth birthday on September third."

Sophy's face wrinkled more deeply as she concentrated. "That would make the dates right. I wondered about your mother at the time, but she was a plump girl, was Beatrice, and with them it's not so easy to tell. And in those days we wore the crinoline. You couldn't hide a swelling belly so easy now, could you, in those ridiculous sheath dresses?" Her voice was becoming slurred. "O' course, ordinary servants didn't wear big crinolines, but your mam was Miss Edwina's maid and was allowed to dress in fashion. And a clever girl could lift the crinoline frame higher over her middle if she had the need."

The glass of wine almost slipped from Sophy's grasp and a few drops slopped on to the quilt. Rhonwen reached out to steady it, and Sophy snapped with sudden vigour, "Let me be! Just because my body's warped some folk think my mind's the same. It isn't so—it isn't so!" But her eyes were clouding over, and Rhonwen knew she was about to slide into deep alcohol and drug-induced sleep and felt frantic.

"Mrs. Parry, Sophy, please try to help me. I want to belong to someone. I have no family, so far as I know—no one—"

Sophy's eyes opened as she dragged herself back to consciousness. "And you brought me gifts hoping I could help, eh? Well, I don't think I can. Beatrice Morgan kept her secrets. Poor Miss Edwina never could understand why such a devoted maid left so suddenly without a word. Yes, and if rumour's true, she took things with her that didn't belong. It was all long ago, and now there's only my old Mervyn and me remember."

Her heavy lids closed over her slumbrous eyes, but her voice went on in a sing-song monologue. "Poor Miss Edwina. She was a sad, lost soul herself in those days. She'd had bad news from somewhere. Some say a lover died. A letter came and she went racing to her room and fell and hurt herself. Don't know how. Kept to her bed for months. Beatrice tended her. No one else allowed near. There was jealousy, so there was. 'Member the housekeeper sneered when Beatrice Morgan ran away. I was sorry for her, though. So white and ill she looked, but Miss Edwina's illness came to a crisis and Beatrice never left her side . . . stayed by her . . . loved her . . . then ran away without a word . . ."

She took a shuddering, indrawn sigh. "Poor Miss Edwina . . . poor Beatrice . . . tormented by her guilty secret, I daresay . . . good Methodist she was . . . lucky there was crinolines . . . what do girls do nowadays to hide their misbegotten babies . . . ?"

She subsided into snoring sleep, and Rhonwen removed the wine glass that was slipping sideways and placed it carefully on the bedside table before a sound from the doorway made her look round. Cristin Caradog was leaning on the door jamb, and his face held that watchful expression she was beginning to know.

He spoke softly. "So you found what you came here for. Come, I'll walk you to the castle. I have sent the footman away."

Rhonwen rose and walked past Cristin into the outer room where Mervyn was preparing a cupboard bed. He looked up. "Is she asleep? Why, miss, you don't look well. Will you sit awhile? Can I get you a drink of something?"

Rhonwen shook her head. "No, thank you," she said in a thin voice." Miss Caradog must be wondering why I have taken so long. I am sorry your wife is so ill, Mr. Parry."

The servant looked embarrassed and stared at the floor, and Cristin put his hand beneath Rhonwen's arm and led her outside, where she breathed deeply of the cold mountain air. "Did he not want me to speak of Sophy's illness?" she asked tonelessly, trying to keep herself from dwelling on the fact that her private hopes and dreams had been destroyed.

Cristin's voice was unexpectedly kind. "Parry is not used to being addressed as 'mister' by anyone from the castle. It does not matter."

They began to walk slowly along the path and Cristin said, "I tried to warn you, Miss Morgan. Reason supposes that if your mother made such efforts to hide herself, and you, she must have something of which to be . . ."

"Ashamed?" supplied Rhonwen. "Yet we do not know the circumstances of my birth. And now I shall never know! Oh, I wish Mother had thought fit to tell me. I would have cared for her still! Why did she not trust me?"

Her distress reached Cristin, who stopped walking and held the lamp high to illumine her face. "It was all long ago. You must forget. Try to think only of the future." He leaned closer. "You could marry easily and start your own family. You are very beautiful, though I daresay many men have told you so."

"No, sir, they have not. Only one—your brother, Bryn." The memory of Bryn's words and looks on the night they had dined surprised her into sudden warm speech, and a frown crossed Cristin's face. "Mother did not allow me to associate with anyone," continued Rhonwen. "She was particularly careful to guard me."

"From what? Did she not desire to see you settled into some respectable alliance?"

"I do not know. What does it matter now, anyway? And what 'respectable' man will want a girl whose father is unknown to her? I would be obliged if you would escort me back to the castle. Your cousin will be wondering."

He lowered the lamp and they walked in silence until Cristin asked, "Have you received any training for work?"

"Not really. I can do plain sewing, and I have been taught by a woman of gentle birth who was a governess. But pray, do not suggest that I should take up teaching. I am not fitted for it in temperament or accomplishments, and, anyway, no acceptable employer would consider me with my background."

"They might if you had a reference from Miss Caradog."

It was Rhonwen's turn to stop. "But why should she help me? Do you think she would? No! She does not know me!"

"You are answering your own questions." Cristin's face was in shadow, but she knew he was smiling and she laughed reluctantly. "I think I am generally more logical, but tonight—I have had a shock."

He tugged gently at her arm and they resumed walking. "You have had too many shocks of late. Poor child. Yet I feel sure we could find a way of helping you. Your mother appears to have been singularly irrational in your upbringing."

They were entering the hall as he spoke and the footman stepped forward to take the shawl, giving her no chance to utter the swift defence of Beatrice that had risen to her lips.

As they approached the drawing room there was the sound of an expertly played piano. Cristin opened the doors and the music stopped abruptly, and Frances allowed her hands to fall into her lap. Rhonwen caught her look of hastily veiled suspicion. "You have been an age," she said in bored, patently false tones.

"Do go on playing, dear," begged Edwina, who sat in her fireside chair, her hands busy with the interminable embroidery. "I was enjoying it. Neither Bryn nor Cristin are experts on the pianoforte, Miss Morgan. They leave it to Idris Betho, their cousin, who is away at school. Dear Idris. How I long to see him. The term seems an age. But Cristin paints well, does he not, Frances?"

An insensitive person might have thought her speech mere rambling, but Rhonwen became aware that Edwina's eyes were moving from one to another and that she was trying to stem the undercurrents of emotion of which Rhonwen was dimly conscious. Castell Craig was proving to be an uncomfortable place.

Frances did not resume playing but strolled across to Edwina, her ivory gown shimmering in the candlelight. She sat by her hostess and examined her sewing. "Why, this is exquisite! For what is it intended?"

Edwina looked at Rhonwen and said, "Pray sit near the fire, Miss Morgan. You must be chilled from your walk. This is *appliqué* work to decorate a shawl I have finished, Frances. And how was Sophy?"

Rhonwen spread her hands to the warmth of glowing logs. "She seems very ill and she was sleepy, but she welcomed the gifts, Miss Caradog."

She felt a fraud as Edwina gave her a sweet smile. Naturally she had felt genuine pity for Sophy, but her motive in visiting her was selfish. She caught Frances's dark stare. Her brilliant eyes seemed to penetrate her mind, and they definitely held hostility. What could she have done to generate such dislike?

"The Caragog men feel most protective towards you, Miss Morgan," said Frances mockingly. "First Bryn decided he must go to make sure you were properly guarded, only to be ousted by Cristin, who claimed the privilege as the elder, though he did not mind allowing his younger brother to carve at table, I recall. You seem to have bewitched them both."

"Don't be silly, Frances," Bryn interposed in clipped tones, which brought a faint flush to deepen the rose in Frances's cheeks. "You are making Miss Morgan uncomfortable. It matters nothing who escorted our guest so long as proper attention was paid to her. My brother and I would not have permitted only a footman to attend her had we known of the proposed visit."

"Now they criticise you, Edwina."

Edwina carefully snipped a thread. "You are making much of nothing, my children. You must know, Miss Morgan, that having been reared almost as brothers and sister they sometimes squabble as if they were back in the schoolroom. Then the boys went away to school. Cristin enjoyed his time at Harrow, but you did not, did you Bryn? He wanted nothing more than to be here in his home. Even now he takes care of our people while Cristin manages the business matters."

Again Rhonwen recognised Edwina's adroitness in manipulating the conversation along smooth lines, and she wondered if Castell Craig was always like this or if she herself had sparked off an antagonism she did not understand.

A porcelain clock on the mantlepiece struck ten and Rhonwen said apologetically, "Miss Caradog, would you think it unmannerly of me if I asked to take my leave now? The Evans family must rise so early they usually retire before this."

Edwina smiled, "How thoughtful you are, Miss Morgan, in so many ways. Of course I do not mind."

Both Bryn and Cristin stood with her, and Rhonwen feared there would be an altercation about who was to take her home. She saw by the quick glances directed at the men by Frances that she had the same idea, but Cristin simply bowed and said, "Good night, Miss Morgan. Your visit has been most—interesting and enjoyable. I daresay we may not have the pleasure of your company here again. No doubt you will be moving on. Returning to London, perhaps."

"Well, I hope you enjoy the remainder of your holiday," said Edwina, while Frances contented herself with a nod in Rhonwen's direction and a murmured farewell. For an instant it seemed as if she dropped her guard of brittle flippancy and showed relief in her face.

Bryn escorted Rhonwen to the hall where she was helped into the shabby jacket, and she looked round at her sumptous surroundings as Bryn himself shrugged into his coat, before taking her to where the gig and horse were waiting.

Then she was seated beside Bryn, who guided the pony with skilful hands through the gates of Castell Craig to the road back to the village, and suddenly she felt sick with disappointment. She had arrived with far higher hope than she had dared to admit and that hope had been destroyed by a few words.

"Of what are you thinking?" asked Bryn.

"N . . . nothing. I . . . I seem to have forgotten Mary's basket!"

"It is under the seat—and I do not believe that it was the basket that gave you the forlorn look you have been wearing since you returned from visiting Sophy. And what did my brother mean when he said you might be moving on? You said nothing to me about leaving."

"Why should I tell you of my plans?" Her voice was sharp with the need to fight down unexpected tears.

"I thought we were friends!"

She was silent, staring at the steam rising from the pony's nostrils and wreathed in the light from the carriage lamps, before she replied, "Yes, we are friends, Mr. Caradog. I beg your pardon. Your brother assumed I would be leaving. I do not know why."

The lie sat uncomfortably on her lips and she felt Bryn's disbelief. "Cristin followed you to the Parry's cottage tonight. He was adamant to the point of—one could almost say violent argument—that he, and not I, should fetch you. I wonder why."

Rhonwen could find no answer. She could not bring herself to lie to Bryn again, even had she thought he would be taken in. He seemed to have an uncanny knack of understanding her.

"Has my brother hurt you in any way, Miss Morgan?" Bryn's tones were quiet, but there was a steely quality to his voice that made her realise that he was a man to be treated with respect.

"Your brother has been kind to me," she answered bleakly. "Tonight I . . . I needed someone."

The tears would be stayed no longer and she sobbed helplessly. Bryn pulled the pony to a standstill and turned to her. "Miss Morgan—oh, damn formality—Rhonwen—don't cry. What ails you? Cannot you tell me?"

"There's not much to tell." She wiped her eyes with the large handkerchief he offered. "I have not been nice at all tonight. I took the presents to Sophy because I wanted an excuse to talk to her, and your cousin thinks I am so kind and I'm not at all and . . ."

"Steady! You can't have done anything so very dreadful. You simply are not the type." Bryn's laugh sounded in the darkness. "Honestly, Rhonwen, you are about as fitted to be out in the world alone as—as that kitten I compared you with. Can't you tell me anything? I might be able to help."

"No one can!" She sobbed again but gulped back her emotion and in a few words explained her reason for coming to Wales, without mentioning the box, saying simply that she had found the two drawings. She ended by telling him what Sophy had said.

"Oh, my poor girl! And your sad mother, too! She must have missed her home desperately to have hung on to those badly executed pictures. And I didn't help you, did I, jumping to conclusions and trying to make you admit to a family—the one thing you do not seem to have. Forgive me, please."

He slipped an arm about her waist and she let it lie, sensing his friendliness and warmth. "You came to Wales looking for kinfolk and have found nothing."

"That is not quite true," protested Rhonwen. "I have made good friends. Though it isn't the same!"

"No, I must agree with you there. I love my people and my home. I would never underestimate the need to belong; but, Rhonwen, you will meet someone who will love you as you deserve and you will begin your own family."

"Your brother said much the same thing."

"Did he? Then for once we are in agreement."

They were quiet for a while. The cloud thinned and a few stars lightened the sky to silhouette the treetops swaying in the breeze.

"What can I be thinking of?" exclaimed Rhonwen. "I must go home!"

"Is that how you think of the Evans's cottage—as home?"

"Well, it is at present—and they make me feel wanted," said Rhonwen.

Bryn gave the reins a light jerk and the pony began to jog along the track. "So perhaps you will decide that after all you did not come to Wales in vain and will not think of leaving us."

Was his voice a shade too casual? Did it matter to him if she stayed? Suddenly she knew that in spite of his wealthy family connections he, too, was lonely. The thought was startling. It had never before occurred to her that such a thing was possible.

"If Mary and Owen will have me I would like to stay," she admitted, "though I must find a way to earn my bread. I wondered if there was a position I could fill at Castell Craig. I would not mind if it were humble. I am willing to work and to learn."

"No!" Bryn's vehemence startled her. "Sorry, Rhonwen, but it would not do."

"I fail to understand why!"

"You have been a guest in my home."

"Yes, that is true, but from what I've seen one could work forever in the kitchen and never meet the family."

"No, Rhonwen, I repeat—it would not do. I value you as my friend and want to keep you that way."

"And you could not befriend a humble little kitchen maid born on the wrong side of the blanket!"

"Now you are being ridiculous! Oh, God, why do we rile one another? If you were a scullery skivvy it would not matter to me any more than it does that your mother was—" He stopped abruptly and shook the reins so that the pony leapt forward and Rhonwen clutched the side of the gig.

"Go on! Why don't you finish? My mother was not married to my father. And that makes me a—"

"Be silent! How in hell did the conversation get here? Rhonwen, my little friend, please take it from me that it would be better if you did not seek employment at Castell Craig—certainly not in any humble capacity. I—like you—indeed, I like you very much and I know my Cousin Edwina does. She could want to meet you again—as an equal—and if that sounds impossibly snobbish to you I can only apologise. It is the way of the world."

They were turning into the village street and the only light came from the smith's cottage. The door opened as they stopped and Mary appeared, smiling at them. "So you have brought her safe home then. Will you come in, Mr. Bryn? No? Well, I daresay you will be wanting to get back."

The two women watched Bryn turn the gig and give a final wave before they went in to drink hot chocolate while Mary insisted on knowing at once what had happened.

"Ah, so you've been disappointed, bach. Well, it is sorry for you I am. Yet you have a shine to your eyes. Do you like Mr. Bryn?"

Rhonwen laughed shortly. "Like him? Yes, I like him—and I find him infuriating at the same time. He has a most—direct way of speaking."

"He always had. He was the one who got into trouble when he was a boy, while Mr. Cristin was even more mischievous, but stayed quiet and did as he pleased. They were a regular pair of imps before they went away to school and came back tamed into gentlemen."

Rhonwen made no reply as she sipped her drink, but remembering the cross-currents at Castell Graig she wondered how deep the taming had penetrated.

Chapter 7

RHONWEN HAD TO fight a feeling of depression as she dressed the following morning, but she resolutely determined to try to forget the past and think only of the future.

Mary and Owen were at breakfast though they had been up for some time and were clearly pleased when Rhonwen asked if she might extend her stay.

"But in future you must call me when the rest of you get up," she insisted. "I must take a full part in the work."

The younger children were away at their lessons, but Tomos and Hugh laughed at the rich chuckle that came from the smith's deep barrel chest.

"Is it the forge you will be working in then, Rhonwen?"

"Hush your foolishness, Owen. She will help me."

"That I will, with pleasure, Mary, so long as I can find a way to pay for my bed and board."

At Owen's frown she begged, "You must allow me my independence, please. I would so much like to spend the winter with you."

Owen's frown did not relax but Mary said briskly, "The child is right, so she is, and you would be the first to say so if one of our own were in her position. Rhonwen is as good a cook as ever I met, and her stitches have got so tiny you can hardly see them. Rhonwen, you shall earn your keep by helping me with the baking for the inns, and there is often sewing to be had from some of the big houses. That way you will be able to keep your little nest egg safe."

Owen nodded his agreement and Hugh said, "It will be like having another sister." Then he blushed and hurried out.

Tomos stood before her, his huge bulk blocking the light so that his face remained in shadow while he smiled his slow, sweet smile and his opaque dark eyes almost vanished in a maze of lines. "Rhonwen will stay. That is good. I like you. Pretty Rhonwen." He put out a hand, which could have broken her with a blow, and touched her hair with almost imperceptible gentleness. "Like the fire in the forge," he mused. Then he stumped out.

"You'll not be afraid of him?" asked Mary anxiously. "I've never known him to harm even an insect."

Rhonwen shook her head. "I shall not fear him."

She was kept busy that day, but she said little and Mary wisely left her to the thoughts that frequently brought a shadow over her smooth brow. Then shortly before the others came in to their evening meal, as Rhonwen was laying the platters of bread on the table, Mary said, "Try not to be sad, bach. Life is too short to mourn the things we cannot have."

"I know you are right. I had not realised until my hopes were destroyed how much I had been banking on finding my own kin. And I still have not given up entirely. Sophy may not be the only one with memories."

Mary looked at her gravely.

"The name of Morgan is so common in Wales that to find anyone of your own after so long with almost nothing to help may prove impossible. Your mam could have come from anywhere—a tiny village in the far south, perhaps. You will break your heart. You know, we have a proverb in Wales. It goes: 'A man takes after his own kin'—and, to judge by you, your father must have been real nice—and your mother, too, even if she was strict and not very happy. Life can be cruel to some. Why not make yourself content and look to the present?"

She drew a reluctant smile from Rhonwen, but the very physical act of smiling went a long way toward shifting the heaviness in her heart and she resumed the table laying with a springiness in her step.

The beef stew, which had been simmering for hours, was demolished in minutes and Mary cut into the marrow pie. Owen sniffed the aromatic scent of nutmeg and sank his teeth into the pastry that was almost too short to serve, while Tomos chased currants about his plate before handing it up for a second portion.

With her arms deep in the washing-up suds Mary said, "With such a cooking skill you will be able to get a place as a cook if you want it—or win a husband," she finished softly.

"My mother always seemed to want to turn my thoughts away from the men in London."

Mary glanced at her, her eyes alight with laughter.

"That will not be the way of the young men hereabouts. When they get to know you I warrant they will lay a trail to our door to beat the one Megan inspired."

She may have been right, but they were both astonished when Rhonwen's first invitation came from Cristin Caradog. The day was glowing with autumn hues and the foliage shiny with the drops of moisture that the early mist had left on trembling cobwebs. Rhonwen was standing at the cottage door, listening to the rhythm of the hammers from the forge and breathing the country aromas when a horseman turned into the village street and reined by her side.

Hugh came running, "Has he cast a shoe already, Mr. Caradog?"

Cristin smiled to dispel the anxiety in the boy's face as he swung himself down.

"Your father does his work too well for that, Hugh, but you may stable him for me, please."

As Hugh obediently led the stallion away, Cristin said, "Good morning, Miss Morgan. It is you I have come to see. I wonder if you will do me the honour of walking a while with me."

Rhonwen flushed. "Why, I do not know—I had not expected—"

Cristin stopped near enough for her to catch the male scent of shaving soap and tobacco, and she felt her heartbeats increase at the nearness of so handsome a man. Mary appeared and favoured the idea of a walk.

"It will do you good, Rhonwen. You still have some of the peaky look of the city about you. Please come in for refreshment when you return, Mr. Cristin."

Rhonwen found herself walking by the Artro with Cristin

before they began to climb a path into the hills, leaving the river far below. They made polite conversation about the scenery, but Rhonwen sensed that Cristin had deeper matters to discuss. She longed to question him as to whether or not he had learned more of her mother yet feared to hear his answers. They came to a place where the grass grew as close as velvet and boulders were shrouded in brilliant green moss. A small tributary stream leapt and sparkled over rocks; oak trees, twisted and stunted by the altitude, their roots intertwining and clinging to granite rocks, leaned at crazy angles. Cristin removed his coat, laid it on a flat rock and patted it.

"Sit here, please! I commend you upon your forebearance. Most females would have deluged me with questions."

Rhonwen sat meekly, her hands folded to still their nervous shaking, and Cristin, one booted leg upon the rock beside her, stood looking down at her.

"After you left the other night I could not rest for thinking of your disappointment. I discovered that the head housemaid was scullery maid at the time of your mother's departure. She says she remembers Beatrice Morgan."

Rhonwen licked her suddenly dry lips as Cristin continued, "I am sorry I bring you no good news, my dear. It seems that Ettie almost never saw your mother, who, as Cousin Edwina's personal attendant, ate her meals with the upper servants while the juniors were at table in the smaller hall. But the talk at the time of your mother's flight was so great as to be unguarded, and she recalls clearly that it was strongly suspected that Beatrice was with child and that is why she ran away. There was never any mention of a husband, but quite a lot of speculation as to who could be her lover."

The waterfall sounded loud in the ensuing silence and the harsh bark of a raven echoed through the trees and made Rhonwen start. Cristin said softly, "I had hoped to bring you news that would make you happy."

Rhonwen looked up into his handsome features. "It is not your fault that you failed. Thank you for what you tried to do. It seems I had best give up my dream."

"Dreams are not easily relinquished."

"This one must go. I will do as Mary Evans advises and look to the present."

Cristin strolled to the side of the stream where he stared for a moment into the water before returning to sit beside her and cover her cold hands with his.

"What I am about to say may seem odd—even presumptious —but because your mother was a respected servant in service with my family and must have come to grief beneath our roof —though I do not remember her—I feel a measure of responsibility."

"There is no reason why you should," Rhonwen returned sharply.

"Nevertheless, I do. And that is why I have decided to help you."

Rhonwen felt immediate proud rejection of his authorative manner. She sensed a cool, but implacable, determination to involve himself with her affairs and as he continued to speak, she searched his face for hidden meaning until surprise overcame all else.

"My family has many financial interests, Miss Morgan, some of which include property. The lease of a small shop has become vacant through the death of a childless tenant. Would you like that lease?"

"I? But I know nothing of shops, sir."

"You could learn. Clearly you are intelligent."

"What kind of a shop is it?"

"Ah, that is better. Now you show interest. It is a small general store that sells butter, bacon, things of that sort. However, it is in competition with other food stores, and I have long thought that the village needs a shop that caters to other needs of the womenfolk. Someplace they may purchase cloth, hats, fripperies to enhance their femininity."

He gave her a teasing smile, though the watchfulness stayed in his eyes.

She said slowly, "Mary believes I could acquire more skill at sewing and I do love pretty things."

Cristin looked approving. "You have behaved just as I hoped. I will set the wheels in motion at once."

"I have not said I will accept your offer."

"But you are going to give it serious consideration, are you not, and can come to only one reasonable conclusion."

"Is it near? In Llanbedr? Or Harlech perhaps—though

Megan's new family have a good haberdashery there!''

''Oh, no, surely you cannot wish to remain where people know your mother's sad story! The shop is in a village near Swansea, in South Wales. I have not seen it, but my brother says it is a pretty place near the sea. I am sure you will like it.''

''And is Mr. Bryn Caradog also sure I will like it?''

Cristin's brows rose. ''Bryn? I have not discussed the matter with him. Why should I? Cousin Edwina leaves these things to me since I am the heir and all will one day be mine.''

The idea of going away suddenly tore at Rhonwen's sensibilities.

''I will not go! I will not leave this place!''

''Now you are being heedless, Miss Morgan.'' His tone was soothing as if he addressed a wilful child. ''I had taken you for a sensible creature.''

She sprang to her feet. ''Well, now you know I am not. I love Glyn Dedwydd and the mountains. I *know* my mother came from these parts—I feel I belong—I feel it here!''

She struck her breast with her fist. ''And I love Mary Evans and her family and they . . . they are fond of me. Why should I destroy my contentment?''

Cristin shrugged lightly, but his face was dark with anger. ''If you do not mind accepting their charity . . . !''

''Who dares to say that! I work for my keep.''

''Indeed! It proves that you are an infant in the ways of the world, if you believe that. A man with a healthy wife and sons and daughters scarcely needs another pair of hands—or another mouth to feed.''

Rhonwen felt stricken and sat down again heavily. ''Surely you are wrong! They do need me—they do!''

''I am sorry, Miss Morgan. I spoke unkindly in my wish to make you understand. And I feel rather let down. I pondered long last night on your dilemma and thought I had at least solved the matter of an income.''

Rhonwen put out her hand.

''Sir, you are kind and I am being churlish, but I cannot say that I will go to your shop in Swansea. Not yet! I cannot come to grips with the idea of leaving this place. I . . . I will talk to Mary . . .''

''Who will continue to insist that she needs you,'' interposed

Cristin gently. "I am offering you independence."

"Yet I will talk with her. I know she will be honest with me."

Cristin said no more, but his shrug was expressive. Rhonwen rose and turned her face towards the path to hide the tears suddenly filling her eyes. How dare he try to spoil the first real family atmosphere she had known. How should he comprehend her tormenting need of family love—he who had so much?

Cristin moved to her side and held out an arm which she ignored. She hurried forward, anxious to return to her room where she could think. Her foot became trapped by a tree root, her impetus carried her forward and she fell clumsily. Pain shot through her ankle to her knee and she cried out once, then bit her lip.

"That is what comes of behaving precipitately, Miss Morgan. Do you never stop to consider?"

His words were unsympathetic, yet as he spoke he had knelt by her side and was releasing her foot and probing with a sure but careful touch.

"Can you stand?"

He raised her, but when she put her foot to the ground she cried again irresistibly and he lowered her to a rock.

"Sit still. There is no break, but you have a bad sprain. You'll be going nowhere for a few days, that's apparent. I'll fetch help, but meantime I think we should remove your boot. You can put your foot into the stream. The cold water will reduce the swelling."

Rhonwen clenched her teeth as he tugged off the boot and waited for her to roll down her black woollen stocking. He knelt and eased it off, then stopped moving as if transfixed, his gaze riveted to her toes. She followed his look, flushed and attempted to draw her foot back beneath her skirt. Living with her deformity she had tended to forget it and pain had made her thoughtless; but now she saw her toes as if for the first time, as a stranger would see them. Her foot was slender and shapely and the toes long and well-formed—except for the smallest. Where there should have been a fifth toe there was only a tiny bone with skin and no nail. Nature had fashioned her to perfection save for this flaw. Cristin still did not move and had a look on his face that made her nervous.

"Will you help me to the water," she demanded, her voice too loud.

"Is . . . is your other foot as this one?"

She was amazed at his tone. One might almost believe he was afraid. But of what? She remembered too late how often Beatrice had warned her not to flaunt her deformity. "There are folk that hate anything not made perfect and some scared by it." It was as if her mother spoke the words aloud in the glade. Cristin must be one of those folk. She felt desperately vulnerable as she tried again to hide her foot from his mesmerised glare.

Then he looked up at her, his eyes narrowed, his lips pale. "You did not answer me! Is your other foot the same?"

She pulled the remnants of her pride together.

"How dare you! How dare you look at me as if at some sort of . . . of freak! It is so small a thing—so slight a difference. What right have you to question me so—?

She gasped as he grasped her arm, "Answer me!"

She cried, "All right, sir, if you will have it. My other foot is exactly the same. What a pity I am injured! You should have been spared such an ugly sight!"

Cristin passed his hand over his brow then spoke in a voice he could not quite hold even.

"Oh, God, I am sorry. Forgive me, Miss Morgan! I . . . I was taken by surprise."

His hand was unsteady as he stood and brushed the small twigs and leaves from his knees before helping her to the bank of the stream. He made her as comfortable as possible, placed his coat over her shoulders and left her dipping her foot into the cold, clear water as it cascaded down the rocks.

Tomos returned with him, his face creased with anxiety as he crouched by Rhonwen.

"You are hurt. That is bad—very bad."

He looked round at Cristin and something flickered in the depths of his strange eyes.

"You hurt Rhonwen."

"Don't be a fool, man, of course I did not. Pick her up and let's get her to Mary. She needs proper care and warmth."

Tomos frowned at the contemptuous tones, but bent and lifted Rhonwen as if she was a child, carrying her with great tenderness until he placed her on her bed, leaving Mary and Marged to bathe and bandage, soothe and minister. After they had gone, the air was filled with the soft odours of cammomile and bittersweet emitting from the ointment Mary applied. It was invented by Mary's grandmother and fulfilled her promise to help the pain.

Rhonwen lay remembering the look on Cristin's face when he saw her foot. Mary and Marged must have noticed the deformity, yet their expressions had not altered. There was a world of difference between them and the great Caradog family; she felt even more strongly that here was a refuge where she could feel wanted and secure. But as she drifted into a doze, Cristin's words returned to revive her doubts. Perhaps Owen did not really want another person to care for. Her throbbing ankle and worries engulfed her, and suddenly she was back on the dream staircase with fear tearing at her from behind and a locked door in front until she was shaken into wakefulness by an alarmed Mary putting her arms about her.

"There, there, bach, what is it then? There is frightened you look. You must have had a dreadful dream. Ah, it's the pain, but it will pass."

Rhonwen clung to her, still floundering in the horror of the nightmare. "I want to belong! I do, I do! I do not want to leave."

"Leave? To go where? Who has been putting such ideas in your head?"

Rhonwen was fully awake now and she drew a deep breath. "I'm sorry I worried you. My mother always used to say I cried out in my sleep. But now you are here I would like your advice."

She told Mary of Cristin's offer of a shop and the smith's wife began to look grim.

"Swansea is far away, so it is, and we would never see you. Though I must not be selfish, Rhonwen. It is a fine opportunity for you—a better one than you may ever get again—and you will be wanting to take it."

"Yes—no—I don't know, Mary. I have to make my own way . . ."

"Are you not happy here?"

"Oh, you must know I am. I love your family and your home.

I feel a part of you—but independence—you said yourself it is important."

"And so it is, but loving friends are better. Oh, yes, you would make new ones, I have no doubt; but we all want you to stay with us. It's as if . . . as if you belong here. You feel it, don't you?"

Rhonwen nodded, delicate colour running up beneath her skin. "I should consider Mr. Caradog's offer. He thinks—I think that I do not earn my bread."

"Not earn your bread!"

Mary's voice grew shrill with indignation.

"You spend every waking hour in the service of this family. I've a good mind to give Cristin Caradog a piece of my mind if that's the nonsense he's been filling you with. And not only are you a big help to me but you have made my little Marged quite different. I honestly believe that she will be content to stay at home until some fine local boy comes after her. I'll tell that Cristin Caradog what I think of him, so I will."

Rhonwen smiled into Mary's cross face. "I will speak to him myself, thank you, Mary."

She saw Cristin three days later. She was able now to hobble about and was sitting outside the cottage enjoying the blessing of a burst of late autumn sun while she prepared brussels sprouts for the midday meal when a shadow blocked the light. She looked up in surprise.

"Mr. Caradog. I did not hear your horse."

"You were very far away, Miss Morgan. I trust your ankle is better and that your cogitation was upon the new life we have planned for you."

"Much better, thank you. What new life?"

"Why, the one in the shop, of course. I have instructed my agent to hold the lease for you and given orders that the food stocks be sold off and any necessary repairs and painting be put in hand at once. You will go to a finely decorated place and will have great fun choosing stock. I have asked Miss Kendrick to help you, by the way, and she was kind enough to say she would."

Rhonwen stared at him.

"But I have made no plans with you, sir. I was to be given time to consider . . ."

"Oh, come, you cannot mean to tell me that a sensible creature like yourself can have reached any decision but the correct one. It remains only to determine the date on which you leave and your mode of travel."

"You almost leave me speechless. You have no right to order my life! Just who do you imagine you are?"

"As to that I am in no doubt of my identity, Miss Morgan, unlike you, I must remind you. I am giving you a chance such as comes to few low-born persons, and you behave as if I were trying to seduce you."

She coloured. "You are offensive, sir," she replied in low tones.

Cristin sat beside her and removed the vegetable knife from her hand and tossed it into the bowl.

"I beg your pardon. In my anxiety to see you well settled I spoke wrongly. You are surely courageous enough to face facts."

"Facts can be without soul, and love is more precious to me than anything. I am staying where I am wanted."

"You disappoint me—upon my word you do! But I shall not give up easily. The offer remains open and I will call again."

He rose and Rhonwen picked up the knife and began to trim a sprout. "What does your brother think I should do? Have you told him?"

Cristin sounded angry.

"Yes, I have told him, but that has nothing to do with the matter. If he were at home I am sure he would add his persuasion to mine, but he has gone to one of our coal mines in the south. There was an accident—not serious, thank heavens—but the circumstances left our safety regulations in doubt. Bryn is insistent that the security of the men be paramount. He left within an hour of the news."

"Did he leave a message for me?"

The question left Rhonwen's lips almost, it seemed, without volition and she was not surprised at Cristin's amazed look.

"Good God, no! Why should he?"

"No . . . no reason. It is only that we are friends. But if he believes I am to be here when he returns it does not signify."

"Then I regret having to disillusion you. I fear you lay too much stress on lightly formed friendships, Miss Morgan. Bryn thinks that you will have left for Swansea by the time he returns since he is likely to be away for some time. We have other business for him to transact in Cardiff."

"I see. You are probably right. I suppose I read more into relationships than is actually there. Friendship is doubly precious to me because I have known nothing of it before."

She tried to smother her dismay at Bryn's defection as she watched Cristin ride away.

Four more times he visited her. Her ankle healed and they were able to walk together. He used many arguments to persuade her to depart, but Rhonwen remained adamant. She refused to leave a place she considered a home and in the end, to everyone's surprise, Owen took a hand.

"Mr. Cristin, it's sorry I am to appear disrespectful, but Rhonwen will not be going from here. We want her and she will stay."

Cristin was defeated at last by the smith's stubborn refusal to discuss the matter further and Mary said with rounded eyes, "Well, Rhonwen, I wouldn't have believed it of my Owen. If there's one thing he hates it's argument. He thinks a lot of you."

Rhonwen was left in peace until Cristin called again on a day when the early chill had left the trees dripping and the sun was drawing November mist from the wet land. She had not seen him for a week and she looked apprehensive.

He laughed and threw up his hands.

"It is all right, Miss Morgan. I have surrendered. I come to ask for your company purely on a social basis. If you insist on remaining I think you had better learn to ride."

Rhonwen looked doubtfully at the pony he held by a bridle.

"I thought it was for shoeing," she said.

"*She*, not it, if you please. Her name is Tansy and as you perceive she has been fitted with a sidesaddle."

The last thing Rhonwen wanted to do was mount the pony —any pony—but having experienced the domination of Cristin's will she settled for the only argument he could not refute.

"I have no suitable clothes or footwear."

He slid from his horse, leaving Hugh to hold the bridle, and handed her a bundle.

"Cousin Edwina is a little shorter than you and slightly more mature of figure, but these will do well enough and she begs that you will make use of them."

Rhonwen took the parcel and stared at the brown paper and string.

"It will not go away," grinned Cristin, and she gave him a reluctant smile.

Mary was on his side.

"Riding is necessary in the hills," she insisted. "All my children can manage a pony. Go on, love, no harm can come of trying."

So within a short time, dressed in garments that were of better cut and quality than any she owned, Rhonwen found herself perched at an unnerving height being led along a forest track by Cristin.

"Did the boots fit?"

Cristin was looking ahead and did not see her slight flush as she answered, "Why, yes, they did. Your cousin must have a narrow foot for usually I have difficulty with my . . . my . . ."

The uncomprising rigidity of his back gave her no encouragement and she stopped, amazed again that he should find it so difficult to accept so slight an impediment in her body and wishing he had not asked the question.

But he taught well and she was quick to learn. He seemed to have forgotten his anger at her refusal to take the shop lease, and she found him a charming and considerate companion. He came every day, leading the dainty mare of which Rhonwen was growing fond, and he was delighted with her progress.

"Tomorrow, Miss Morgan, if it is fine and the air clear, we will venture into the mountains and I will show you a view across to the sea that must delight you. You have been so proficient I have no doubts at all that you can manage the ride."

But when Rhonwen joined Cristin on the following morning, he was holding the bridle of a different animal.

"Where is Tansy?" she demanded. "I am only just used to riding her—I do not want to mount a different pony!"

Cristin smiled with a mixture of condescension and kindness that defeated her.

"Tansy has cast a shoe and a fool of a stable boy has allowed her to go lame. I have brought Zillah. She is also a ladies' mare. Come now, Rhonwen, no more protests, if you please. You are good enough to show Zillah who is in charge."

The mare stood quietly as Hugh held her, and Rhonwen was helped into the saddle by David; but she sensed that beneath her was a creature less gentle than Tansy and her heart beat fast.

"Do not be surprised if we are away for some time," said Cristin to Mary. "Cook has prepared a luncheon for us. I intend to show Miss Morgan as many of our countryside beauties as light will allow. Pray, take off that anxious look. She is a natural on horseback."

Zillah behaved well as Rhonwen cantered her along forest paths soft with falling leaves and damp moss, avoiding the jutting branches of trees. They slowed to a walk where flood water had created slippery conditions, and Rhonwen began to regain confidence in herself as a rider. The path widened and Cristin reined to walk beside her.

"I think, Miss Morgan, it is time we dispensed with formality. May I call you in future by your very pretty name, and will you address me as Cristin?"

She looked up at him, but he kept his eyes on the way ahead as she answered, "Your brother and I have been on first name terms almost from the time we met. Did he tell you?"

He looked sharply round at her. "What has that to do with anything?"

"Why, nothing special, sir. I would be glad to be less formal."

"Then that is settled."

He pressed forward as the track narrowed again through the boundaries of the forest. "Keep a tight rein on Zillah from here, Rhonwen. There are likely to be stones and hollows concealed by the grass."

His warning did not come too soon, for as he spoke Rhonwen was forced to gather her reins as Zillah's hind hoof slithered into a dip and she pranced sideways in a terrifying way. Cristin glanced back, "Well done! I knew you would manage."

Rhonwen smiled at his praise but she knew, and she was sure Zillah knew, that she had to concentrate to control the mare. They climbed higher until first the sparse, wind-twisted trees were left behind and finally all vegetation vanished except the hardiest of mountain grasses clinging to hollows in the granite. The horses picked their own way between boulders broken off from the rocks deeply scored by ancient glaciers.

Rhonwen asked, trying to keep her voice from quavering, "Have we much further to climb, Mr. Caradog—Cristin, I mean? Pray do not forget I am a novice rider. My arms are aching. I find Zillah far more difficult to control."

Cristin turned to smile and she saw that his eyes were shining. He seemed not to have heard her question as he said, "Soon we shall behold one of the finest views in all the world, Rhonwen. Places such as these belong only to God and those who dare to come here."

For a few moments more they climbed until they rounded a vast rock formation and Rhonwen gasped. They were poised on a steep crag from the foot of which rolled miles of forests and hills, green and blue and purple as distance increased, until they reached the sea, glinting grey and silver as the sun sent beams through the drifting cloud.

"Well! Was it worth the climb?"

"Indeed, sir. It is beyond anything lovely."

Again she did not think he heard. "This is Caradog land, Rhonwen. Most of what you see belongs to us—and more—much more in other parts of Britain. One day it will be mine!"

"You love your home, do you not? Oh, how much I envy you —and people like you! Even the humble Evans family have so much."

This time Cristin took notice of her words and turned. "And I have been offering you something of your own. A place where you could perhaps found a family. Where one day you could bear children who will never be cast adrift as you were. Why do you continually refuse me?"

All Rhonwen's sadness was drenched in anger. "Is that why you brought me here? Did you go to the trouble of teaching me to ride simply to get your own way? I remember now that Bryn said . . ."

She stopped, appalled at her tactlessness. She had despised Frances Kendrick for causing dissension, and now she was falling into a similar pit.

"What did Bryn say?" asked Cristin in a voice soft but vibrant.

"N . . . nothing, really," she dissembled. "Just . . . that you are a determined man when you want something."

She recalled that Bryn had used the word ruthless, but this she refrained from repeating. "Please do not be annoyed with me. I appreciate your kindness, indeed, I do, but I have given my word to Mary and Owen that I will stay. Perhaps you are right to think that I do not really earn my bread—I know little of the world—but I do have a good influence on Marged and that is worth something. I owe them loyalty, do I not? Cannot you give me time? Later I might give you a different answer."

"Later could be too late—for this shop, at least. It cannot remain empty. But I will bear in mind what you say."

He gave her a hard stare before he appeared suddenly to lose interest as he pulled out a gold hunter watch from his pocket.

"It is past twelve. Would you care to investigate what Cook has prepared for us?"

Her relief at the change of subject gave her answer an enthusiasm she did not truly feel. Cristin's resignation in the face of her continual rebuffs engendered a desire in her to please him. She watched him turn his mount carefully on the narrow ledge and then look expectantly at her. She realised, with an attack of panic, that she must do the same and lead the way from this hazardous place so that they could ride to a suitable picnic spot.

Chapter 8

SENSING HER stablemate's readiness to depart, Zillah stirred restlessly and Rhonwen tried desperately to remember her lessons. She looked down from the height of the sidesaddle, which seemed to position her to tumble down the steep rock-covered slope, and said, "Cristin, I cannot turn Zillah! I do not know how. Will you not dismount and lead her?"

"What nonsense you talk, Rhonwen! No, I will not lead you, for if you give way to nerves now you might not regain your courage. Pull gently on her mouth with your right hand."

"But then she will have her back to the drop."

"She knows it is there and it is best that she does not see it. She is sure-footed and once you have got her to move, allow her head and all will be well, I promise you."

Rhonwen concentrated hard to master the trembling of her hands, which might convey the wrong signal to the sensitive mouth of the mare, and tugged at the rein. Zillah sidled and danced, and Cristin's face grew tight with annoyance.

"Rhonwen! A child could do better."

"I daresay it could, but I am not a child, sir, and have no experience of riding, as well you know. Cannot you understand that I am afraid . . . ?"

"You must control your fear or you will transmit it to the animal. Now please do as I have taught you!"

Rhonwen licked her lips and looked down the long drop. Fear and anger invaded her.

"I cannot—I will not . . . !"

She tried to bring her leg over the pommel of the sidesaddle in an attempt to dismount, but the length of the riding dress made her clumsy and she found herself leaning over the pony's neck, completely off balance. Zillah turned hurriedly towards the edge, her sharp little hooves slithering and scraping as she tried to keep her feet. At the same second Rhonwen freed herself and slid to the ground, managing only at the last moment to tug her foot from the stirrup. For a few terrible seconds girl and pony fought to remain upright, but first Zillah and then Rhonwen fell terrifying close to the chasm edge. Cristin was off his horse and leaping towards them. Rhonwen put out her hand to him and looked imploringly into his face. Something primitive was in his eyes—something she could not define—then as she began to struggle to her feet, he held out his hand to her and grasped Zillah's bridle at the same time.

The mare scrambled upright and trotted to Cristin's horse, who nosed her gently, while Cristin and Rhonwen stared at one another. The only sound now was the soughing of the wind. As Rhonwen's heartbeats began to slow she was shaken by an enormous rage.

"You had no right to expose me to such danger! You must have known the risk!"

"Don't be a little fool! If I had not cared for *you* I should for the mare. One of the sweetest little creatures I have bought in years and I have not had time even to know her . . ."

He stopped and flushed, then the hectic colour receded, leaving him pale.

"You brought me *here* on an untried mount! You attempted to make me perform a manoeuvre when you did not even know if she was competent!"

Cristin looked out across the mountains, his breathing fast; then he threw his crop to the ground and took Rhonwen's hands in his.

"Rhonwen, I swear to you that I bought Zillah from a man well known to me whose own daughter has been riding her. In fact, she has demanded a more venturesome pony. I respect you and wanted you to keep your courage. How could you believe that I would expose you deliberately to danger? I think far too much of you for that."

"You have a strange way of proving your concern!"

She tried to withdraw her hands but he held them tight. "I want you to do all things well. I need it, Rhonwen! My dear, I care for you . . ."

She was amazed at the depth of feeling in his voice and tried again to pull away. There was an almost febrile quality about him that worried her.

He sensed her alarm and said softly, "Do not fear me. Do not ever fear me. Oh, Rhonwen, I will be honest and admit that I have fought hard against the emotion I have for you. I have used all the arguments. It is not right—not suitable—I even tried to send you away . . ."

He stopped once more, his voice cracking; then he continued with controlled calm, "Do you think you could learn to care for me?"

"Care for you? I . . . I like you—as a friend—your whole family is good to me."

He slid an arm about her waist. "Don't play games, Rhonwen. It is more than friendship I require from you."

Her anger flared, and she went rigid within the circle of his arm. "I am not to be bought for the price of a few lessons in riding, sir!"

He pulled her closer until they were only inches apart.

"Release me," she demanded. "You cannot mean to take advantage of our isolation to . . . to harm me!"

"Never that, my dear. You must trust me. More than that, you must try to love me."

Shock widened her eyes. "Love you?"

"Is it so difficult a thing? Do you find me ill-favoured?"

"I think you are the most handsome man I have ever met, but I am not prepared to begin an illicit relationship with you."

His mouth curved in a smile that lit his eyes. "Oh, my dear, how badly I have expressed myself. Do not you realise that I am asking you to be my wife?"

He drew her closer and his arms were hard about her. She felt the power of his masculinity, the heady success of a woman who has enslaved a man she considered far above her reach, the strength of his protection. In spite of herself she could not stop the dreams that tumbled about her mind. In her grasp lay security, the warmth of a family, undreamed-of tranquility. His lips were on her face. He kissed her lids, her chin, her mouth with great tenderness and she warmed to him, relaxing in his embrace, returning his kisses in almost childlike trust.

"My beautiful little Rhonwen," he murmured against her mouth, "you are adorable. You will give me the happiness I crave! You will marry me!"

She was floating in an unfamiliar sea where harsh reality could no longer touch her. She could not remember saying yes, but Cristin was gazing down at her, his face filled with triumph.

"We will tell the others at once. Oh, Rhonwen, we are going to be so happy together."

Somewhere deep inside her there was a flicker of panic as she stared into the eyes so close to hers. The pupils were enlarged and she needed no experience to recognise passion. Again he bent his head and his thin, mobile lips explored her features until they lingered on her mouth. The flicker died and an upsurge of relief swamped the remnants of her will. She would belong to a family at last—and such a family—and Cristin had opened the door to her. She returned his kiss, and they clung together until the impatient stirring of the horses caused him to release her.

He led the animals until they came to a place where soft grass was sheltered from the wind and they sat down among the boulders to eat. For Rhonwen the rest of the outing passed in a haze in which she heard Cristin's voice outlining his future plans for them, giving her no time for reflection.

"I shall take you to London as soon as I think you are ready, Rhonwen, and your beauty will take Society by storm. You will, of course, be presented to Her Majesty. How wonderful you will look, my love, with the Caradog diamonds displayed to an advantage they have never before known."

Doubts and worries chased exultation in her mind. He was speaking of matters of which she had read only in newspapers. The Season Presentation to the Queen. These things happened only to girls born to wealth and position. Her doubts remained unexpressed because she had no means of understanding exactly the world he described.

But with a jolt she returned to reality when he followed her into the Evans' cottage as the sun was setting. The family had finished their evening meal. Owen and Tomos were seated by the fire lighting their pipes, watched by an envious Hugh who must wait for his eighteenth birthday for his. David was reading, his elbows on a corner of the kitchen table. The little ones were playing in a corner, and Mary and Marged were clearing the dishes. Everyone looked up as Rhonwen and Cristin entered, and before she had time to utter a word, he said, "See, Mary, I have brought her safely back to you, but not for long, for you shall be the first to congratulate us on our betrothal."

His words seemed to seal their bargain with inexorable finality. For a moment no one moved, and Rhonwen was reminded of a waxworks tableau to which Miss Reeves had taken her. Then Marged flew to her and kissed her cheek, and Owen rose to shake her by the hand while the little ones gazed open-mouthed at this unusual display of exuberance from their father. Only Mary was calm, offering her congratulations quietly, nodding and pouring them wine to toast one another. Cristin drank his quickly, bent to brush his face briefly against Rhonwen's, then mounted his horse and led Zillah into the darkness.

When everyone had gone to bed, Mary and Rhonwen sat by the dying fire and Mary said, "I had no idea you loved Mr. Cristin."

She had bent to stir a log with the long iron poker and sparks flew and flared on the sooty chimney back.

"I did not know until today," answered Rhonwen.

Mary sat up and said anxiously, "You are sure, aren't you, bach? In my opinion, spinsterhood is better than marriage without love. But there, I must not speak so, for I know you would not be tempted only by the Caradog wealth. You must care for him. . . . yet. . . . I am amazed that I did not suspect. My wits must have been wandering."

She leaned forward to gave Rhonwen the motherly kiss for which she had been craving, and the two women hugged one another.

"I wish you all the joy in the world, love. It should not surprise me that Mr. Cristin has proposed. You are very beautiful!"

Rhonwen lay awake for a long time reliving the scenes on the mountain, trying to recall what she had said. Cristin was so evidently a man of experience he must have recognised feelings in her that she had not suspected. He loved her and she him, and together they would enter a future bright with true affection and cushioned by the material advantages that Rhonwen knew only too clearly made such a difference to comfort.

The following day found her stiff and bruised by her fall. Tomos stared at her as she carried his breakfast to the table.

"You are hurt," he stated flatly.

"Only a little," she smiled. "I fear I am not an expert horse-woman, Tomos. I fell from the pony."

He scowled and his greying brows became a straight line above his small black eyes.

"That man always hurts you!"

The big man looked first at Mary than back to Rhonwen. "She always falls when she's with him," he declared, his mouth set as stubbornly as a child's.

Owen grinned. "He's right, so he is. Mr. Cristin and Mr. Bryn will try to make you as venturesome as themselves if you don't watch out, Rhonwen. Now eat your porridge, Tomos, and leave Rhonwen alone."

Tomos obeyed, but the sullen expression did not leave his face.

Later in the day Mary gave Rhonwen an expert massage and left her to rest. She was back within minutes.

"Mr. Cristin is downstairs and wants to talk to you. I told him you should keep your bed a while, but he won't take no for an answer. Well, it is natural for a lover to be impatient."

She helped Rhonwen dress, but there was no friendly teasing. Rhonwen felt a coldness inside and sensed that her new position was building a barrier between herself and the woman she had grown to love so much. When Mary had coiled her hair and Rhonwen was ready to descend, she pulled the small Welsh woman close.

"Please, don't change towards me. I could not bear it. We must always be as we are now."

Mary looked seriously at her and shook her head. "No, bach, it will not do. Mr. Cristin will not allow it."

"Nonsense! He could not be so unkind as to deprive me of my dearest friends."

"He will not consider it in that way. You will see, Rhonwen, and, indeed, it will be best, for your life will change completely."

Rhonwen continued to protest, trying to win a smile from

Mary, but when she sat by Cristin in the small parlour that was opened only for special occasions, she found that Mary was right.

"Good morning, my love," said Cristin, briskly kissing her cheek. "Now for our plans. You cannot remain here, of course. Edwina is giving orders this morning that a room be prepared for you, and you can leave here either tonight or tomorrow. You have not many clothes, I daresay, but we shall soon put that to rights. Frances is up to all the new rigs and will advise you, and Edwina will instruct you in the management of a great house."

Rhonwen's voice almost failed her as she viewed her future prospects with apprehension. Was it unreasonable to wish that Cristin had allowed more time for the flowering of their love before he made plans to improve her? Or that he might at least have pretended to find her satisfactory as she was—at least until they were man and wife?

She felt an urgent need to assert herself and said mutinously, "I wish to be married from here. This is my home—I feel it to be so—and Megan's wedding was the most wonderful occasion."

Her voice trailed away as she realised that Cristin was smiling at her as he would at a rebellious child.

"Of course, my dear, you do not wish for a big affair in view of your mourning. That is proper, but you cannot compare the marriage of a smith's daughter to a village shopkeeper's son with ours. Such a position as you are about to fill cannot be entered into in a village chapel, followed by a dance on the grass to music by the local fiddler."

'He has a way of denigrating humble things and making them seem cheap,' she thought, before she stifled so unworthy a suspicion. If he had stormed and argued she might have made headway, but he continued to talk as if humouring a child until her resistance seemed futile and unconsidered. She agreed to go to Castell Craig the following morning. As soon as he had obtained her promise, Cristin gave her another brief salute on her cheek and left. She stood by the cottage door ready to wave, but he did not look back.

Rhonwen half expected a teasing "I told you so" from Mary, but the Welsh woman hastened to assure her that her decision was the right one. Together they sponged and pressed her garments and David polished her boots until they reflected his face. Marged, with enormous concentration, undertook to replace some broken tapes and a missing button. The family met at the evening meal as if all was as usual, except for Tomos, who sat scowling at his plate until Mary sharply reproved him. For a horrified moment Rhonwen thought that he was close to tears, and as she looked round the table, she, too, felt like weeping. She wanted to stay with this family but realised that already there was a barrier between them that made it impossible. Suddenly she felt lonely.

Tomos picked up his knife and fork and muttered, "I don't like Mr. Cristin. I like Mr. Bryn. He is kind. Mr. Cristin isn't."

He then applied himself to his food while Owen tried to pass off the incident with a wink and a grin. Mary said, "Pay him no heed, Rhonwen. Just because Mr. Bryn lets him roam the hills with him and gives him tobacco he has no time for anyone else from the big house."

The following morning the whole family abandoned work. Even the little ones stayed from school to wish her well and wave as she was driven off in the gig by a smiling Cristin. As they turned out of the village street he put his gloved hand over her clenched fists.

"That's that! Now you begin a new life. It will not prove easy, but your intelligence is good and you will soon become what I wish my wife to be."

She pulled her hands away in irritation.

"If I am so full of faults I wonder at your desire to marry me."

She had almost said "your loving me," but Cristin's undemonstrative attitude made her shy of using the emotional word.

He looked down at her and laughed. He was bare-headed, and the early light filtering through the branches of overhanging trees gave unexpected auburn glints to his brown hair.

"There is much about you that is adorable, my sweet, but surely you are honest enough to admit the difference between your life and mine. Do you not wish to enter my world with confidence? I must have a woman who can take her rightful place in society, Rhonwen. Am I not right?"

108

"Yes, you are, sir, but . . ."

He laughed again. "But you thought perhaps I should have ridden to the Evans's cottage on a white charger, carried you off and made violent love to you, is that it?"

"You make it sound very silly, Cristin. Of course I do not expect life to be like a storybook."

"That is a sensible girl."

He dismissed the subject and talked instead of the countryside, pointing out the streams swollen with the rain that had been sweeping the mountain tops. "Winter is almost upon us. It is a time for taking stock. It will be a time for us to grow to know one another in wedlock and for you to prepare yourself for your first Season."

They began to drive through the rocks enclosing Castell Craig. In the daylight Rhonwen could see how impregnable a stronghold the castle must have been in former, more turbulent times. "Is there another way in to the castle?" she asked suddenly.

"Not for anyone but a friend. There is a small, deep lake at the rear, but cliffs rise sheer on each side. My ancestors knew how to make their world secure. And I—I also know, Rhonwen. Never make a mistake about that!"

His voice held a curious significance, almost as if he gave her a warning, and she shivered. For a moment she had felt afraid of him. Then his smile drove foolish fancies away as the gig was drawn up before the great front door.

"Welcome to your new home, Rhonwen. Castell Craig is ready to greet its future mistress."

Rhonwen's hopes that she would be allowed to make a quiet entrance into the castle were dashed. Stable hands came running to take the horse and gig, touching their caps and trying not to stare. When the double doors were thrown open by two liveried footmen she took an alarmed step back: a small army of servants were lined up in the hall, and the stately butler approached her with a bow and relieved her of her shabby jacket as if it had been sable. A formidable-looking woman, dressed entirely in black with an enormous chatelaine at her waist, curtseyed.

"Good morning, miss. May I welcome you to Castell Craig

on behalf of the staff. I am Harris, the housekeeper, and this is Tedder, our butler."

Cristin greeted them carelessly, and Rhonwen envied him his ease as he said, "These are the two with whom you must remain on good terms, my dear, for all our comfort lies in their capable hands, eh, Harris?"

The housekeeper curtseyed again and smirked.

"It is kind of you to say so, Mr. Cristin, indeed, it is; but, of course, miss, we could not manage without the others."

"All trained by your capable self," interposed Cristin and the woman gave him a look that bordered on the affectionate.

"Well, get on, woman," he continued in mock severity, "finish the formalities and let us go to Miss Edwina."

Servant after servant was named by Harris until the bobbing figures and smiling, bashful faces blurred into a whole and Rhonwen felt despairingly that never would she be able even to recall their names, leave alone their duties. Only one made an impression upon her: Ettie, the head housemaid, a tall, grave-looking woman, who, Cristin had said, remembered Beatrice.

As they filed away through a green baize door, Harris said, "Of course, miss, there are others in the basement. Scullery maids, washer-women and so forth who you'll never see; but the ones you have met are the upstairs workers and they are ready at all times to assist you." She gave a deprecatory cough. "Excuse me, but are we to make ready to receive your own maid?"

"Miss Morgan will be selecting a personal servant," said Cristin briefly. "Bring sherry to the morning room, Tedder."

For a moment Cristin and Rhonwen were alone in the hall and she said, "I shall never be able to cope with all those people. You know I have no experience in ordering domestics."

"Oh, don't worry your head about it. Frances will help you and so will Edwina, though frequently she only sees Harris and Tedder for days at a time. You can do the same if you so wish, but I feel a home is best run when the mistress is on terms with all the senior servants. However, you will decide that later."

He guided her to a small room with chintz-covered furniture and a blazing fire. Rhonwen felt more at ease in the homely atmosphere. Edwina laid aside her embroidery frame and held out welcoming hands.

"Miss Morgan—how charming this is. I little thought when first we met that you would return as Cristin's affianced bride."

She drew Rhonwen down and kissed her cheek. Her words and looks were warm, yet Rhonwen felt that the inner core of reserve remained inviolate. Did she truly feel pleasure that her cousin was to marry a nobody? Somehow one could not visualise Edwina speaking or acting without sincerity, and Rhonwen hoped earnestly that one day she might find her way through to the true Edwina and make a friend of her.

"Sit near the fire," she went on. "Ah, here is Tedder with wine. Pour a little for Miss Morgan. She looks chilled."

After the butler had obeyed and left, Edwina continued chidingly to Cristin, "Or perhaps she is cold with nervousness. I admonished him, Rhonwen, when I heard that he had ordered the servants to change into their afternoon clothes and present themselves for your inspection. Poor child! How terrified you must have been."

Rhonwen said with surprise, "How could you understand that? I mean, you are used to such attention . . ."

Edwina laughed. "Certainly I have not lived without servants, but never have I had to enter a house in such a manner. I think I might have run away. It was too bad of you, Cristin. Rhonwen should have become accustomed to them gradually."

Rhonwen was startled by Cristin's heavy frown. *"My* wife will observe all the right formalities at all times," he grated. "Rhonwen will pay her duty to me, of that you may be sure."

The awkward moment passed with some light observation from Edwina, but later that night Rhonwen sat at her window and tried to grasp the enormous change in her life. She had spent a quiet day thanks to Edwina, who insisted that she had had enough excitement for the time being and had been conducted to her bedroom at ten o'clock by a footman. He had carried a lamp through seemingly endless passageways and stairs, already illuminated by lamps and candles in a manner clearly reckless of cost, though by now Rhonwen understood that only immense and ancient wealth could be responsible for the furnishing and upkeep of Castell Craig.

She walked to the bed, sat on it and swung her legs to the

coverlet, then reached out and tugged at the heavy wool curtains. They slid around the bed and back again in a silent glide that spoke of servants who attended to every tiny detail that would make life smooth for the occupants of the castle.

Rhonwen wondered if ever she would become accustomed to a room containing a fourposter bed as substantial as a four-horse coach and almost as big as her room at the Evans's. Sudden nostalgia for the comfort of Owen and Mary's kindness brought tears to blot out the sight of the carved furniture and rich hangings. She dashed a hand across her eyes. What was the matter with her? She must overcome her inhibitions and allow her love for Cristin to flower.

She did not pull the curtains around the bed but lay sleepless, staring through the window across the castellated walls to where a half-grown moon threw light on to the jagged crags of the Rhinogs. Here was her future home; here and in some grand house in London, she imagined. But she would always be with Cristin, always have his love and care to sustain her. They must, or she would never find the peace of mind she associated with a home and a family of her own.

Chapter 9

THE NEXT MORNING Rhonwen drank the tea and ate the bread and butter carried to her by a respectful maid and looked with surprise at the leaping flames in the grate. Someone—one of the little humble skivies—had crept in with amazing stealth and kindled the fire.

She got out of bed quickly, feeling uneasy that a stranger had observed her asleep and feeling pity for the girl who had to begin work so early. Then she was chagrined at the thought of what Cristin and Frances would say if they could eavesdrop on her thoughts. She must begin to think like a great lady. She could not envisage Frances even noticing a menial whose daily task was to climb flights of stairs carrying coal.

Jugs of hot water were brought by two maids, one of whom was Ettie. As they curtseyed before leaving, Rhonwen said impulsively, "Ettie, I wonder if I might speak privately with you."

The other housemaid hurried away and Ettie stood waiting quietly, only her eyes betraying her puzzlement. Rhonwen said, "I have heard that you have some memory of . . . a maid who used to be here."

'She was my mother,' she thought, but she dared not voice the words. Belatedly it had occurred to her that Cristin would not want it known that his bride-to-be was the daughter of a former servant by an unknown man. She should not have shown an interest that could provoke talk.

Ettie was frowning a little. "Did you want to ask me something, miss? I have yet to take water to Miss Edwina."

"I am sorry to delay you. It is only that I . . . I would like to hear of Mrs.—Miss Morgan—when she was a girl."

"I never knew anyone of that name, miss."

"But . . . but surely . . . Mr. Cristin asked you about her and you said . . ."

Her voice trailed away beneath Ettie's calm gaze. "You are mistaken, miss. Mr. Cristin has not had occasion to speak to me for ever so long. I hardly ever see him."

"Are you sure? You cannot have forgotten? Beatrice Morgan is the name—she was once personal maid to Miss Edwina."

"I don't remember her, miss. I've only ever known Grace Bell in the years I've worked above stairs."

"You have been here since you were a child!"

"Yes, I came eighteen years ago, but I never heard talk of anyone of that name."

The maid met Rhonwen's stare unflinchingly. If she was lying she did it superlatively well. But why should she? And if she was telling the truth, then Cristin . . .

"Have I your leave to go, miss? I really should be about my duties."

"Yes, yes, you may go. Thank you."

She resolved to ask Cristin, at the first opportunity, to explain the mystery to her. Then she stood before her open wardrobe surveying her shamingly few, shabby garments, wrestling with the foolish notion that Cristin should have waited to rejoice in acquiring her as a bride before asking Frances's help in improving her. She had been chosen by Cristin Caradog, handsome, cultivated, rich, and she must learn to follow his dictates, which must surely be correct.

With a sigh she took out her blue serge dress, pulled it on, then looked into the long, gilt-edged mirror, trying to see herself from the view of a comparative stranger. Both Caradog brothers had commented favourably upon her looks. And so had Frances Kendrick—not in words, but in the wary way one lovely woman looks at a rival. 'How did I know that,' wondered Rhonwen, then acknowledged ruefully that some truths were born with women. She threw out her arms, feeling suddenly glad that Cristin was not content to leave her in shabby clothes. She would know the sensuous feel of rich materials, and it seemed that among the wealthy it was not considered evil to covet such things.

Cristin had not wasted time. As Rhonwen was finishing her breakfast coffee, Frances was announced. She entered the room, gowned in impeccable riding gear; tossing her hat and crop to an easy chair, she called to Tedder for more hot coffee. Edwina seldom rose for breakfast, so Rhonwen and Cristin had been alone and Frances looked from one to the other.

She smiled, but in her eyes was something that gave Rhonwen an inner qualm as she said, "It seems I have to congratulate you, Miss Morgan, though I know you will permit me now to call you by your Christian name since I have long felt a part of the Caradog family. And you must address me as Frances."

She threw herself in a graceful sprawl in the chair beside Cristin, who said dryly, "Stow it, Fran! You know it is I who should receive congratulations, and proper courtesy entitles Rhonwen to your good wishes."

Frances raised her eyebrows. "Try to ignore his slang, Rhonwen. In the general way, Cristin, that is true, of course; but your chosen bride seems an honest enough girl. She will admit that she has been exceedingly fortunate to gain the love of Cristin Caradog of Castell Craig. At least she will admit it to one who has been almost a member of the family. And expected to be fully so."

The last sentence was uttered in so low a tone that Rhonwen could have thought she imagined it. Frances had turned her head towards Cristin so that Rhonwen could not see her expression, but for an instant the room was filled with some overwhelming emotion, like the heavy atmosphere preceeding a storm. Then Frances turned to her and her lovely face was filled with laughter.

"And this morning I shall begin to help with your *trousseau,* Rhonwen. It will be such a delight to garb so pretty a creature."

The words were unexceptionable, but Frances had a way of barbing the delivery, and two points of colour appeared over Cristin's cheekbones.

"Do not go too far, Frances, or you will answer to me."

"Oh, hold your tongue," returned Frances carelessly. "Women do not require assistance from a male when they choose clothes, do they, Rhonwen?"

Rhonwen reminded herself that these two had been reared in such close proximity that they could throw insults like brother and sister; but she could not join in Frances's lilting laughter. She wondered if ever she would be on such easy terms with Cristin. Perhaps marriage would make her feel different. Everything was so new to her—even the caring. She still could not use the word love. Love was too tender a plant in her life to speak of it with familiarity.

Cristin rose and bowed with mock ceremony. "I defer to your superior knowledge in this field, Frances. Obtain all that is needful for the present and bring the bills to me."

As he left the room, Rhonwen muttered a hasty excuse to Frances and followed him. "Cristin, there is something I wish to ask you."

He turned, smiling indulgently. "You may safely put yourself in Frances's hands, my dear. She is very clever where fashion is concerned."

"It is not that! I spoke to Ettie."

Cristin's face clouded with rage. He looked at the footman who stood at the front door and a maid who hurried through the great hall, the short streamers of her morning cap bobbing behind her. Then he took Rhonwen's arm, none too gently, and thrust her through the door of a book-lined room.

"Now explain yourself!"

"I spoke to Ettie, that is all. I asked if she remembered Beatrice Morgan."

"Did you say what your relationship was?"

"No, I did not, though truly, Cristin, it goes very much against my inner feelings to deny my own mother, even by my silence."

He made an impatient sound and she continued hastily, "Ettie says she never knew my mother. Yet you told me that she even recalled the talk of her pregnancy by an unknown lover. Did you lie to me?"

"You little fool, of course not! Have you no sense of decorum? Or of loyalty to me?"

"That is not fair!"

"Not fair? And what do you think of your own behaviour? Of course Ettie denied having spoken to me. I told her I was making discreet enquiries on behalf of someone who wished to trace a servant called Morgan—naturally I did not mention you. I made her understand that the matter was one of extreme delicacy and gained from her a promise that she would discuss it with no one. What a quandary you must have placed the poor woman in! Either she must break her vow to me or lie to you. You must have made her very curious. If she had not previously connected your name with that of your mother's she certainly will do so now.

"For God's sake, Rhonwen! Are you going to seek out and question all the older servants. Can you not let the past remain buried?"

"You are ashamed of me!"

Her cry rang through the room, and Cristin's face softened as he took her in his arms, smoothing her hair from her brow. "Forgive my anger, my dear. One day you will learn to understand—even, I hope, to share—the great pride I have in my family's name. I daresay it seems over-emphasized to you—how could it be otherwise—but you will learn—I will teach you. Fortunately, I am convinced that any secrets discovered by Sophy or Ettie will be safe, but once allow the lower servants to discover your origins and your name will be bandied about in a way I could not bear. And so will your mother's! Surely you would wish to protect her memory."

Rhonwen said, "You are right, of course. I am sorry, Cristin. I shall not make that mistake again."

He kissed her forehead. "That is my good girl. Now, go to Frances and remember, the past must be left undisturbed."

In Rhonwen's bedroom Frances looked about her. "You have a fine view of the mountains, though I prefer the chambers above the lake. Looking out upon the water made so impregnable by the cliffs I feel so . . . so secure. I love this place."

Her voice had gone bleak as she faltered, and her mouth twisted in what could have been grief. Rhonwen took a step towards her, scarcely knowing what she wanted to say. "Miss Kendrick . . ."

But Frances stepped back. "Come now, you must remember to call me Frances. I have had my maid pack a tape measure. Take off your gown and let us begin. We shall buy materials in Harlech for now—they will be inferior but they will have to suffice. We will order better ones from London and my sewing woman can make up the patterns. When Cristin takes you on your bridal trip, you can purchase gowns from London and Paris to enhance your looks and figure. Cristin Caradog's woman must look like a great lady."

Had Rhonwen imagined the stress on the word "look"? Frances seemed friendly, but there was an undercurrent of an emotion kept rigidly in check.

The two women were later driven to Harlech and entered the draper's shop. As soon as Howell Pugh saw Rhonwen he called to Megan, who ran to clasp her in her arms.

"It's welcome you are, love. Can you stay to dinner with us?"

"You are forgetting your duties, Megan Pugh!" The reproof came from Howell's father, who was bringing a chair to the shop front. "Here is Miss Kendrick who needs to be waited on."

Megan blushed and dropped a curtsey. "Please excuse me, ma'am. I was excited, you see. Go you through, Rhonwen, and I'll be with you as soon as possible."

Frances laughed lightly as she seated herself. "Miss Morgan and I are together, Mrs. Pugh. Please show us some of your best materials—in muted shades, of course, since Miss Morgan still mourns her mama."

Megan looked her astonishment and Rhonwen said faintly, "Mr. Cristin Caradog and I are to be married, Megan."

"M . . . married? Well! Well, I hardly know what to say. I didn't know, but I haven't seen anyone from home—Glyn Dedwydd, I mean—for a day or two. Well, it is surprised I am, but happy for you, bach."

Impulsively she kissed Rhonwen and would have said more, but she was quelled by the icy looks from Frances.

Mr. Pugh tutted and said, "Go to your kitchen, Megan. It will be best if Howell and I reach down the bolts of cloth. They are too heavy for you at present."

Megan scurried into the back, and as Howell and his father climbed ladders to the high shelves, Frances raised her brows in amusement and said softly, "Megan Pugh's lusty young husband has wasted no time, it seems."

Her meaning dawned on Rhonwen. "Do you think that Megan is with child? They have scarcely been wed . . ."

"There has been time enough. People of their class seldom seem to have difficulty in procreating."

Delicate colour ran under Rhonwen's skin, and Frances raised her brows again. "Oh dear, I have said the wrong thing, have I not? Do forgive me, Rhonwen dear. You must allow me time to become accustomed to our different backgrounds."

Howell and his father brought many different cloths before Frances selected three. Rhonwen's suspicion that Frances was being deliberately difficult to please and would end by choosing something unbecoming was banished when she was asked to approve of lavender-grey cashmere, shimmering black silk and peat-brown velvet. She needed no one to tell her that the shades and textures would flatter her. After they had bought soft white lace to relieve the black, satin ribbons of a matching shade for the velvet and three dozen tiny pearl buttons for the grey wool, Frances rose with the obvious intention of departing.

Rhonwen said before anyone could intervene, "I must say goodbye to Megan. She is my friend." She slipped through the house door but soon joined Frances in the carriage and kept her face averted.

Frances said, "It was a mistake to go to Mrs. Pugh, was it not?"

"She curtseyed to me. To *me!* She was awkward and treated me as if . . . as if . . ."

". . . as if you were far above her," supplied Frances. "And so you are. She recognizes it even if you find it difficult."

"Surely she cannot think I would so glibly relinquish our friendship."

"She knows she cannot aspire to be the intimate of the wife of a Caradog," said Frances and continued dryly, *"He* will never countenance familiarity with people of lesser breeding, and the Evans and the Pughs of the world are aware of that. If you wish to retain his love you must conform."

Her voice grew low and took on the brooding quality Rhonwen was learning to dread. "He must want you badly or he would not have proposed marriage to one who . . . ." She stopped.

". . . one who is of lesser breeding," finished Rhonwen. "That is what you are thinking even if you will not say it. Honesty compels me to admit I was surprised when Cristin proposed to me. I did not expect it, you must know. I did not seek for it."

The other woman's voice was vibrant though still low. "So, you did not seek for it! You can scarcely expect me to believe that! You look so youthful and innocent—and beautiful—it is no wonder that Cristin desires you. Oh, do not suppose that I was unaware of his visits to you. How I laughed! But you were too clever for him, were you not? You held out against his importunings—his blandishments—you drew a proposal of marriage from him. Now I will have to endure the amusement of our friends."

Rhonwen felt flayed by the implications. "You are inferring that Cristin's intention was to seduce me. That if he had succeeded he would not have offered me marriage. But you are wrong. He has never tried to lay seige to my . . . my virtue. He has never even kissed me in a way that is not chaste."

"What's that you say?" Frances's head whipped round so fast that she had to clutch at her fashionable beaver hat. "You cannot expect me to believe you! I *know* Cristin Caradog!"

Rhonwen stared back at Frances. "I . . . I do assure you, ma'am, that Cristin has behaved to me with the utmost propriety."

"Then he *does* love you—he must—Oh, I had not thought it was . . . !"

Her distress caused her to raise her voice above discreet tones, and Rhonwen glanced through the wind shield at the coachman's back. "Hush, Frances, he may hear. Why are you so upset? You already know that Cristin and I are betrothed to . . ."

"Betrothals can be broken!"

Rhonwen managed to keep her voice low though she was badly shaken. "Are you telling me that you believed Cristin to be using an engagement as a means of gaining his way with me? That is revolting! It is unforgivable of you to suggest it! What grounds have you?"

"What, indeed? Cristin Caradog has lain with so many women I have lost count, but always he has returned to me. Naturally, I believed you to be yet another in the line—more difficult to obtain and consequently more desirable—and that he would pay you off and we would resume our usual relationship. Or so I thought until now. Oh, God, I cannot bear it!"

Rhonwen was savagely angry. "You have been helping me to select materials to please a man you thought was to be my . . . my betrayer. Where I was reared we had an ugly name for people who procured—an ugly name for a disgusting occupation!"

Frances's fury matched her own. "And no doubt you had a name for women who use their beauty to ensnare men. How is anyone to be sure that you have not been on close terms with other men? We know nothing of you! How can Cristin be such a fool? I still cannot accept his love for you. Perhaps you are simply a convincing liar—and yet . . . yet . . . he would not offer you marriage if he had already taken your body—and you say he has not even tried—can he truly love you?"

"Frances—the coachman!"

"Damn the coachman! And damn Cristin Caradog and all men like him! Ever since I can remember I have wanted Cristin and he has desired me, but never would I yield. I have known that my chief hold was to keep myself for marriage and turn a blind eye to his amorous adventures, which were, after all, only the amusements of any virile man. And now you have come along—a penniless ill-bred chit—and robbed me of the only man I could ever love! Do you think I would have remained so passive had I thought my future in danger?" She gnawed viciously at her glove, tearing the soft kid with her small white teeth. "How dare he! I am twenty-five years old and have spent my youth waiting for him. And now I find I am to lose him. You have stolen my man!"

Rhonwen knew she must hide the pity she felt in spite of Frances's insults. She said quietly, "He is not your man, Frances. He was not obliged to offer for me, and he must love me as I . . . I care for him."

"Care for him? A milk-and-water expression to match your flimsy nature, I daresay! I love him—adore him—I have so much to give him. Oh, Cristin . . . !"

The carriage was turning into the drive to the castle. Frances stared ahead of her, while Rhonwen prayed that the coachman had not overheard enough to set the servants' hall abuzz with speculation. As he drove to the stables, Frances stood for a moment at the foot of the steps leading to the door being opened by a footman. She was pale and her breathing was uneven, but she said in almost normal tones, "Rhonwen—my disappointment—my anger at Cristin's behaviour to me has led me into indiscretion, and I overstepped the boundaries of what is due to you. You . . . you did not deserve such treatment. Pray, try to forget what I said. I will continue to help you, as Cristin desires. Do not heed my words of his past. Many men behave in such a fashion, but they become model husbands."

She began the climb the steps, seeming to require no answer, taking it for granted that if Cristin wished for some course of action all would obey him. Rhonwen followed slowly. Apparently she was expected to accept Frances's revelations about his conduct without a murmur.

Memories of obscure allusions by her mother and Ida Blake to the behaviour of some of the gentry flashed through her mind, and for the first time their meaning was understood by her.

After lunch Edwina applied herself to her sewing and Cristin decided to take Rhonwen on a tour of part of his home. Frances joined at his invitation. Cristin explained, "Frances knows as much about the family possessions as I do, Rhonwen, and often more."

She was guided in and out of sumptuous rooms, through corridors and ante-chambers; shown treasures collected over centuries until she was bemused, both by the quantity and the value. She had gained some knowledge of such things through her visits to London museums and galleries with Miss Reeves. She had always felt drawn to beauty, and she appreciated still further the tremendous difference in her background and that of her fiancé, while Frances was so much at home in Castell Craig that it might have seemed to a stranger that she and Cristin were husband and wife displaying their mutual possessions.

Back in the small drawing room Edwina asked, "Did you get as far as the gallery, Rhonwen?"

"No! There is much left for her to visit," interposed Cristin. "She can meet the portraits of our ancestors some other time."

Edwina, Frances and Cristin fell naturally into a discussion of great houses known to them, and Rhonwen went to sit on the window seat, leaning so that she was almost concealed by the heavy brocade curtains, feeling a need for a moment of seclusion. She was still overawed by the marvels of Castell Craig and felt humble at the realisation of what Cristin was offering her. One day she would be mistress here. Cristin would take her to other parts of the world, but from now on her life would be bound into this place. She recalled the rooms overlooking the lake where she had stared out at the dark water shadowed by vast cliffs and scree-laden slopes and stirred restlessly, wondering why she felt as if the mountains were closing in, giving her the claustrophobic sensation of a prisoner.

Lost in her own imaginings she became suddenly aware that someone had entered the room and was talking to the others. Bryn Caradog!

"We had not been expecting you, Bryn!" That was Frances whose voice had taken on the mocking tinge she so often used when both brothers were present. "I thought that Cristin had given you work enough to keep you away for weeks."

"I have completed all I thought essential. How are you, Edwina? Stop frowning at me, Cristin. I dismissed the mine manager, as we thought might be necessary, since he has been misusing the money we sent him for safety precautions. But as there is no question of embezzlement, I decided that to lose his post was punishment enough. The injured man is recovering and has our promise that he will be paid until he is fit and can earn his bread again."

Rhonwen stayed still, acutely embarrassed. The others seemed to have forgotten her presence and she was as shut out as if she did not exist. Frances would never be found in such a predicament. She would simply have revealed herself and immediately dominate the company. Rhonwen's new status had not yet given her such self-assurance; and besides, she could not understand her sudden irrational nervousness at the idea of confronting Bryn when he received the news of her forthcoming marriage.

"What of our business in Cardiff?" Cristin sounded far more annoyed than the situation warranted.

"I have been to Cardiff and found matters to be nowhere near as urgent as you represented them, my dear brother, and I have a particular reason for wishing to be at home just now."

Frances gave her silvery laugh. "How mysterious! Dare I

wonder if your reason is connected with a woman?"

"With a lady, if you please, Frances; but that is as much I will tell you. All will be revealed in time."

"Cristin! You are forgetting our honoured guest!" That was Edwina. "Your brother has a most pleasant surprise for you, Bryn."

The moment could no longer be postponed and still with baffling reluctance Rhonwen pulled aside the curtain, rose and walked to the others who were grouped near the fire.

She looked first at Bryn and smiled, and his thin face lit in an answering smile. "By all that's wonderful! This is *indeed* a pleasant surprise. I had not expected to see you so soon, Rhonwen."

He took impatient strides to her and clasped her hand in his. "But you are cold. You should not sit so far from the fire." He bent his head and said softly, "No mud or flour on your pretty nose tonight, though it is somewhat pink from the draught."

Cristin moved quickly to them, and as Bryn released Rhonwen's hand, he took it with obvious gesture of propriety. "Bryn, I believe you have already met your new sister. Rhonwen has done me the honour of accepting my proposal of marriage."

Shock widened Bryn's eyes, and for an instant she felt a stab of fear at the expression that crossed his face, before he gave a small bow and said, "My felicitations to you, Cristin. And to you, ma'am. It seems you have both been busy while I was away. Pray excuse me, Edwina, while I wash the dust of my journey from me. I wasted no time in coming home."

He was gone and did not return. Shortly before the dinner hour Edwina said, "Cristin has shown you part of our home, Rhonwen, and now it is my turn. Are you too fatigued to visit me in my own small domain?"

She led the way through the castle until they reached a stairway Rhonwen had not seen. Edwina said, "No one except my servants comes here except at my express invitation. I have never shared my home with another woman. I feel strongly, Rhonwen, that you and I are destined to be friends."

She opened a door at the head of the stairway, and a maid who was tidying a chest of drawers looked over her shoulder in surprise. "I have brought Miss Rhonwen to have a little talk.

This is my own dear maid, Grace Bell, who has been with me for eighteen years—ever since . . ." She stopped as a spasm twisted her mouth. "You are to wish Miss Rhonwen joy, Grace, for she is to wed Mr. Cristin."

The maid showed her obvious amazement, and Rhonwen felt hard put to summon a smile as Grace recovered herself enough to offer her good wishes. The sooner everyone knew of her betrothal and accepted her, the better pleased she would be.

After Grace Bell had left Rhonwen looked around. Edwina's quarters were in one of the square turrets and were furnished in a well co-ordinated mixture of styles in which Tudor oak predominated. "As you see, Rhonwen, I care most for the old things. They are heavy, but their simplicity of design and deep, lovingly executed carving appeals to me." Her fingers explored the sculptured wood on an oak chest, and Rhonwen was reminded of her mother's box and recalled in the same instant that Beatrice had almost certainly stolen it from these rooms when she ran away from Castell Craig.

She felt suddenly overcome by guilt and sat down heavily. Edwina looked startled, then her face softened, "My poor dear, you must be exhausted. After your recent sufferings we have asked too much of you. I am being entirely selfish. Another day would have done as well to visit me."

"No," cried Rhonwen unable to control the emotion that sprang from a sense of her mother's shame. "It is not that. Miss Caradog, I . . ."

"Oh, make it Edwina, dear. You will lose your nervousness in time, never fear."

Tears filled Rhonwen's eyes and Edwina handed her a delicate, lace trimmed handkerchief. "I will make tea for us. I have a tiny kitchen of my own, you know. Sometimes I do not join the others for meals, and Grace and I are very cosy together. Frances frowns upon this, saying I should not hobnob with my inferiors, and Cristin agrees with her."

Frances and Cristin—always their names linked! There seemed justification for Frances's rage towards her. Had she truly stolen her lover from her?

Edwina placed a tray of porcelain cups and saucers and a dish of buttered oat cakes on a small table and began to pour tea, glancing up to give a reassuring smile.

Rhonwen felt she could not endure such unquestioning acceptance. "Edwina, there is something I must tell you. I . . . I feel I am with you under false pretences."

Edwina replaced the silver teapot on its stand. Even now, dispensing tea in the seclusion of her own quarters, she maintained her air of remoteness. She folded her hands and waited for Rhonwen to speak.

"Edwina, the reason I came to Glyn Dedwydd was to try to trace my mother's people. She was Beatrice Morgan—the maid who left you so suddenly."

Her words, dropped into the well of silence, broke Edwina's tranquillity at last as the ripples penetrated her understanding.

Her brown eyes were filled with bewildered distress. "You are the daughter of *my* Beatrice? I cannot credit it—you do not resemble her at all. Yet why should you come here and lie to me?"

She breathed deeply, trying to compose herself, and Rhonwen grew even more nervous as it dawned on her that Edwina might suspect her of being an interloper who had discovered some of Beatrice's past history, including her loving relationship with her mistress, and wonder if she had journeyed to Wales with the intention of trying to gain some profit from her knowledge.

"I am speaking the truth, Edwina. I . . . I can show you drawings I found after my mother's death. They are signed by Cristin and Bryn. I had never seen them before."

Her voice cracked, and Edwina gave her a long stare. "I want to believe you, Rhonwen. I liked you from the first." She was silent for a moment. "Tell Grace where you keep the drawings and she can bring them here."

Rhonwen thought of them lying in Edwina's own box and said, "It would be better if Grace could simply direct me to my room. I have other evidence there."

Edwina gave her another searching look. "Very well, Rhonwen. So be it."

Grace waited by Rhownen's door while as she hurried inside and contrived to unlock her carpetbag and extract the papers from the box without lifting it. She locked the box and bag once more, replaced the keys in her purse and fetched other articles from her dressing table drawer.

She handed everything to Edwina, who looked at the childish scrawls and marvelled, "She kept them all these years. It all makes her flight seem more strange. I know she loved this place."

She picked up Beatrice's brooch. "This was her favourite and she wore it often. How clearly it brings her back to memory. And what is this? A photograph!"

"Mother took me to have our likenesses taken when I was eight. She said every child should have at least one record of childhood." Rhonwen looked over Edwina's shoulder at the sepia-coloured picture. Her mother stood, holding herself unnaturally rigid, her face showing her suspicion of the photographer and his tricks. She wore her best black gown and there, on the front, was pinned the precious brooch. One hand lay on the back of a chair where sat Rhonwen, youthful but unmistakable, her feet not quite reaching the floor, her ringleted hair adorned with a large bow of ribbon, hands demurely clasped in her lap.

"I couldn't keep still," she confessed, "and the man had to fix an odd wire contraption behind my head, but Mother didn't move an inch. The man complimented her on her excellent control. Fancy remembering that. I thought I had forgotten that day."

"Beatrice was a most strong-minded woman," murmured Edwina, looking at the photograph. "So strong and determined, but so very good to me." She handed Rhonwen her possessions, her eyes moist. "Thank you. I did not wish to doubt you, but I had to be sure. I recall her so vividly. I thought she loved me too well to leave me." She asked in calmer tones, "Why did she go? What happened to cause her to break the habits of a lifetime and . . . ?"

. . . steal from me?—the words were unsaid, but they were in Edwina's mind, Rhonwen felt sure.

She said evenly, "Mother never talked to me of the past. After she died I felt desperate for a family of my own. That is why I came." She would not produce the box—not yet. The evidence Rhonwen had given Edwina had convinced her of her identity so why resurrect her mother's crime to no good purpose? Perhaps one day, when she was a part of the Caradog family, she would find the right way to give Edwina back her box.

"What of your father's people?" asked Edwina. "Could you not have gone to them?"

Rhonwen swallowed. How would Edwina take the remainder of the bitter truth about the girl who was to marry into her family? "Mother always spoke of him as if he were dead; but since coming to Glyn Dedwydd I have found reason to assume —that is, I am sure—that I was born out of wedlock. That is why she fled. She was already pregnant. Sophy Parry told me."

"Oh, how dreadful!" The shock in Edwina's voice made Rhonwen sick with apprehension, but she need not have feared. "My dear, dear Beatrice! To have gone without a word and for such a reason. She knew I loved her. She must have known I would shield her—I above all others! Why did she not confide in me? I failed her—I must have done . . ."

She sprang to her feet and began to pace the floor, her hands writhing together in agitation. "I must have failed her," she repeated. "And after all she did for me!"

She stopped abruptly and flung a question at Rhonwen. "Does Cristin know this?"

"He knows."

Edwina walked the room once more before she seated herself beside Rhonwen. "Then this family can make reparation through you. Your poor mother came to grief beneath this roof. I am glad to know that Cristin is so selfless—he must love you very much, Rhonwen. His pride in his family and home is an obsession with him. I believe true love to be a jewel of inestimable value and set it above birth. I am glad that in your case Cristin agrees with me."

They drank tea while Edwina plied Rhonwen with questions about her life with her mother, often interrupting to exclaim her pity at their hardships, wondering aloud why Beatrice had not asked for assistance.

"She cared well for you though, Rhonwen, and has brought you up in a very fine way. In spite of appearances, Beatrice was a good woman. Her rigid notions did not permit her even to take table beer—alcohol was abhorrent to her. What could have made her give herself to such an undeserving man?"

Rhonwen tried to visualise her mother through Edwina's eyes. No wonder she had become racked by guilt when she and Ida drank too much or indulged in bawdy jokes and raucous laughter. Beatrice had tried hard to blot out her past but had never truly succeeded. Life had been harder for her than Rhonwen had suspected.

Before Rhonwen left the turret room, Edwina opened a carved chest, and the air became redolent with the scent of cedarwood and sweet herbs. She drew out an exquisitely crocheted, long-fringed white shawl. "Your mother finished this just before she left. I was kept to my bed, but she sat with me, her hands always busy. She made such lovely things. I would like you to have it."

Rhonwen brushed the soft wool against her face and thanked Edwina, who said, "How wonderful it will be to have you here, my dear. It will be like having a daughter. I always felt I would like one." She flushed. "How silly that must sound—an old maid wishing she had a child."

Rhonwen would have tried to offer reassurance, but she sensed that Edwina had retired once more into her impregnable fortress of reserve, and she followed Grace Bell back to her room.

That evening she wore her black sateen gown with the shawl draped over her shoulders. When she entered the drawing room, Frances was sipping wine while Cristin and Bryn leaned on the mantelshelf talking of business. Cristin smiled and led her to a seat near Frances, but Bryn's expression and greeting were cool, and Rhonwen felt a stab of hurt.

Frances's eyes immediately perceived the shawl. "Did you make it? How clever you must be!"

"It is a gift from Edwina."

"Really! Were you long in her rooms? How splendid that you have won her confidence so quickly."

What sharpness she had in her tongue! She could make a seemingly innocuous remark sound like an insult. She was wearing a shot silk gown of orange and scarlet, with dark garnets at her throat and ears and slender gold and diamond bracelets on her wrists. On most women such an outfit would look horribly garish, but it enhanced Frances's dark beauty and made her appear as if her body was encased in shimmering flames and pinpoints of light. Rhonwen was not surprised that the eyes of both men were drawn often to her.

With a shock she gathered that Frances had not been home

to change and, therefore, must have a supply of clothes in Castell Craig—perhaps even a permanent room. Would she continue to regard the castle as her second home after Cristin's marriage? Would Rhonwen have to compete with Frances, always at hand, immaculate and self-assured, her mere presence reminding Cristin of his wife's humble upbringing and *gauche* ways?

Edwina joined them and dinner was eaten in an atmosphere of celebration and gaiety that seemed forced and unreal to Rhonwen. Later, while waiting for the men to finish their port, she sat at the small writing desk in the drawing room and wrote to Miss Reeves and Mr. Baker, telling them her news. Then Cristin and Bryn entered, and Frances walked to the piano where she began to play in her accomplished style.

"Do come and sing, Cristin. Rhonwen must know how we Welsh love to sing. I daresay your mama has told you—or sung to you. One day we must hear you. Perhaps your voice deserves to be trained."

Cristin hesitated, gave Rhonwen a deprecating smile and moved to the piano. Frances began to play again, talking over the music. "This is *Hob y deri dando,* Rhonwen. It has some good sentiments in it."

She and Cristin sang in Welsh and Rhonwen saw that there was yet another barrier between her and the others. When they reached the last verse, Frances began to sing in English and Cristin fell silent as her contralto voice carressed the words: *"Did we know that fancy fails us, Even we? And that only love avails us? Ah me, whispered she, I would live and die for thee."*

Frances made no attempt to conceal the look of passion she directed momentarily at Cristin, and Rhonwen saw that he accepted it as normal as he kissed Frances's fingertips and thanked her for the music.

Chapter 10

RHONWEN LAY sleepless that night in the great four-poster, thinking of the prospects of her life with Cristin. Frances's presence was making her feel increasingly uneasy, and she wondered if she would receive any support if she tried to make the other woman's visits fewer and of shorter duration. Bryn might help. The thought presented itself, then was quickly suppressed. His reaction to the news of her betrothal and his later attitude towards her left no doubt that he disliked the engagement. Was his anger born of his antipathy towards his brother? Or was he jealous? This unexpected idea was thrust into the recesses of her mind. Bryn would surely learn to accept her as a sister.

Edwina might prove a good companion if only she would not continually put up barriers between herself and those about her. Rhonwen felt suddenly homesick for the warmth and uncomplicated affection of the Evans's and then a longing for her mother who was certainly unpredictable but never wavering in her protection of her daughter.

Rhonwen had a premonition that tonight she would suffer again, she struggled against sleep until suddenly she was lost in the nightmare, which ended with a terrifying difference. At one moment she was on the staircase, scrabbling with desperate hands at a locked door; the next she was inside the room and could hear the frantic scratching on the wooden panels and knew that danger lay both inside and out. She woke crying aloud, reaching blindly for the comfort of her mother's flesh, until she was fully awake and able to find the matches and light her bedside candle with shaking hands. She lay until dawn watching the play of light on the intricately embossed ceiling then fell into a heavy dreamless sleep from which she awoke with a severe headache.

Edwina came to enquire after her and brought remedies of her own, which helped to kill the pain.

"I suffer myself with headaches, Rhonwen. They can be devastating. Pray rest for as long as you need and ring for anything you require."

She paused at the bedroom door and returned to stand looking down at her.

"My dear, it must be wearing on your nerves to be alone among strangers. I know you have Cristin's love, and we will become friends in time; but is there no one you would like to invite to be with you? She would be most welcome."

"I . . . I have no acquaintances of my own age," said Rhonwen. "In fact, the only person I can think of is Miss Reeves, my teacher. Perhaps she would come. I daresay she would enjoy visiting here. She was born into a good family though she is now in straitened circumstances."

It was agreed that Rhonwen should ask her, and as she felt well enough, she rose to joined the others for dinner. There was no sign of Frances and when she and Edwina retired to the drawing room, she wrote her letter to Miss Reeves, which was given to Tedder to be taken out with the morning mail. Cristin begged to be excused for the remainder of the evening, pleading unavoidable business. Rhonwen looked down at his softly waving brown hair as he bent to kiss her hand, before pressing his lips to her cheek, and wondered if his business concerned some local girl. She wished that Frances had not told her of his past adventures. Words spoken by her mother came to mind. "A man takes his pleasures wherever he can get them, but a woman must remain pure." Poor Beatrice! It seemed as if she had proved the truth of her words by her own bitter experience.

Edwina retired early, leaving Rhonwen and Bryn alone together. For a while they were silent, as Bryn read a newspaper and Rhonwen tried to concentrate on a book, until Bryn flung his paper down, jumped to his feet and came to stand by her.

She looked up into his glowering face. His brows were a straight line above his eyes.

"It's no use, Rhonwen, I have to speak. I must ask you why you are marrying my brother. When I went away there was no question of such a possibility. Do you love him?"

Rhonwen was shaken by his devastatingly direct approach.

"Why, sir, you have no right to demand any such knowledge. Would I marry Cristin if I did not love him?"

"Can you have given your heart so suddenly?" Without giving her a chance to reply he said, "Yes, it is entirely possible. I know it to be so! Yet you do not behave as lovers."

"What a dogmatic statement! Would you have us parade our love in a vulgar manner?"

"Vulgar! The girl I met on the station would never have coupled the words 'love' and 'vulgar'. She would not have scorned to show emotion. I have always been sure that when a man and woman truly care there is something about them— a kind of aura—that tells the world their good news. I do not sense it in you or my brother."

Rhonwen held on to her temper. "There are degrees of affection. I am not experienced, but . . ."

"Degrees of affection, indeed! You are not fashioned for such lukewarm sentiments, Miss Rhonwen Morgan. I do not believe you care for Cristin as you should for your future husband. You saw Castell Craig and tasted the idea of wealth and life-long ease. I had not thought it of you!"

Rhonwen leapt to her feet.

"How dare you suggest that I would sell myself for material gain! That would make me no better than . . . than certain creatures I met in London. I would not be human if I did not relish the idea of life protected from an incessant struggle for existence, but I would never marry for money! You are unjust!"

"I see that *you* believe in your sincerity, Rhonwen. Well, perhaps what you feel for Cristin is enough to build a marriage on. And although I find it incredible, I must accept that he loves you."

"This is insufferable! First Frances and now you express your astonishment that a man could love me enough to offer marriage. You are cynical—and cruel . . ."

She tried to push past him, but he seized her wrist. "I am not the cynical one, madam. Both Frances and I have known Cristin since boyhood, and nothing in his nature has led us to expect him to look upon a woman without status and fortune as anything but a passing fancy. For your sake I hope he proves all that you need. And you are sure of your own feelings, are you? Marriage to the wrong man would prove disastrous for such a nature as yours."

"What do you know of my nature?"

Bryn's grasp on her arm tightened, and she set her teeth to avoid wincing.

"I know more about you than I think you know yourself, Rhonwen. I understand you because I care more for your welfare than my own."

"Sir, your choice of expression is . . . immoderate, and you express sentiments in which I find it hard to put credence. How can you have the temerity to accuse Cristin of cynicism when you, who professed to be my friend, left Castell Craig without bothering to send me a message although you knew I would have left when you returned?"

Bryn released her arm and stared at her. "What do you mean? I gathered from you that you were settled with the Evanses. Where did you propose to go? And, in any case, I sent you a letter. Because I was called away so suddenly, I gave it to Cristin and asked him to make sure it came to you. It explained everything."

"But—but I received no letter. I assumed you had gone without a word."

"Did you truly think I could do so? Oh, Rhonwen, if only I had taken time to see you—but Cristin informed me of the mine accident just before I had time to get a train south."

Awareness dawned on them both, and Bryn's angry eyes searched hers. "Cristin had designs on you all the time and I did not suspect. How fortuitous the accident must have seemed to him. I wonder what excuse he would have used otherwise to get me out of his way.

"I suspected nothing. If I had thought about it at all, I might have conceived the idea that he would try to make love to you, but I would have placed my faith in your virtue. So he has won. You have accepted his proposal." He gave a sharp laugh. "You

will be my sister, Rhonwen. Come, sit beside me, sister."
He pulled her none too gently beside him on to a sofa.
"You said that you had intended to go away. Where were
you going?"
Rhonwen explained Cristin's offer of a shop and Bryn said,
"How incomprehensible he is. First he tries to get rid of you,
then he offers marriage."
"Why must you always denigrate Cristin? He was simply
trying to help me, then he realised he cared for me. And you
did *nothing* to help."
She hurled the last words at him in an inexplicable desire to
wound him and regretted them instantly.
He said quietly, "I believed you to be happy with Owen
Evans and his wife. They are a very good set of folk in that
cottage. I respected you for your independence. I did not expect you to fall helplessly into the arms of the first man who
came to court you. Rhonwen, you know nothing of life—of
Cristin—and I hope he does not teach you some bitter lessons."
"Whatever they are they will not prove half so bitter as the
ones I am learning from Frances and you. All you both have
done is to run Cristin's character down to me. You are a pretty
pair! Perhaps Frances should console herself with you, for you
would make a fine match."
For an instant she felt fear as she stared into the blazing eyes
so near her own; then she stood up and said, "Pray do not ever
speak unworthily to me again of your brother. I will not tolerate
it."
Bryn rose and looked into her flushed face.
"Will you not, my kitten? Well, don't assume that marriage
to Cristin will prevent me from speaking my mind when I see
the need. Though that will not be often, I fancy. You will soon
learn that Cristin's pride in his ancestral home can be satisfied
from the distance of London, Paris or Rome, or wherever the
frivolous have their being, while I shall remain to tend our land
and our people because I truly care for them. You will go
Cristin's way, Rhonwen, and I, mine."
He swept her an ironical bow. "Your servant, ma'am."
Then he was gone and Rhonwen sank back on to the sofa
struggling with a sudden desire to weep.
During the next few days, Rhonwen was allowed little time

to mourn the loss of Bryn's good will. Her new gowns were made up by the sewing woman provided by Frances, who also supervised the fashioning of hats by her personal maid and the cutting of shoes by the local shoemaker, where Rhonwen felt thankful that modesty forbade the removal of her stockings. The two women pored over fashion plates and fabric samples; an order was despatched to London, and in an astonishingly short time a large parcel arrived at the castle.

Rhonwen unpacked it and stared at the profusion of silks and satins, brocades and velvets; at the yards of delicate lace and feathers of all sizes; at the linen and cotton to be made into her bridal underwear and nightgowns. She picked up a length of lawn and held it to her body, looking at herself over its white purity in the cheval glass. She tried to picture herself in Cristin's arms, but her imagination refused to carry her so far. She wandered over to the window, still clutching the fabric as she gazed at the mountains whose summits were wreathed in November mist, visualising her future husband, holding the image of his tall form, his handsome face and dark eyes, remembering the touch of his hands, his gentle kisses, trying to reconcile his behaviour toward her with the things others said of him.

Frances arrived and glanced at the materials and then at Rhonwen, still holding the nightgown fabric to her breast. A spasm crossed her face before she smiled bleakly.

"Do you picture yourself in your husband's arms, Rhonwen, enjoying his carresses?"

She had so expertly gauged Rhonwen's thoughts that she denied it with embarrassed vehemence and Frances laughed.

"You protest too much, my dear; and why should you not think of love? You will be so happy, I am sure. Cristin is an experienced lover."

"How should you know that?"

Frances answered coolly, "No, he has not bedded me, though not for want of trying. His kisses have held promise of his skill, and there are many women, oh, so respectably married now, who gaze at him with the ghost of rapture in their eyes. How impossibly dull their clodhopping husbands must seem to them after such a lover."

Rhonwen tossed the material onto the bed. It was useless to cross swords with Frances on this issue, and Beatrice had warned her of the liberal passions of many men. Yet she could wish that her future husband had been less lavish with his amours.

"Has Bryn such a reputation?" she asked, surprising herself as much as Frances.

"Bryn? Heavens, no! I daresay he must have had a woman or two—he would not be a man otherwise—but he uses a good deal of energy on the estates, chopping down trees and similar vigourous pursuits. He does it for fun. He is a strange man."

"He and Cristin sometimes seem to . . . to hate one another."

Frances yawned behind white fingers. "They are not compatible, that is all. Cristin is highly civilised, and Bryn retains the unbridled ways of his forbears."

"It seems to me that it is Cristin who does that."

Frances emitted an exaggerated sigh. "You automatically associate undiscipline with the human needs of a real man. It is typical of your class."

The words hung between them, and it seemed that for once Frances had not meant to be unkind, for colour tinged her skin and she said, "I beg your pardon. That was thoughtless of me."

Rhonwen had no answer, and the two women began to decide upon the type of gowns that would best suit Rhonwen's slender figure.

"It is a pity," remarked Frances, "that mourning prevents your wearing any but dark colours, though the deep shades of green and blue become you admirably."

"I do not miss lighter colours," answered Rhonwen, "since I was never allowed to wear them. Mother always said . . ."

"Ah, yes," interrupted Frances, "that is a matter I have been meaning to raise with you. When you use the word 'mother' as a name you really must learn to say 'mama'. There is nothing so *déclassé* as the misuse of the word 'mother.' Do try to remember."

Rhonwen bit back a retort. If she was to please her future husband, she supposed she must assume Frances's guidance to originate in him and follow it accordingly.

Frances came before dinner to supervise the maid sent to assist Rhonwen and watched closely as Susan brushed her mistress's hair and drew it back to form soft coils in the nape of her neck.

"Have you no jewellery, Rhonwen? You should wear eardrops of jet or pearl, or perhaps a necklace of ivory or gold—either would be suitable for your state of mourning."

Rhonwen thought of the gold chain and locket still hidden in the box, the key of which she could now carry in one of her dainty new reticules, but she shook her head.

"We were poor," she said.

"Well, you will have to do as you are," said Frances. "Go and look at yourself in the full-length glass."

Rhonwen stared at the unfamiliar image. Against a shimmering black silk sheath gown, her neck and arms appeared whiter than ever and her hair shone with red-gold gleams. When she and Frances entered the dining room, Cristin's gaze widened and held an expression that made her wish the sewing woman had not cut her gown so revealingly.

He came to her and said, "While you have been busy I also have been buying."

He drew out a slim leather case from his pocket and opened it to reveal a necklace of pearls, which seemed alive in their luminosity, and matching pearl eardrops the shape of falling tears. He fastened the necklace around her slender throat and watched her as she used the mantelshelf mirror to push the gold loops through the holes in her ear lobes, thanking Beatrice in her heart for her insistence on the ear-piercing so long ago. Cristin took the tiny silver wire "sleepers" she had removed and tossed them into the back of the fire.

"You will never need these again. I shall expect my wife to wear suitable jewellery at all times."

Rhonwen had half-raised her hand in a gesture of protest but she was too late to prevent his action, and she was forced to close her mind to the memory of her mother's struggle to find the necessary money.

Cristin could not help behaving in so autocratic a manner, and she had to admit that the jewels were the finishing touch she needed. The mirror told her without reservation that she was beautiful, and she saw that Frances knew it, too, and in spite of the help she had given, hated her for it.

Edwina paid her compliments and so did Miss Watkins in her nervous way, but Bryn stared with apparent hostility, and she lifted her chin and kept her eyes averted from him. Frances was gowned in crimson velvet and Edwina in soft cream cashmere; the men wore impeccable evening dress and white cambric ties; the dinner was served by soft-footed servants whose voices were never raised above a murmur and the food was lavish and superb.

Rhonwen had a sensation of viewing the scene from outside and felt the unreality of the change in her life. She wondered what pithy comment Ida Blake would have made, and as if her wandering mind had conjured an image, Edwina asked, "Have you received a reply to your letter to your former teacher— Miss Reeves—is it not?"

"No, I have not," replied Rhonwen, "and it is unlike her to be so remiss. I do hope nothing has happened to prevent her coming."

Cristin looked at her sharply. "What is this? Have you sent this woman an invitation here?"

Edwina said, "She did so at my suggestion. Rhonwen must feel strange among us. I think it a good idea for her to have a companion, and I understand Miss Reeves is well born."

"Why was I not consulted?"

Cristin made no attempt to conceal his anger, and Edwina looked surprised.

"I do not have to consult you as to whom I invite to my home, Cristin. You forget yourself."

Cristin waved away a dish of persimmons with a furious gesture and made an obvious effort at control.

"No, of course you do not, Cousin Edwina. I beg your pardon. But pray remember that Rhonwen is to be my wife and my responsibility. I desire only her good. We know nothing of this Miss Reeves. She may prove totally unsuitable."

Edwina smiled. "Rhonwen seems to me to have good judgement. I am prepared to trust it."

She caught the eyes of the other women and rose, and Frances, her companion and Rhonwen followed her to the drawing room.

"Do not look so worried," said Edwina. "Cristin is sure to like your Miss Reeves and has probably already forgotten his irritation."

But when the men joined them, it was obvious that Cristin was waiting only for the servants to depart before resuming the subject. Frances was at the piano picking out a tune with an expert touch, and Bryn joined her in singing. Cristin came to Rhonwen's side. He glanced at Edwina, who was threading a needle, and said quietly but in a voice hard with suppressed emotion, "Rhonwen, I must express my extreme displeasure at the underhand way you set about inviting this woman from your past to my home. I thought you *must* know that I desire you to sever all such connections."

"I have *not* been underhand—in fact, the suggestion came from Edwina—and Miss Reeves cannot prove in any way detrimental to me. She is truly a lady. She simply is not wealthy, that is all."

"All! Soon enough you will discover that to be poor is to be nothing! It may be regrettable, but society will have it so. I insist that you write at once to stop her from leaving London."

Rhonwen looked into his face, dark with anger. His eyes were cold, and she said abruptly, "Cristin, you do love me, don't you?"

"For heaven's sake! What kind of an answer is that? Have I your promise that you will prevent this proposed visit?"

"I will try to obey you in all ways that are just, but please do not insist upon this. Miss Reeves is my friend; she remembers Mother—Mama. I need someone to talk with."

"You must show more self-control, Rhonwen. As my wife you will take your place among great folk who will rend you like wolves if they once suspect you to be of questionable birth. Naturally, it scarcely needs to be said that it does not matter to me."

"Then you will withdraw your objection? When you have met my friend, I know you will like her."

Cristin shrugged, but his face still held anger. "It is clear that you are determined to oppose me in this. Very well, have your own way if it means so much; but in future I shall expect to be consulted upon all matters concerning your life, and you will pay me the deference a husband has a right to expect."

The singers at the piano fell silent; then Frances said, "How very pretty you look, Rhonwen, when you are flushed. Are you annoyed? Cristin, you must not upset your chosen bride. He is a bully, is he not, Edwina?"

She seemed determined to fracture any hope of an amicable

atmosphere as she continued, "Where is your mama's betrothal ring, Cristin? I am surprised you have not produced it. You were always used to declare to *me* that it should grace the hand of your affianced lady."

Cristin looked even more angry, but he forced a smile and touched Rhonwen's head gently. "That was until I was captivated by this beauty. Rubies and red hair do not go well together. I shall purchase something suitable for Rhonwen."

"Quite right," approved Edwina. "Perhaps Bryn's bride may wear the ring."

Neither man vouchsafed a reply, but Frances's fingers stroked her dark hair in an apparently unrelated gesture, and a shiver shook Rhonwen.

Edwina patted the chair beside her.

"Come closer to the fire, Rhonwen. Our ancestors must have been a hardy race, for some of the draughts they endured still elude our efforts to cure them."

She rang the bell, and a footman was despatched to request Susan to bring Rhonwen's shawl. Edwina thanked her, but Cristin said, "Susan, do not send your mistress downstairs without adequate protection from the cold. In future, remember that your sole purpose in life is to serve Miss Rhonwen."

Susan withdrew, her face scarlet, and Rhonwen's cheeks went pink in embarrassment and sympathy.

Frances said, with a shade too much kindness, "Do not take to heart a reprimand to a servant, Rhonwen. They must be kept in their place at all times. One cannot afford to allow them to relax for an instant."

"I daresay I have much to learn," she cried, "but you must give me some time. I cannot help thinking of Mother—I mean, Mama . . ."

In her confusion her eyes filled with frustrated tears, which she blinked away. Even Miss Reeves had explained that well-bred women did not betray emotion, save in the privacy of their rooms. She realised that Bryn had moved to her side and was offering her his handkerchief. For an instant she thought of the room at the inn where they had laughed together, but there was no mirth in his face now.

"What is this nonsense about 'mother' and 'mama'?" he demanded.

Cristin's voice was weary. "Do not interfere, if you please. You know that Rhonwen must learn our ways if she is to take her place among us."

Bryn continued as if his brother had not spoken. "There is no word so beautiful in our language as 'mother'—though if you must destroy all Rhonwen's natural freshness, which to my mind is the best of her, I cannot prevent it; but for God's sake show her some patience."

"I do not require someone who mixes freely with any village lout to teach me humanity!"

"And I do not require someone who behaves like a mincing fop to teach me etiquette!"

Frances looked on in amusement as the brothers glared at one another, and Edwina sighed and laid down her sewing.

"Stop quarrelling! I order it! In your own ways you are equally correct. Bryn must remember that Rhonwen is Cristin's to guide, and you, Cristin, must show her forbearance. She is intelligent, pretty and biddable, and will soon learn."

She patted Rhonwen's hand and although the brothers refrained from further acrimony, the uneasy atmosphere persisted until the company parted for the night.

As Susan unbuttoned Rhonwen's gown, she apologised in a chastened manner for her lapse.

"If you could overlook it please, miss, I shall get used to being your maid . . ."

Rhonwen said, "I have not given it a thought, Susan. To tell the truth, I have many lessons to learn about my new life. We will study together."

Susan looked gratified, but Rhonwen realised that Cristin and Frances would be scathing had they heard her. She stared at her reflection as Susan brushed her hair with long strokes before twisting it into two thick plaits.

"There, Miss Rhonwen! My, but it is beautiful you are! No wonder Mr. Cristin forgot everyone but you."

The maid's ingenuous words struck at Rhonwen's heart. Cristin's affairs must be common knowledge. She resolved to make his life so pleasing after they were married that he would not wish to stray. She would give no room to the realisation that with him she felt no release from the inhibitions fashioned by the years with her mother.

Susan answered a knock and came back with a small parcel. "From Miss Kendrick, miss."

Rhonwen pulled off the wrapper to disclose a slim volume entitled *"Mixing in Society."* It proclaimed itself to be a manual of manners written by an anonymous countess. For a moment Rhonwen felt blindly angry, then she tried to tell herself that Frances might have meant the gesture kindly.

She climbed into bed and Susan raised her hand to draw the heavy woollen bed curtains, but Rhonwen said, "Leave them, please. They shut out the air. I do not care to be enclosed. And do not blow out the candle. I shall read a while."

Susan looked doubtful.

"If you say so, Miss Rhonwen, though I think the night air is bad for you. I think it's much better to be tucked away. I miss my cosy wall bed at home. You ring for me now if you change your mind."

Rhonwen lay back on the feather pillows and picked up the book, riffling through the pages, before she began the first chapter. In spite of herself she became interested, and she pulled the candle a little closer. The fire was dying and the room growing cool, so she snuggled into the bedclothes and continued to read.

She woke with a jerk. A sharp object was pressing into her eyelid. The book had fallen over her face. Breathing was difficult—unreasonably so—and she realised with sudden horror that she was enveloped in darkness and suffocating smoke. Gasping and choking, her eyes streaming, she tried to leap from the bed; but something imprisoned her—something heavy that held her back and poured more smoke into her mouth and nostrils as she beat her hands against its softness. Her rapidly clouding senses told her that she was struggling with the drawn bed curtains, and with a desperate lunge she drew one along the rail and fell, gulping in the purer air close to the floor. But now, as the wool smouldered, the killing smoke was increased and began to swirl about the room. She ran in a half-crouch to the door and twisted the handle. The door would not open, and she pulled and tugged with both hands as she heard the crackle of flame. She began to scream—strangled cries for help.

There were footsteps, voices, then the door opened from outside and she fell into Cristin's arms.

Pain and confusion followed as she gasped and retched. She was carried to a room where Grace Bell and Susan helped Edwina tend her. Edwina did not leave her side, and Rhonwen felt the compassionate strength that flowed from the older woman.

Rhonwen was given an extensive examination by a doctor. "No lasting damage" was his verdict. "You are a lucky young woman. Moments more in that room and your lungs and heart could have been damaged beyond redemption. I wish I had a guinea piece for the number of times I have advised people not to leave candles too near combustible material."

Rhonwen knew that she had not drawn her candle too close for safety and that she had not pulled the curtains. She tried to explain, but the effort tore at her sore throat and chest and she began to cough.

The doctor shook his head warningly.

"I shall leave a soothing draught for you. Stay still and do not try to speak."

Edwina gave her a dose of the medicine, and she and Grace Bell left Susan to sit with her mistress. Rhonwen was beginning to feel drowsy when she heard Susan protesting as she answered a knock on the door.

Bryn entered, followed by a still-grumbling Susan who declared that Miss Rhonwen should not be disturbed.

Bryn came into Rhonwen's vision. He motioned Susan to stay back as he bent over the bed.

"I shall not be a moment. I had to come, Rhonwen. Are you all right now? My sweet little idiot—you might have died! I could not have . . ." He stopped, his lips pressed together. "Rhonwen, my friend, you must take more care."

She tried to speak, to explain that everyone was mistaken in the assumption that she was responsible for her close brush with death; but the doctor's drug finally imprisoned her mind and tongue and she fell into blackness.

Chapter 11

RHONWEN MANAGED to eat a few mouthfuls of the light breakfast carried to her by Grace though her throat and lungs felt rasped and sore and her eyes hurt. But she was otherwise well and protested that she was being spoiled.

"Nonsense!" declared Edwina as she entered. "I was most dreadfully anxious for you last night. We all were."

Rhonwen was embarrassed that she had found herself in Edwina's own bed, but the older woman laughed.

"Do not worry. I was perfectly comfortable on the couch in my dressing room, and I was able to supervise your care here."

"Do you know, Miss Rhonwen, my mistress tried to insist on sitting with you herself, but Susan and I promised to take turns and call her if necessary."

"Grace is a fearful bully," said Edwina, but she gave her maid an affectionate smile and Rhonwen wondered why her mother had not felt able to trust such a good mistress with the guilty secret that had driven her from Castell Craig in such panic.

Rhonwen was permitted to dress, and she looked from the turret window far above the water of the lake. The Rhinogs seemed to loom over the castle, and Edwina divined her thought, for she said softly, "I am as happy here as I could be anywhere, Rhonwen. The mountains are bleak and the lake deep, and they suit my soul."

At Rhonwen's startled glance, she gave a laugh holding no humour. 'She is moody,' thought Rhonwen, and a vivid recollection of her mother filled her mind.

"I hate a moody person," Beatrice had yelled when she arrived home in a towering rage at some vagary of a temporary employer. Perhaps when Beatrice had needed Edwina most she had withdrawn into the protective cocoon Rhonwen sensed again.

Edwina said remotely, "I have lived my life at Castell Craig. I daresay only a Caradog could feel so at one with the atmosphere. The castle, the rocks, the mountains and water are in our blood and bones. This place is my refuge from life, and my work is my shield."

She walked to a tall cupboard and flung open the double doors with a gesture that did not invite comment, and Rhonwen stared at the shelves stacked high with articles Edwina touched with long white fingers before pulling out some pieces to display. There were embroidered cloths and pillow slips, knitted shawls, crocheted garments of all sizes, even, Rhonwen noted, feeling a little sick, some baby clothes. Edwina drew out a long drawer in the base of the cupboard in which lay piles of handmade quilts. She dragged one out and threw it across the bed, where it lay in a marvellous display of brilliant hexagonal designs.

Feeling compelled to make some response, Rhonwen breathed, "They are all so wonderfully made. But do you not envisage a use for them?"

"They have served all the use I need when I have completed them. It is the actual work I require, not the finished product."

She smiled at Rhonwen with a flash of warmth.

"Perhaps I will let you choose something for your bridal collection."

As abruptly as she had dropped her guard she raised it again; Rhonwen felt a desolate sense of loss and the questions she wanted to ask about the previous night remained unspoken.

Bryn and Cristin rose as Edwina and Rhonwen entered the morning room, and Cristin came swiftly to her side.

"How pale you look, my dear. What a fright you gave us!"

He led her to a chair, and Rhonwen asked, "Where is Frances?"

Cristin's brows rose slightly.

"She has returned home. We had no need to accept her offer to sit with you last night, and upon hearing of your complete recovery, she decided to go to her own estates to see her bailiff. She was much concerned for you, of course."

Concerned or guilty? wondered Rhonwen. Frances had been outside her door with the others last night. Had she been there before? Long enough to draw silently gliding bed curtains and to push a candle a little too close. Did Cristin really believe that Frances had relinquished him so easily?

"How came my bed curtains to be drawn?" she asked abruptly. "I was reading, and the next thing I remember is being almost suffocated by smoke. I actually forbade Susan to close me in. I like the air."

"That must have amazed her," said Cristin. "Are you sure she did not decide she knew best and creep back later?"

"If she had done so she would surely have removed my book and blown out the candle," argued Rhonwen.

Edwina said gently, "Do you dream vividly, my dear? I know I do. Can you be certain that you yourself did not pull the curtains while asleep?"

"I am certain," persisted Rhonwen. "There is something here I cannot understand. It . . . it frightens me."

Bryn said gravely, "You are raising some very disturbing speculations, Rhonwen. Are you positive of what you did? Perhaps there was something in your novel that troubled your mind."

"It was not a novel," said Rhonwen. "It was a book of . . . of etiquette."

Bryn gave a wolfish grin. "And where did you purchase such a gem?"

"I did not. Frances sent it along to my room."

"Well, I'll be damned! I beg your pardon, but that really is the limit! Is Frances trying to turn Rhonwen into a Society doll?"

"It is scarcely your affair," said Cristin.

"So it was your idea!"

"No, it was not, but it was well thought of by Frances. And Rhonwen was sensible enough to read it."

"All right," said Bryn, "have it your way. Ruin the girl, if you must. It is more important to discover the truth about the events of last night. Just how did Rhonwen become trapped in what could have been a tomb for her?"

"Always so immoderate in your choice of phrase," said Cristin wearily. "I thought it had been agreed that for some reason Rhonwen became confused and created the emergency herself. Her brain was so fuddled she could not open the bedroom door."

"Because it was locked from the outside," cried Rhonwen. "I tugged and twisted the handle. I had been locked in!"

Cristin came to put his hand on her brow.

"You are feverish. You should not have left your bed. Do you know what you are implying? I can assure you that your door was not locked. There was not even a key there. In Castell Craig we have never had occasion to believe that our rooms would be entered without the courtesy of a knock."

"I am not feverish," declared Rhonwen. The impossibility of making anyone believe her dried up further speech. She was beginning to doubt herself.

Edwina said gently, "It is natural that you are still upset, Rhonwen. Why not wrap yourself warmly and take a stroll in the garden? It will help to clear your head. And I will go and see what progress is being made in the move to your new room. Your former one will need a great deal of repair."

Cristin looked at his watch. "Nothing would please me more than to be free to take a turn with you, Rhonwen, but I have a business appointment I must keep."

Rhonwen felt wretchedly that she had disturbed the tenor of life at the castle. "It does not signify. I can walk alone."

But Bryn came to put a comforting hand beneath her arm and raise her to her feet. The compassion in his eyes moved her.

"You are not yet fit to be on your own. Your nerves are jangled. I will be glad to accompany you, if you will permit me."

They paced slowly between flower beds where gardeners were cutting away late-withered blooms, which dripped after the first of the winter frosts. Above the grey stone walls surrounding the gardens the hills rose into clouds of mist hanging motionless in the damp air.

Rhonwen's voice shook a little as she asked, "Was everyone outside my door last night? Did I imagine I saw Frances?"

She half-expected a reproof from Bryn for raising the subject again, but he answered quietly, "She was there. Your cries aroused us all. Except Edwina, whose quarters are too far away for her to have heard. She came later."

"And Cristin reached my door first?"

"As to that I cannot say. My room lies furthest from yours. By the time I arrived, Cristin had opened the door and you were tumbling into his arms. Thank God you were not hurt."

She thought his voice assumed a significant intensity, and she longed to pour out her fears and suspicions. She had even begun to wonder about Edwina. Was she secretly angry that a girl from nowhere had become betrothed to the heir of Castell Craig? She tried to thrust the idea from her. Had Frances, unable to bear her rival, tried to destroy her?

She had opened her mouth to speak as Bryn kicked at a pile of crackling leaves, when Mervyn Parry hobbled from behind a tall shrub.

"Up to your old ways, are you, Master Bryn? Never could keep a pile of leaves when this young devil was around."

The abrupt switch from her dark thoughts to an old man's memory of a mischievous small boy threw Rhonwen off balance and she laughed.

" 'Tis no laughing matter, miss. It's hard work enough as it is to make the fools who call themselves gardeners nowadays to understand that the leaves have to be collected separately."

"Why do you not want to mix the leaves?" asked Rhonwen.

"You come along with me and I'll show you."

They followed him to a walled garden where winter vegetables were rooted, and he pointed proudly to a series of small brick enclosures.

"Compost," he announced, as if displaying gold. "And the best of all is this. Beech leaves—as rich and dark as tobacco. And the stupid louts who reckon to take my place laugh at me."

His eyes watered a little as he stared into the distance. "Miss Edwina depends on me, so she does. She knows I'll always take care of what's hers. Wickedness, that's what it was!"

His voice had grown so bitter that Rhonwen and Bryn were startled, and Bryn said gently, "Come, man, mixing the leaves can scarcely be called . . ."

"Wickedness!" interrupted Parry. "I don't know what the world's coming to when such things can happen. Who could

have done it, that's what I'd like to know? Tampering with
matters that don't concern them."

Bryn's eyes narrowed.

"What is it that 'they' have done? If someone has hurt you
they will answer to me."

"It's Miss Edwina that could be hurt."

His voice had taken on a quality of real anguish before he
turned and stumped off, ignoring Bryn's further questions. As
he went he called back, "If you've a mind to visit my Sophy,
miss, she'd take it as kindly meant."

Rhonwen and Bryn stared at one another.

"I wonder if Sophy knows what he was talking about," said
Bryn. "I think we'll accept his invitation."

Entering Sophy's cottage gave Rhonwen a comforting glow.
Small rooms and simple furniture had been so much more a part
of her life than the grandeur of Castell Craig. Yet she noticed
that the rooms appeared to have shrunk, the cushions were
much darned and the grate had not been swept. The castle had
spoiled her unquestioning acceptance of a humble dwelling;
and she felt despairingly that whatever direction her life took,
she would always feel herself set apart from her fellows.

Automatically she picked up a brush and shovel and began
to sweep the ashes, and Sophy said querulously, "Leave it be!
The maids will come and do it later. It ain't fitting for you now,
Beatrice Morgan's daughter."

"I've almost finished," said Rhonwen. 'There was something
to be said for tending a fire,' she thought as she laid down the
tools with a small sigh of satisfaction. She used tongs to replen-
ish the fire with shiny coal from a black scuttle, then straightened to find Bryn watching her with an expression that startled
her before he said with a laugh, "Come along, Rhonwen. I
think Sophy is becoming impatient."

But she felt that his words had been used merely to fill a void,
for Sophy was lying still, her twisted hands clasped, and her
voice was unexpectedly gentle as she said, "I wonder how you
will fare in Castell Craig, bach. Mr. Cristin will not allow you
to undertake menial tasks. There are servants for everything up
there."

As Rhonwen sat by the bed in a chair brought by Bryn, she
continued, "When I was a slip of a girl and working my heart

out in the kitchens, they would ring above stairs if they wanted a handkerchief picked up from the floor. No matter what we were doing someone had to take off a working apron, put on a white one and skip up the flights of stairs and arrive looking clean and calm. Well, never mind; it did no harm, I suppose. I ended up as head housemaid, and if these cursed rheumatics hadn't got me, I'd have been housekeeper now. Isn't that true, Mr. Bryn?"

"I reckon it is, Sophy." Bryn's voice was sympathetic. "Miss Edwina always says you were one of the best servants she ever knew."

"Ah, she's good, is Miss Edwina. There's many a mistress would have turned us off—me and my old man—when we got old and I was useless. I think it's lucky we are and that we'll be gone before the castle gets taken over by someone else. I wonder if Mr. Cristin . . . but there, I daresay he means well."

Her voice began to drone.

"He's not like Mr. Bryn. Mr. Bryn's the good one. He goes to the mountains to care for his shepherds and his sheep. 'Feed my lambs,' that's what the Good Book says."

Her bleary eyes cleared suddenly.

"Your mother was a great one for the Bible. I wonder what devil could have persuaded such a decent girl as Beatrice Morgan to lose her virginity without wedlock."

Rhonwen clenched her fists and looked from the window at the bare branches of a rowan tree. For an instant she wished with all her heart she had stayed in London where folk did not talk about the past. The moment was gone as she felt Bryn's hand on her shoulder. It lay there for only seconds, but she sensed his sympathy and understanding and was comforted.

"Sophy," said Bryn, "we just saw your husband. He seems troubled. He talked of wickedness."

Sophy's eyes flew wide open.

"Yes, that's what it was! Some might even think of black magic! Who could have done it? They must know how Miss Edwina reveres her little dog's grave. She's never kept another dog since that one died."

Rhonwen and Bryn were silent in surprise, and Sophy went on, "Miss Edwina loved her little dog. It was always ailing, so they said, and never left her room. It died young and Miss

Edwina had it buried in her favourite garden. You know, Mr. Bryn, the one where the special scented flowers and shrubs grow."

Bryn nodded. "My cousin puts a posy of flowers on the grave on the anniversary of the animal's death. I don't remember it myself, but I was little more than a babe at the time."

"That's right. Well, my man went to the garden a few weeks back and he found that some dreadful person had dug up the grave."

"What!"

"Well might you be shocked. We were, I can tell you."

"It's horrible," choked Rhonwen. "Oh, how hurt Miss Edwina must have been."

"*She* doesn't know," said Sophy irritably. "You don't think my Mervyn would let that dear lady suffer! He was so upset he nearly called for an under-gardener, but he thought of the gossips and got his senses together and sent everyone to the far side of the grounds while he looked at the little grave. He said it was clear that someone had tried to make it appear undisturbed, but my man's been a gardener all his life and he knows if an earthworm's touched the soil. He said he believed someone had dug the grave right out and then tried to hide what he'd done."

She stopped speaking and took a drink of water. Rhonwen felt cold prickles running down her spine.

"It's ghastly! Why do you think it happened, Sophy? Does Mervyn know?"

"Neither of us can make it out. At least . . ." She hesitated, then went on slowly, "*I* know nothing, but my man hasn't been himself since. He's had a sick look in his face, and I've heard him cry out in his sleep so loud that even my sleeping draught can't hide it from me."

"What does he say about it?"

"He says nothing. He won't talk to me about it. If he hadn't come home so grievously upset, I don't think he would have mentioned it at all."

Sophy sounded weary and her voice was weaker.

"Why should my good old man look so sad? What harm did he ever do? The world's a cruel place, miss; it is to be hoped you don't find that out for yourself. What harm did my Mervyn do . . . is there anything else you want to ask . . . ?"

She spoke with an effort as her eyelids drooped and her tongue grew thick. Bryn touched her crippled hands kindly.

"No more, Sophy. Sleep now—and thank you for your forbearance."

Sophy allowed her grip on reality to slide as she fell into heavy slumber, and Rhonwen made the covers neat while Bryn checked the fire and they left. They walked in silence, Bryn's face set in such rigid furrows that she did not dare to ask questions. The old woman's words had increased the sense of oppression that had been growing in her since she came to Castell Craig as Cristin's betrothed. She hurried along slightly behind Bryn, who pushed through the shrubbery heedless of the showers of droplets spattering their clothes and trickling in tiny rivulets into their boot tops.

They arrived at the head of a short flight of stone steps which curved down, and Rhonwen exclaimed with pleasure at the sunken garden with its paved walks, alpine slopes, and a rock and water pool, where a flash of gold told of fish darting to cover at their approach. Herbs growing between the paving stones were crushed beneath their feet, releasing scents like the memory of summer, and red-berried shrubs and winter foliage brightened the dull day.

"Edwina's garden," announced Bryn, and there was a movement from a corner and Mervyn Parry rose into view.

"I'm just putting leaf mould round the marjoram," he explained distantly.

Bryn strode to where the old man's bent back was just visible above a clipped cypress.

"Come out here, if you please! What's all this I hear about some maniac digging up Miss Edwina's dog's grave?"

"Why can't my old woman keep her mouth closed? I never should have told her, but I was that shocked . . ."

"And so am I! Have you any idea who did it, or why?"

The old man's eyes slid past Bryn's gaze, met Rhonwen's briefly, then stared out to where the Rhinogs dominated the sky.

"No reason I can think of. Probably some young devil's

prank. Some of the lads we take on now would never have set foot here in the old days and . . ."

"Then you cannot help me?"

"Not I, Mr. Bryn. I wish I could. Can I go now?"

"One last question. When did this outrage occur?"

Parry scratched his head.

"Mmmm, now let me think. I'd been planting the alpine seedlings and went to check like I always do and found the grave had been dug up. That would be near the end of October. Fair turned my stomach it did."

"With good reason. Could it have happened some time before you noticed?"

"Not a chance of that," declared the gardener crossly. "I thought everyone knows I tend Miss Edwina's garden better than anywhere and that's saying something. And I've just remembered I promised to prepare some flowering pot plants for her room. She'll be wondering where they are."

Bryn nodded his dismissal, and the old man hurried off, leaving his spade where it lay.

"He was lying," said Bryn. "Did you not think so, Rhonwen?"

"I agree with you, but why? I don't understand and I . . . I think it is all too horrible to be borne."

Her sore throat constricted, and her voice cracked and trembled.

Bryn said sharply, "No hysteria, if you please!"

Anger steadied her. "Is that all you can say? Is Castell Craig always like this?"

"Like what?"

"How can you ask? I've almost been suffocated—or burnt—in my bed and now—grave robbers. And you seem surprised that I am upset!"

"Your term is absurd. Grave robbers, indeed! A dog's burial place is not hallowed ground."

"No, it isn't; but it *is* a place beloved of your cousin and as such should be sacred to those about her. Where is it, anyway?"

Bryn took her to a corner where winter jasmine climbed above a stone bench. To the side of the bench was an orderly patch of white and silver foliage, and in the middle was a small strip of velvety grass enclosed by white stones.

"But it is beautiful!" exclaimed Rhonwen. "Silver leaves and even the stones are like stars."

"It's asteriated quartz," explained Bryn. "I gather Edwina sent for it from abroad." He bent to look more closely at the tiny grave. "You make me see it with fresh eyes, Rhonwen. I have always taken it for granted as being part of Edwina."

"But how barren of love her life must have been if . . ." She stopped, appalled.

"I beg your pardon. That was an unforgivable thing to say. I know some folk set great store by their pets."

"Don't apologise for saying what you think—not to me at any rate. As for the love in my cousin's life, I know nothing really. There was some tale of a distant relative who came from America. He was the grandson of Mari Caradog, who wed an American and went to live in her husband's homeland. It is said that he was Edwina's lover and died before they could be married, but she never speaks of it. In any event, it is her own business."

"I agree, though it is very sad if it is true."

"I seem to recall a miniature of Mari somewhere in the long gallery. I am surprised Cristin did not take you there. He is fond of our family portraits, and he and our young cousin Idris have spent hours there. Idris has taken water-colour copies of some. He would like to paint as a profession, but Cristin insists it is not a gentleman's occupation."

"Is Cristin his guardian?"

"No, but Edwina allows my brother to take charge of most family business. It will all be his to command one day."

"I would like to see the family portraits. If Cristin has no time to show me, I daresay Idris will do so when he comes home for Christmas."

Moved by a sudden tenderness towards Edwina, Rhonwen bent to touch the soft, damp grass of the dog's burial place, then straightened with a sigh.

Bryn said in a voice tinged with harshness at odds with his words. "You are very sweet, Rhonwen. So full of trust and with so much love to bestow I pray you will not be wounded."

Rhonwen stared at him. His thin, dark face was filled with concern, his eyes inexpressibly kind.

"Oh, Bryn, how gentle you are beneath that tough exterior.

Why are you so mistrustful of your brother? He has shown me nothing but thoughtfulness and . . . affection."

Again her tongue stumbled over the word love.

"Will it be enough for you, Rhonwen?"

"I shall have much more than I have been used to."

"Was not your mother good to you?"

"She cared well for me after her fashion. I think she was deeply fond of me. It was not her way to show her feelings."

"That is not how Sophy remembers her."

"My poor mother was hurt by someone. I wish I knew more of her past. I wish she was here so that I could show her more love than I demonstrated. Now I have time and leisure to think back, I wonder if she was not more lonely than I. She must have been, for I knew no other existence."

They walked back to the castle in a companionable silence, and as they ascended the steps to the front door, she wondered why she felt so dissatisfied and troubled. As Tedder relieved them of their outdoor things, the sound of raised voices reached them from the small drawing room. The butler's face was impassive as he turned away.

"What's up, Tedder?" demanded Bryn, "and don't try to fool me you don't know."

The butler coughed behind his hand.

"It seems, sir, that Mr. Cristin has given his permission for young Mr. Idris to spend Christmas away from Castell Craig, and Miss Edwina does not care for the arrangement."

"What! I'll lay any odds she doesn't!"

Bryn walked swiftly into the drawing room, calling Rhonwen to follow him.

"You are part of us now and may as well join in the family upsets."

Edwina turned a white face to them.

"Bryn, did you know that Idris had been invited to spend Christmas at a friend's home and that your brother has accepted without reference to me?"

"I most certainly did not! For heaven's sake, Cristin, what nonsense is this? You know full well how Edwina looks forward to the school vacations and that Idris is miserable away from his home. If it were not for you he would have had a tutor."

Cristin threw up his hands in mock despair, but his eyes were furious.

"All this fuss over nothing! I suppose you would have our cousin spend his life hiding from the world. The invitation has come from Lord Barnwell and, of course, I accepted. Naturally I assumed you would all be delighted that Idris has made such a suitable friend as the son of a peer. It may help him in his future."

Bryn retorted, "You know that Idris sees no future but that of a working landowner here."

"Landowner? How so? I must recall to your memory that this estate belongs to Cousin Edwina and will—forgive me, Edwina —one day be mine. The question of ownership scarcely applies to Idris any more than to you, Bryn."

Bryn reddened. "Castell Craig belongs to all Caradogs for all time. The eldest member has always held it in trust for the others. That is how it has always been."

Edwina asked shakily, "Do not you believe that, Cristin?"

Cristin walked to Edwina and lifted her hand to his lips. "Of course I do, my dearest cousin. Bryn possesses a devil's power to make me lose my temper and say things I do not mean. And I am truly sorry I have hurt you. I thought you would be pleased by Idris's good fortune in going to a house that is to be filled by young folk near his own age."

Edwina said uncertainly, "I had not regarded it like that. Do you suppose Idris has felt the need for such people? Has he not been content here?"

"Of course he has!" exploded Bryn. "Cristin knows that— he is not such a fool."

Cristin bowed to his brother. "Thank you so much for those kind words. And since I am not a fool, might I be correct in assuming it is not wise to allow Idris to depend so much on we who are older?"

"You may be right," said Edwina. "Yes, I daresay he is, Bryn. I was so sad at the thought of not seeing my dear boy I allowed myself to be selfish."

Bryn's mouth opened and closed, and Rhonwen saw that he bit back words that would only have added fresh ire to the charged atmosphere.

"I suppose there is no chance of changing the arrangement," he suggested.

"None whatsoever," declared Cristin. "In future, though, Edwina, I shall refer to you before accepting an engagement on Idris's behalf."

He turned to Rhonwen. "Forgive me, my dear, for not greeting you as I ought. This brother of mine is so tempestuous. I hope you are recovered. You look well enough."

He succeeded in making Bryn sound like a naughty child, and Rhonwen felt a surge of indignation. Perhaps after they were married she would have some influence over Cristin's behaviour. He seems sometimes to lack sensitivity, she thought; but marriage will change that. Of course it will!

Chapter 12

THE FOLLOWING DAY brought an answer from Miss Reeves. It was carried to Castell Craig at lunch time, and when Rhonwen read it she gave a cry of distress.

"Miss Reeves tells me that Mr. Baker has died. I had no idea he was so ill, but his severe dyspepsia was caused by a malignant disease. They knew it but they kept it from me. Oh, poor, dear Mr. Baker. How I wish I could have repaid some of his kindness."

"I am so sorry," said Edwina, gently. "Would you like to go to London to pay your last respects?"

"Surely that will not be necessary," interposed Cristin. "He was only someone who tutored you, was he not?"

"Well, yes; but when Mother died he did so much to help me and he must have been in pain." She glanced down again at the letter. "But I shall not need to go to London, for Mr. Baker died over a week ago and Miss Reeves has attended to the obsequies and even placed flowers on his grave from me. She thought that the ordeal of so melancholy an occasion would be too harrowing for me after what happened to Mother, Mama, I mean."

"What a truly thoughtful woman she must be!" exclaimed Edwina. "Does she accept our invitation?"

Rhonwen read on. "Yes, she does. Oh, I am so glad. She will be writing again soon."

Rhonwen sensed Cristin's annoyance as he said, "So it is settled and this person will come here."

Rhonwen looked up, stifling an apology. She hoped that when he met Miss Reeves he would recognise her for the lady she undoubtedly was.

Edwina said, "You will be communicating with your Miss Reeves, expressing your sorrow, Rhonwen; so why not ask her to join us for Christmas?"

"Oh, that is good of you. She is a lonely person." She paused, then said tentatively, "May I ask her time of arrival so that she can be met at the station?"

"Do not be absurd," said Cristin. "Do you imagine we allow our guests—welcome or otherwise—to fend for themselves?"

"I will meet Miss Reeves," said Bryn. "Anyone who has engaged Rhonwen's affection must be well cared for."

"We shall decide when the time comes," said Cristin. He rose. "Rhonwen, I believe Frances made sure you were provided with a warm suit and walking boots. I would like to show you the beauty of the hills before winter sets in. Would you care for that?"

"Oh, Cristin, I would! How very thoughtful of you." In her release from tension her voice was too shrill, and Bryn's brows went up.

"Do not make her walk too far the first time," warned Edwina. "She must grow accustomed to the steep climbs."

Cristin bowed in his cousin's direction, and Rhonwen sped to her new room near her fiancé's. It was a charming apartment with golden satin wood furniture and blue-grey hangings, and she liked it better than the other, perhaps because she slept in a bed of shining brass with not even a hint of a fitting for curtains. Her locked carpetbag lay in the bottom of her wardrobe, and she checked it at intervals.

Within an hour she and Cristin were leaving the road to Castell Craig and walking up a mountain track. Cristin looked relaxed, and she resolved not to do anything to upset him. She would allow herself to be guided by him—and Frances, who had advised her well in her choice of clothes. Her suit was of brown and blue-flecked tweed, and her stout leather boots cradled her feet.

"Are you happy, my dear?"

She turned her face, glowing with health and exercise, to

Cristin. "Indeed, I am. I never knew how much I would love hills and forests until now."

"I am glad you like my home. You will be content when we reside here."

"I think I shall never want to leave it."

Cristin smiled. "That would not do at all. We will have commitments in Society. You must understand that."

"I do. I will try, I really will, to please you."

Cristin held her elbow as he guided her across a patch of marshy ground. "Keep to the tufted grass and you will find footholds," he cautioned. He was equally solicitous in handing her round boulders that sent the narrowing track close to the edge of chasms where streams, heavy with autumn rain, tumbled over falls and flowed through deep pools on their way to the sea.

The trees became sparser until Cristin stopped and told her to look back. She gazed down at a familiar view. The drawing in the box had been wrought by a child, but this was unmistakably the same scene. There was Castell Craig and, in the distance, the sea.

For a moment she was back in the two rooms she had shared with her mother. She felt again the sense of loss and apprehension as she had examined the contents of her mother's box. In memory she could even smell Mr. Baker's peppermints. Against her will a dry sob escaped her.

Cristin looked at her sharply. "I thought you said you were happy!"

She longed to confide in him, to rest in his strength. "I am —it would be ungrateful of me not to be happy—yet—I still have such a sense of incompletion. I have no background—no true place in life."

"That might once have been so. Now you are about to become my wife. My family and its history will be yours. Is that not enough?"

Rhonwen wanted to cry. No, it is not! I do not know who I am! He still looked enquiringly at her, and she said slowly, "I know you think I am foolish, but I cannot help yearning after my own people."

Cristin moved impatiently and his boot touched a stone that went spinning into space to crash down through the bare tree branches below. "You must curb these notions, Rhonwen. Your mama is dead. You do not know if you have a family, and, to be frank with you, I think it would be best if you forgot your probing and were satisfied with what life is offering you. Surely to God it is sufficient!"

On the last words his voice grew harsh and angry and Rhonwen replied nervously, "Yes, oh, yes, I am sure you must be right. Shall we walk on?"

But the mood was damaged and they returned to Castell Craig.

That was the first of several walks, and Rhonwen's rapport with the mountains increased. She began to comprehend the meaning of tranquil solitude and asked Cristin, "Would it be safe for me to walk alone up here?"

He gave her a long look before he smiled quizically, "Bored with my company even before we are wed?"

"Oh, no, indeed, I am not, Cristin. But you cannot devote all your time to me—you have duties to perform. I wondered only if I might indulge my enjoyment of the hills on my own."

Cristin looked steadily at her before he turned his attention to the path. "Why not? One must, of course, remember that although the mountains permit you to love them they are merciless to the unwary. Never venture on them without suitable clothing."

"Oh, I won't," agreed Rhonwen. "What does one do if an accident should befall?"

"To begin with, always mention to a responsible person that you are going out; then, if ever you are in a dangerous situation —lost, perhaps—you might find a stream and follow it down— or take what cover you can and wait for rescue. We Caradogs and our shepherds know every inch of the hills."

Once they glimpsed Bryn in the distance, riding his horse as if man and beast were one. A black-and-white sheepdog trotted at the horse's heels. Another time, she and Cristin met Bryn on foot. They stopped and there was a short uneasy pause before Rhonwen put out a hand to the dog that remained still until a command in Welsh from Bryn freed him to move. Rhonwen stroked the smooth head and ears and patted his thick coat, and the dog nuzzled her.

"He likes you, don't you, Tipyn," said Bryn.

"Where are you going?" asked Cristin.

"The old ewe is missing from the flock. Tipyn and I are going to search for her."

"A waste of time," said Cristin shortly. "If the dogs did not round her up then she is most likely dead."

"I daresay you are right, but we do not know. She has been such a good animal. Just think, Rhonwen, she has given us twins every time and once, triplets. That was the only occasion when she could not nurse all her babies. She deserves our attention if only to ensure that she does not die a lingering death on the mountain."

Cristin shrugged. "Have it your way, but I doubt if you'll find her. If she is dead, the birds will have picked her clean."

Rhonwen flinched inwardly at the look Bryn gave his brother, who either did not notice or did not care, and she and Cristin watched for a few moments as Bryn began to climb, using rocks and stunted bushes to pull himself higher.

"He's a sentimental idiot," said Cristin. "Or maybe he does this sort of thing to emphasise the fact that I gave him charge of the sheep."

Rhonwen felt a prickle of anger on Bryn's behalf. "I thought Edwina was the owner of Castell Craig. Does she have no say in its running?"

Cristin looked coldly at her. "Such remarks are not calculated to assist our relationship. It is not for you to criticise me in these matters."

Rhonwen flushed. He was right, but still she wished she knew how to defend Bryn.

He returned after the others had finished dinner, disappointed at not finding the ewe.

Edwina said anxiously, "Will you give up now, Bryn? I have every sympathy for the poor creature, but cannot countenance your taking unnecessary risks at this time of year. The weather can be treacherous."

Bryn kissed her. "Don't worry, I can look after myself, and Tipyn reaches parts inaccessible to me. I have only one last place to search. I think she must be there."

"Bryn loves the mountains," Edwina said to Rhonwen. "Are you enjoying your walks with Cristin?"

"I am indeed. I feel so much at home up there."

Cristin laughed. "She takes to it better than she did to riding."

"It was not her fault that she was thrown," said Bryn. "From what I hear, you expected too much of her. A novice should not have been in so dangerous a spot, especially on an untried mount."

"Nonsense! Rhonwen has a natural seat on a horse."

"I cannot agree! Only someone who has ridden from childhood can acquire such consummate skill. Rhonwen may do well, but never superbly. She should not ride on the mountain so soon, anyway."

"So now you set yourself up as judge of my fiancée's equestrian ability!"

As the brothers glared at one another Rhonwen was dismayed to find herself the subject of acrimony.

"Please . . . ," she began.

"I care too much for my . . . my future sister to think of placing her at risk," interrupted Bryn.

"Are you implying that I do not care enough for her?" demanded Cristin.

Bryn glanced at Rhonwen and controlled himself with visible effort. He bowed in her direction. "Forgive me, ma'am—and you, too, Edwina. I have not the right . . ."

Abruptly he turned and walked from the room.

Edwina said gently, "Do not let these foolish boys of mine upset you, Rhonwen. They were always at loggerheads."

Rhonwen tried to smile, but she felt uneasy. Was it always to be like this? Both brothers loved Castell Craig too much—that seemed to be the basis for their quarrelling. Suddenly she feared for Bryn. Cristin would one day have the power to turn him out, if he so desired.

Edwina retired to bed soon afterwards and as the door closed behind her, Cristin said, "Come, Rhonwen, sit beside me here on the sofa. We must talk of our future."

Rhonwen felt a stab of alarm as she obeyed. "I am having quite a task learning to live with the present, Cristin." She tried to speak lightly, but her apprehension must have shown, for Cristin raised his brows.

"Is it so dreadful a matter—being engaged to me?"

"Oh, no, I did not mean . . . my life has changed so much."

"Yes, I realise that, Rhonwen, but you are young and will soon learn. I feel I could help you so much more if I had more right to direct you. In short, my dear, we must name the date."

"The date!" repeated Rhonwen foolishly.

"The day of our wedding, my dear. I want to hold you as a man should hold his wife. Do not you share my needs?"

He slipped an arm around her waist and, turning her face to his, cupped her chin in his hand. Then he kissed her on the lips. She tried to respond, but could not. Almost she attempted to pull away from him.

Cristin laughed softly. "You are cold, my love; but I will teach you warmer ways. Your mother must have guarded you well to have kept you innocent in so drab a part of London."

"She was very strict," agreed Rhonwen.

Cristin released her chin and drew a finger down the pure line of her cheek. "You are amazingly lovely, and there must have been those who would have tried to use you wrongly. A ghastly place to be reared!"

"You talk as if you know the district."

Cristin shrugged. "I am a man of the world, and one seedy part of town is much like another." He removed his arm from her waist. "What do you say to December twenty-sixth?"

"Do you mean for our wedding day? But that is less than two weeks from now."

"Well, why not? It will have to be a quiet occasion since your mother is so recently dead. The dressmaker has your measurements and can soon run up a simple white gown—I know you will not require anything fine in the circumstances. Only family members will attend—and Frances, of course."

Rhonwen, trying to control the panic that assailed her, seized upon the only part of Cristin's speech she felt she could readily attack. "Why has Frances to attend? She is not family."

"The sooner you understand that she is as close to us as any sister, the better, Rhonwen. Has she not been good to you, guiding and helping you?"

"She has, but . . . but I do not think she likes me."

"What nonsense! You must curb your imagination."

Rhonwen stared at him. Could he be genuinely unaware of how much Frances wanted him? She could not blurt out such a truth. "It seems to me that since I arrived here I am assumed to imagine a great deal," she said angrily. "Including matters to do with burning bed curtains and a locked door."

Cristin gave her a smile she felt to be patronising. "Come now, Rhonwen, you need to control yourself. Soon you will be mistress of a large establishment. You would do well to emulate Frances. Do you know, we lived quite placid lives at Castell Craig until recently!"

Rhonwen's temper flared. "It was *not* my fault that I almost burnt or suffocated. And I did not imagine the disturbed grave. Neither did Bryn and the gardener."

She cried out as Cristin grasped her shoulders and turned her to face him. "What is this? Of what do you speak?"

"Let me go. You are hurting me!"

"Answer me, Rhonwen. I command it!"

"S . . . someone dug up the dog's grave in Edwina's garden. Mervyn Parry told Bryn and me."

He released her abruptly. "Is that all? A dog's grave! One of the garden boys playing a prank, I daresay."

"It would not seem so to Edwina," protested Rhonwen, but Cristin did not answer and she was surprised to see that he had lost colour.

She touched his arm. "I beg your pardon, Cristin. I should have said immediately that I spoke of an animal's grave. It is no wonder you are shocked—it is commendable in you."

He turned to her and she saw that she was not forgiven as he said icily, "When I need your approbation I will ask for it. I think it would be best to end our talk and go to bed. The sooner we are married, the earlier I shall be able to shape your mind. We shall make it December twenty-sixth."

Frances arrived the next day complete with her maid, her timid little companion and several pieces of luggage. Rhonwen must have looked surprised, for Frances said with a smile, "I have spent Christmas with the Caradog family since I was a little girl."

"I see. I did not know."

"How should you? You are a newcomer, but I will be able to devote much of my time to helping you. I daresay you think me early for the festive occasion, but Edwina has always welcomed my assistance. Of course, in future you will be able to manage, but I do not think you are capable yet, do you?"

Rhonwen shook her head. "You know I am not, though I had best learn quickly, for Cristin tells me—that is to say—Cristin and I have decided to be married on the day after Christmas."

"So soon!" Frances's voice rose, and she swallowed before continuing, "Well, why not? If the deed is to be done, let it be quick."

She speaks as if something dreadful were going to occur, thought Rhonwen. If I were her I would go to my own home. I would not stay to be so humiliated. Has she no pride? Or is she determined to cling as long as possible to hope, however remote? Then Rhonwen remembered the burning bed and the locked door and felt a tremor of fear.

Edwina offered unstinted good wishes as she kissed Rhonwen. "Now you will be truly one of us. Perhaps marriage to such a beauty as you will tame my headstrong boy."

Frances gave a tight smile before she looked away, and Rhonwen glanced at her, noting the nervous movement of her jawline. Could Edwina be unaware of Frances's disappointment, or was she so locked in her fortress of reserve that she could shrug off unpleasing facts?

The whole family was at lunch and Rhonwen marvelled at the apparent ease with which it cloaked its emotions before the servants. Had her life taken a different direction, she could have found herself on the other side of the green baize door, waiting at table or toiling in the kitchen, a distant spectator of what appeared to be an existence of unalloyed pleasure. Instead she sat at the silver- and crystal-laden table, beautiful in a gown of ash-grey Merino wool, and felt edgy and depressed. She was startled at this realisation because the change from poverty and work to riches and ease should have lifted her to heights of happiness.

In the drawing room the four ladies discussed fashion in a desultory manner as Edwina's crochet hook darted in and out of fine white wool while Miss Watkin's knitted something in ecru cotton.

Miss Watkins said, "I have read that as many as forty thousand humming birds are sold at auction in London simply to provide aigrettes for the decoration of ladies."

It was clear that she was nervous and had spoken only to keep up a semblance of conversation, and Frances said coolly, "If you have nothing more interesting than that to impart, you may as well remain silent. To supply our food and raiment the earth's lower inhabitants must inevitably die."

An unbecoming shade of red flooded Miss Watkin's face and thin neck, and Edwina said kindly, "You are tenderhearted, Miss Watkins. I would not have God's creatures killed for our adornment, but it has long been the custom."

"And it is certainly not a subject to raise in a ladies' drawing room," snapped Frances. She rose to her feet, expertly kicking aside the heavy pleating of her ruby silk half-train, and went to stare from the window before she wandered to the fireplace and picked up and examined a small Dresden figure.

"You are restless," said Edwina. "Perhaps we could make up a game of cards, or you might like some music. I daresay Cristin will join us soon."

"What is keeping him? I suppose he and Bryn are arguing again."

"Oh, dear, I do hope not, but you may be right. Bryn insists on making a final attempt to locate the ewe, and Cristin accuses him of wasting his time."

"Cristin should not use energy in arguing with his brother. Bryn is so stubborn."

Rhonwen was prevented from springing to Bryn's defence by the entrance of Cristin, who looked annoyed. "He will go, Edwina. He chooses to ignore the business he should conduct in Harlech."

"Don't become agitated," said Edwina. "We welcome your company. Frances feels the need of diversion."

Cristin glowered at Frances. "You could have gone to any number of livelier house parties."

"I have always come here at Christmas," said Frances.

She looked unexpectedly vulnerable, and Rhonwen said impulsively, "I am sure Frances would be sadly missed if she were to break with tradition."

She was rewarded by furious glares from both Cristin and Frances, who wandered to the piano and began to play. Cristin joined her and sang to her accompaniment, and Rhonwen wondered if they were aware of how they had immediately joined ranks against her at her faint hint of criticism.

"That was delightful," applauded Edwina as they finished. Frances gave a little bow of acknowledgement. "Cristin must hire teachers for Rhonwen. I daresay she has musical ability since her mother was Welsh."

"Yes, I recall that Beatrice was one of the stalwarts of the choir at her church," said Edwina. "I wonder if you have inherited her talent."

"Perhaps her father had no vocal beauty for her to inherit," said Frances.

Cristin gave her an angry look as Edwina said quietly, "We cannot know that. Have you discovered anything of your mother's past, my dear?"

"Enough to know that it is best forgotten," intervened Cristin smoothly. "She will be a Caradog soon and will have a background of which she can be proud."

Rhonwen said, "I am proud of my mother and the way she struggled to give me a decent upbringing."

"And very proper, too," agreed Cristin. "However, Edwina, I would deem it a favour if you would not refer to Beatrice. She is gone—it is all finished and best forgotten."

"It is not possible to kill what has gone before," said Edwina. "It *will* intrude no matter how hard one tries."

Her eyes were on her work, but her voice was edged with some emotion that dominated the others for a moment. Then Edwina asked, "Have you written to Idris yet, Cristin?"

"I have, and he is pleased to learn that he will be acquiring a new cousin." He bowed and smiled in Rhonwen's direction.

"And so my youngest boy will be home for Christmas after all," declared Edwina. "I have you to thank for that, Rhonwen."

The two women smiled at one another, but their mutual satisfaction was destroyed when Cristin said, "But I saw no reason for Idris to change his plans. He will still spend the vacation with Lord Barnwell and his family."

"What can you mean?" demanded Edwina. "How can you think he will wish to absent himself from such an important occasion? His lordship would understand. I insist that you write at once and explain. No, I will do it myself."

She rose and was halfway to the door when Cristin stopped her by taking her hand. "Wait a moment, please. Pray consider!

Rhonwen is in mourning, which demands a quiet ceremony. There will be no festivities. In fact, in a way, it could be rather a sad, poignant experience for Rhonwen to wed so soon after her mother's demise. Idris is young; he will have a much gayer time at Barnwell's place. He has a large and beautiful house renowned for the size and jollity of its parties for young folk. Would you have Idris miss all that for the sake of a few minutes in church and an uneventful family wedding breakfast?"

He turned to Rhonwen. "Do help me in this. Can you deny that the thought of our wedding day may make you even more grieved over the recent passing of your mother?"

"I would have so loved her to be present," said Rhonwen, "and I do not wish you to make our marriage an excuse for upsetting Idris, but Edwina . . ."

"Then that is settled," interrupted Cristin. "Idris will stay where he is and can look forward to meeting his new cousin at the Easter vacation."

"Cristin," cried Rhonwen, "allow me to finish. A family celebration must be held of more consequence than a house party. Surely there will be many other such opportunities for Idris."

"You see," said Edwina, drawing her hand away from Cristin. "your future bride agrees with me."

Cristin scowled. "Edwina, to incite my intended wife to defy me is scarcely what I would have expected from you."

Edwina looked stricken. "I did not mean to do so. You have twisted my meaning."

"I see. So now you accuse me of dishonest argument."

"Cristin, please . . ." Edwina put her hands to her face. "Give me time to think."

"May I remind you that there is no time? I accepted Lord Barnwell's invitation in good faith, assuming it would please everyone. It is a fine chance for Idris to meet people who cannot fail to enhance his position in society. It cannot have escaped your memory that his personal fortune is not large. Now you desire me to retract my permission. I daresay the numbers are already made up at Barnwell Towers."

"If the house parties are so large, surely there can be no problem in altering one small arrangement," protested Rhonwen.

Cristin glared at her. "That is where you display ignorance, my dear. But you, Edwina, should know that one simply does not change plans at the last moment without good reason."

"You call our marriage no good reason!"

"For God's sake! I have already given my explanation. Why should Idris's pleasure be spoiled? You see, Edwina, how easily my bride is moved to rebel against my wishes."

Edwina looked uncertainly from one to the other. "I do not know what to say. You *seem* logical, Cristin. I suppose I am allowing my longing to see Idris to cloud my judgement."

Frances had so far taken no part in the altercation. She still sat on the piano stool, her dark eyes moving to follow the talk; but now she said, "Edwina, dearest, Cristin is right, you know. I comprehend your feelings and agree that in the ordinary way Idris should come home, but only consider his disappointment. He is fourteen, almost a man—at least he will reckon himself so—and would probably feel that to be called away from so glittering a gathering to what will seem to him something so boringly incomprehensible would cause him to lose face in the sight of his comrades. Boys who will be his friends through life, remember."

Rhonwen felt deeply angry. She did not think Frances cared at all whether or not Idris returned for the wedding. She would do, or say, anything to gain Cristin's approbation, and Rhonwen noted the gratification in her face when Cristin gave her a look of warm approval.

"Well said, Frances. You have expressed it better than I. Now do you agree, Edwina?"

But Edwina proved unexpectedly stubborn. "Frances may have a clever way of putting things, but it all makes me wonder if she—if either of you—possess a proper awareness of family solidarity."

Frances leapt to her feet. "That is an abominable remark, Edwina. Cristin, is not that a dreadful thing to say?"

Edwina set her lips and stared ahead. Cristin spoke in low tones. "You owe us an apology, Cousin Edwina."

Edwina did not speak, and Rhonwen sensed the deep pain and the struggle against tears that held her silent. "Leave her alone! Give her time to compose herself."

Cristin turned on her. "I hope you are satisfied! Perhaps this will teach you not to oppose me!"

Rhonwen looked at him, and at Frances. Both stood close to Edwina, and she sensed the power of their combined wills. She heard Edwina gasp an apology and wondered how she would support marriage to Cristin if Frances were always to be present.

The atmosphere of the room, the air of recrimination, became suddenly unbearable and she said, "Please, excuse me, I . . . my head is beginning to ache. If I neglect it I shall be ill. Edwina, would you mind if I went to rest?"

Edwina was touchingly sympathetic. "My poor girl, I know well how you feel. Of course you may retire. Can I bring something to you?"

"No, thank you. Truly, I would much prefer simply to lie quietly on my bed."

She sped to her bedroom and leaned for a moment against the door, her heart pounding. It had not been untrue to say that her head ached, but here in tranquil silence the pain was eased.

She walked to the window and leaned her arms on the sill, watching a bird soar high in the cold, clean air, and she became possessed by an urgent desire to know such freedom. Giving herself no time to think she changed into her tweed suit, selected a heavy black wool cloak and kicked off her house shoes, exchanging them for her laced boots.

She ran down the stairs. There was silence from the drawing room, but as she crept past the door, it opened and Miss Watkins sidled out and closed it behind her. She must have been a spectator of the whole scene, marvelled Rhonwen, and I did not notice her. Poor Miss Watkins—a timid mouse of a woman, who spent her life as an onlooker.

To Rhonwen's surprise the little woman did not scurry away but hurried to Rhonwen and whispered, "Try not to be upset by them, my dear. They are high-tempered people, but do not mean to be cruel."

Her eyes widened as she looked at Rhonwen more closely. "You have changed your apparel. Are you going for a walk? It will do you good. In fact, I would not myself mind . . . if you desire company . . ."

"No!" Rhonwen was abrupt and a part of her curled in shame at the way Miss Watkins recoiled. She kept her voice low as she apologised. "I meant no unkindness, but I . . . I need to be alone for a while. I intend to walk a long way."

"A long way? Where will you go?"

"I crave solitude to collect my thoughts." She recalled Cristin's instructions. "You may tell my fiancé I have gone to walk in the mountains."

She did not stop to listen to the whispered reply from the companion but ran through the doors opened by a footman, down the steps, along the driveway and between the massive iron gates bounded by rock. She kept running until she reached the mossy woods. Then she began to climb.

Chapter 13

SHE REVELLED in the exercise, the sustained physical need to concentrate on keeping a foothold on a track that was slippery with sodden leaves and treacherous with hidden stones, which could turn an ankle. It had happened once to her, but Cristin had been there to help. Cristin! She thought of him and her approaching marriage and forced herself to greater effort, but no haste could close her mind to the apprehension that possessed her when she imagined Cristin as a husband with all the rights that entailed.

All girls have these fears, she reasoned, and wished that she had a woman with whom she could talk. Edwina? Not with her reserve. Perhaps when Miss Reeves arrived—but she had never been wed. Mary Owen? Rhonwen could not imagine her ever being nervous of her husband, and, besides, Rhonwen knew that Cristin would never forgive her if she talked so intimately of him to a woman he considered his inferior.

Her mother could have helped. She must have been familiar with the needs of the flesh, for she had allowed her lover to take her even without marriage. But if Beatrice had lived Rhonwen would not be scrabbling up the sides of a Welsh mountain trying to escape from inescapable thoughts.

The rough path petered out among the first of the scrubby trees and she paused, looking back at the roofs of Castell Craig, out over the valley in which Glyn Dedwydd lay hidden, to where sea and sky merged into one grey whole.

Below her, at the foot of a sheer rock face, the river flowed fast and she gazed into its peaty brown depths, knowing that she should return to the castle yet feeling that she could not yet relinquish her solitude. She began to climb again. The grass was sheep-shorn between the huge boulders, and she kept a wary look out for the vegetation that would warn of peat bogs. The impregnable summits of the Rhinogs towered over her. She decided she would set her sights on a low peak and stand triumphantly on it before returning.

She arrived panting for breath, her hands sore from dragging at the granite rocks, knowing that if she had not been motivated by inner disturbance she would have admitted defeat. Now she stood, holding her cloak about her in the penetrating cold, and looked around.

The view she had hoped for was not visible, and she realised that mist was wreathing up from the valley to join the dripping rain clouds. It was high time she found the path back, and she went down the rocky slope so fast that she half slid, scoring marks in the leather of her boots.

She hurried on, following the track until, without warning, the heavy cloud mist swirled about her and she stopped, unable to see more than a few feet ahead. She searched her memory for landmarks, but in her haste she had noted nothing. She remembered Cristin's advice to follow a stream. It had seemed eminently sensible from a secure point of view, but now she recalled the steep cliffs and boulder-strewn streams and deep rivers with fear. And any step might take her into a bog.

Reviling herself for her idiocy in venturing so far, she considered her position. She had told Miss Watkins she was going to the mountains, so Cristin would know where she was. She had best follow his second piece of advice, to find shelter and await better weather or rescue. It was with relief, as she put one foot carefully before another, that she stumbled upon a sheep track and was able to follow it to the lambing pen she had hoped for. It had only four open walls with one small corner roofed by a large stone slab, but the ground within the pen was lower than the outside and there was straw. She settled herself beneath the little roof, nestling into the straw and wrapping her cloak around her; then she leaned back to wait.

At first she was preoccupied in thought and kept calm, but as the cold winter darkness began to close in, she shivered and wondered if this truly was the right thing to do. Then she recalled the quaking bogs and hidden precipices and tried to relax, drawing her hood over her face to temper the icy air she breathed.

The thick folds of the cloak muffled the scrabbling sounds until they were upon her, and she scarcely had time for fear before a soft, wet nose snuffled at her hands.

"Tipyn!" she cried. "Oh, Tipyn, you wonderful, clever darling. Is your master with you?"

The dog licked her hands before giving a sharp bark, and Rhonwen heard the tread of feet and rose shakily to come face to face with Bryn.

"Rhonwen! What in heaven's name are you doing there? Are you alone?"

"Have you not come out to search for me? I knew someone would."

"Maybe so, if they know where you are, but I have not yet returned home. What are you doing . . . ?" He had put his hand out to steady her as her numbed legs caused her to stagger, and he exclaimed, "You are soaked! And trembling, too! My God, Rhonwen, but you have a facility for finding difficulties."

Rhonwen's head went up. "Can you guide me home?" But her voice wavered, and Bryn frowned.

"No, I can't! Tipyn and I might make it safely on our own, though even that is doubtful. In this kind of weather the mountains are friends to no man, even those who love them."

"But won't someone come looking for you?"

Bryn laughed shortly. "They would if I did not return for a day or two, but my family know I make for shelter in suddenly adverse conditions. Edwina was right when she warned me to be careful."

Rhonwen staggered as she tried to walk. Bryn put his arm about her, and she was too grateful for his presence to question the fact that they were going higher. She trusted his judgement so implicitly that she was almost unsurprised to arrive at a stone hut with a slate roof and a stout wooden door that opened at a push.

"An old dwelling used by shepherds at lambing time," exclaimed Bryn. "The men sometimes stay on the mountain all spring. We shall be safe here."

Rhonwen sank onto a wooden bed and watched as Bryn gathered dried bracken and sticks from a corner and arranged them in the fireplace. Reaching into a cupboard he drew out a box of safety matches wrapped in oiled cloth, and moments later Rhonwen was crouched near the flames, steam rising from her clothes, her teeth clenched against the pain of life returning to half-frozen toes and fingers.

Bryn stood so near she could smell the wet leather of his boots. "What possessed you to be so foolish? You can die quickly of exposure on the hills. Dear lord, Rhonwen, but you take chances with your person since your mother died."

She had to throw back her head to look up into his face, and her hair fell in disorder down her back.

"You are too ready to condemn me! I took the precautions Cristin advised. Someone would have discovered me soon. Even now I daresay there are men climbing the mountain. I realise that I was wrong—that I should not put lives in jeopardy —but you need not address me as if I were an imbecile."

She felt apprehension at the anger in his eyes. "Cristin told you you might venture alone on the Rhinogs in winter? And simply wait if you came to grief? Nonsense!"

Rhonwen's anger flared to match his. "He did not tell me simply to wait. He advised me to follow a river downstream, but I . . ."

"You sound more and more preposterous. Follow a river indeed! That way you could choose between death by drowning or falling. As if Cristin would say any such thing!"

She rose and glared at him. "How dare you accuse me of lying! How could I be so mistaken in such an important matter? I am not such a fool as you think!"

"I do not think you a fool at all, but Cristin knows that in certain circumstances even I would not venture down the mountain. The mist lays traps—changes landmarks. You must have misunderstood him."

"I did not—I did not! By now he will have begun to search for me—I know he will!"

She was close to tears in her efforts to make him believe her. "You are allowing your hostility towards your brother to lead you into injustice! He thinks I am resting with a headache, but when he discovers I am not . . . are you saying that he will not look for me?"

"No, of course not! He will, in time, gather men together, and they will come with ropes and might have found you. More likely they would have carried down your lifeless body. It takes a very short time to die sometimes, Rhonwen."

"That I know," she muttered.

She sat down shivering and Bryn touched her shoulder gently. "Forgive me, please. You must be remembering your mother. I had not meant to remind you."

She heard him open the cupboard and then go outside, but she kept staring into the fire. She was convinced her memory of Cristin's words were correct. Yet Bryn seemed so sure she was wrong. She thought of other occasions on which Cristin had advised her. First the walk through the meadows, though that had ended in she and Bryn laughing at her ludicrous appearance and their intimate dinner. Then there had been the fall from the pony. She herself had been partially responsible for that; and worst of all was the fire in her bedroom.

She gave herself a shake. There could be no link between that and the other incidents. Cristin could have no wish to harm her, but Frances—

She watched Bryn, who returned, put a small pan of water on the fire. "There is never a shortage of water on a Welsh mountain," he said. "I shall make you a hot drink. I usually bring something to stay me when I am out for hours."

He took a bar of chocolate and a folding knife from a pocket and began to shred the chocolate finely onto a tin plate. When the water boiled he removed it from the fire, tipped the shreds into it and stirred the liquid with his knife blade before pouring it into two mugs. "How's that for improvisation?" he grinned.

Rhonwen sipped, and the hot, sweet drink trickled warmly into her body. "You are very clever," she admitted. "Oh, Bryn, how thankful I am that you found me. I was beginning to feel cold and frightened."

"With good reason!"

"I cannot understand it. Is Cristin a thoughtless man?"

Bryn swallowed a mouthful of hot chocolate as he considered. "He is far from thoughtless. In fact, I would say he calculates every move he makes."

Rhonwen was silent as the implication of his words penetrated her understanding. "Then I seem to be having a number of strange accidents lately."

"Perhaps falling from your pony is not unusual, though I do not know why Cristin chose to make you learn in so difficult a place. And I suppose the fire could have been your fault . . ."

"Why will no one listen? I fell asleep over my book. I did not pull the curtains. I did not!"

"Softly, Rhonwen. You seem to be having a run of bad luck lately, it is true."

She thought his voice lacked conviction, and it gave her the courage to say, "I need someone to talk to, Bryn. I have been thinking some awful things. I have wondered if Frances is trying to destroy me. She regards me as her enemy, I know."

"That is too strong. A rival—yes—she had her heart set on marrying Cristin. She may be jealous of you, angry with you—but to hurt you deliberately—never!"

"And there is no one else who would wish me harm, is there?" She could not bring herself to formulate in words her nebulous doubts about Edwina.

"I can think of no one."

He was silent, staring into the fire, which was growing low as the flames ate rapidly into the kindling. Rhonwen's teeth began to chatter, as much from nervous agitation as from cold, and he looked sharply at her.

"I must make up the fire and you will take off your wet clothes. There are blankets here. I'll warm them."

"But I would prefer not to undress!"

"Rhonwen, for pity's sake—do you want to get pneumonia? Don't act like a ridiculous pride. I will turn my back."

Stung by his mockery Rhonwen rose and glared at Bryn's back before she divested herself of her cloak and suit, then followed them by her rain-soaked petticoats. She then grabbed the blankets, which lay before the fire, and wrapping herself round, sat on a small stool and stuck her feet out to dry her stockings.

"You may turn now," she said.

He bowed. "Thank you, ma'am." He hung her garments and his Norfolk jacket on hooks on the chimney breast and piled more wood on the fire. "Why do you not remove your stockings?"

"It is not necessary. They are almost dry."

"You have straw in your hair," said Bryn, but the criticism was uttered as softly as an endearment, and she felt a sudden awareness of him that startled her.

She drew the blankets closer in an involuntary movement and did not look at him as he leaned forward, pulled the straw from her hair and tossed it into the fire. Still she stared into the glow where the pieces of straw crackled into bursts of smoke and flame. He touched her hair again. "Such beautiful tresses, Rhonwen."

Now it took all her will to remain motionless as she was swept with an insane longing to turn to him. His hand followed the length of her hair, caressing her neck through its softness. She must stop him—she knew she should act now if she were to retain control over the situation. Words, phrases whirled in her brain, but they were meaningless beside the power of her intoxicated senses.

His hand was on her waist, his arm was about her, and instead of pushing him away, she placed her fingers over his and looked at last into his eyes.

His muscles tensed, his face was close to hers, his eyes seemed to penetrate the depths of her mind and relay secrets of which she had not been aware.

"I love you," she breathed. "It has been you all along."

"I have known it," he murmured. "I love you." The words blazed like a banner of truth.

She was aflame with ardour as their lips met and parted and met again. All the passion of her suppressed nature overwhelmed her. How could she have mistaken the pallid emotion evoked by Cristin for this glory of need; this ecstasy of desire; this demand to love and be loved? The memory of Cristin was as insubstantial as the smoke from the fire. The only reality was a stone shelter on a bleak mountain, herself and Bryn.

A log hissed in the grate as a long-imprisoned gas was released, and in the ensuing flame she saw Bryn's eyes alight with a fire as hot. Her body swayed to his then she slipped from the stool into his arms and, with hands that shook slightly, he tenderly tugged the blankets from her body, touching her soft skin and murmuring endearments. She found words of response she had not realised she knew; then eyes, lips, caresses became all that were needed as they soared into heights where love was paramount.

They lay in peace together in the flickering firelight, Rhonwen's head cradled in Bryn's arm, her red-gold hair spilling across his chest. Bryn said, "What a glorious creature you are, my love. I think I knew you were mine from the moment I saw you trying to hide your muddy self back in the inn. Or maybe I knew even when you stepped off the train, so haughty, so determined to make your own way, and so vulnerable."

He kissed the top of her head and Rhonwen said, "What a fool I have been to mistake my wish for security for love! Why did you not speak before?"

"How could I? I returned from Cardiff intending to court you with all speed and fervency"—he paused to kiss her again —"and found you betrothed to my brother. That was the most dreadful shock of my life. I could have sworn you cared for me."

"I realise now that I did, but I did not recognise my feelings. Oh, how thankful I am that we discovered the truth before it was too late."

Bryn's lips travelled over her hair and cheek. "Cristin must be told immediately. I will speak to him as soon as we return."

"No!" She put her hand over his lips to still his protest. "The task is mine. I have been a fool but will not be a coward. I owe it to Cristin to make my own confession."

Bryn said nothing for a moment. "I should tell him. I know we snipe at one another, but there is a family affection between us. I will let him down lightly."

"Allow me my way in this, Bryn. I have been running from reality—taking the easiest road—let me face up to this."

"If you put it that way . . . but I shall remain near . . ."

Again they were silent and Tipyn, who had lain obediently on a pile of sacks, whined softly and Bryn put out his hand and murmured something in Welsh. The dog trotted over to lie beside his master.

"Will you tell Cristin everything?" asked Bryn abruptly.

Rhonwen felt her colour rise. "I think it best not. Not because I am ashamed—never think so—I love you too much for that."

Bryn said simply, "It had not occurred to me. You are my

wife in the eyes of God as soon you will be in the sight of man."

"I never before understood the meaning of true love." She felt she could understand Frances's bitterness now. "I will tell Cristin that I cannot marry him because I love you. I do not want to share the full wonder of today with anyone. It is like a secret jewel—for our pleasure alone."

Bryn rolled himself onto one elbow and smiled down at her, and she felt weak with love. "Cristin will not hurt you, will he, Bryn? He seems violent sometimes!"

"Oh, no, Cristin hates physical violence and will avoid it whenever possible. But I think we may have to leave Castell Craig."

"Oh, must that be? You love your home—it is your life. I had not realised. Bryn, I cannot be responsible for causing you such misery."

"Nothing is so important as your love, my darling."

He lay back, grinning a little. "And perhaps it will not be for long. Cristin is far too indolent to undertake the more arduous duties attached to running the estates, and he knows he can trust my judgement. Who can tell—he may find consolation in Frances, and they can spend their lives roving the pleasure spots of the world while you and I . . . Shall you like being the wife of a humble country squire with a modest income?"

"It is what I want above all things," Rhonwen assured him fervently.

Bryn kissed her and rose and stretched himself, and Rhonwen saw the tautness of his body. A tremor ran through her, born of pleasure—passion—a sense of belonging at last, and she jumped up and threw her arms about him. "I love you!" she cried. "Oh, how different the world looks to me now."

Bryn held her close as they walked to the window. "Look, dearest, the rain has stopped. With the aid of the starlight and Tipyn we can go home."

"And we shall probably meet search parties," said Rhonwen as she put on her dry clothes.

They saw no one, and Bryn guided her safely down to the castle. They reached home a little after ten o'clock. There was no sign of bustle or urgent preparation, and Rhonwen said, "It seems as if they have not even missed me. I might have needed to make my own way down—if I was still able."

A footman took her cloak and she asked Bryn, "Shall I just slip up to my room? It might save a deal of explanation."

Bryn addressed the footman. "Have any search parties gone from here to the mountains?"

The man looked surprised. "No, sir. I haven't heard of anyone being lost."

Bryn frowned as the footman took Rhonwen's cloak away. "Rhonwen, you said you told someone where you were going."

"I mentioned it to Miss Watkins—I am sure I did. I know I was upset at the time, but I could not have imagined it."

Before Bryn could reply, the drawing room door opened and Frances emerged. Her eyes widened. "Rhonwen! We all believed you to be in your room with a headache." Her eyes narrowed to slits as she looked from Bryn's to Rhonwen's muddy boots. "Have you been out together?"

Bryn replied with an angry question of his own. "Are you telling me that no one has been to enquire after Rhonwen's health?"

Frances flushed. "Moderate your tone, sir. It is not for me to direct this household!"

"I have not noticed you backward in the past."

"That was indeed in the past," retorted Frances. "Things have altered."

Rhonwen said, "Please—I am hungry. I have not eaten for hours."

"Neither have I," said Bryn. "Sorry, my . . . my dear." When Tedder answered his ring he ordered, "Have soup and sandwiches sent to the morning room. Miss Rhonwen and I have been stranded on a very cold mountain."

"What!" Frances almost ran back into the drawing room, and Bryn gave an exclamation of annoyance as he followed her. Rhonwen walked after him to hear Frances telling the others. "All this while we thought Rhonwen was ill it seems she was —cavorting on a mountain with Bryn."

"For God's sake!" shouted Bryn. "Must you always make trouble? I came upon Rhonwen taking shelter in a sheep pen, and we went to an old shepherd's hut until the mist had cleared. Would you have had me leave her? It seems that no one here has bothered to see if she was well or ill!"

Edwina stood, her needlework falling unheeded to the floor. "My dear girl! Have you been in danger and we did not know? Come to the fire. What happened?"

Briefly Rhonwen explained. "I waited for help as you instructed, Cristin," she finished, "but it seems as if I would have waited in vain."

"Cristin, did you not send to enquire after Rhonwen?" asked Edwina.

Cristin kept his glittering eyes on Bryn as he replied, "I was under the impression that you had done so."

"I? But I gave you no reason to suppose—and I thought—there seems to have been a sad misunderstanding."

"There seems to have been several," said Bryn harshly. "I can only be thankful that Rhonwen did not try to follow a river down in the mist. Are you not thankful also, Cristin?"

Cristin bowed in his brother's direction, his face sardonic. "What a quaint idea. Rhonwen did the right thing to wait in safety for clearer weather, or rescue."

"Which apparently was not to be forthcoming," said Bryn. "Where is Miss Watkins?"

The companion was half-crouched in a chair, her face white, her eyes dilated. She tried to speak, but failed. Bryn's voice softened. "Did you forget to tell anyone of Rhonwen's proposed walk?"

"I told . . . I thought I told . . . someone . . ."

Her eyes flew to Cristin in appeal. "You certainly did not mention it to me," he asserted. "If I had known I should not have ignored my fiancée's danger."

"But, sir, do not you remember? When Rhonwen did not appear for dinner I came to you and said she had gone walking —that I feared she might be in the hills—I am sure I did so— I think it was you . . ."

"I have no recollection of it," said Cristin.

Miss Watkins twisted her hands. "I know I get confused but . . . how fearful . . . if something dreadful had happened to Rhonwen . . . please, sir, try to recall that I spoke to you."

Cristin said impatiently, "Well, if you did, you must have misrepresented the facts; but I have no memory of your saying anything."

"I feel so convinced . . ." wailed Miss Watkins.

"Nonsense!" said Frances crisply. "You are an addlepate! You are always imagining you have done this thing or said that. Go to bed, if you please. Your foolishness could have cost this family dear."

Still protesting, Miss Watkins scurried from the room, and Cristin came and put his arm round Rhonwen's shoulders. It was all she could do not to flinch beneath his embrace. "Are you all right, my love? It seems we have sadly neglected your welfare."

"I am perfectly well, thank you. Bryn and I . . ."

She was grateful to be interrupted by Frances, who said, "That idiot of a companion! If I did not need a chaperon and if she were not a distant relative, I would not be plagued with her another day."

Edwina looked closely at Rhonwen. "Are you positive you do not feel ill? Your eyes are so bright and you are flushed. I think you had better eat, then have a hot bath before you retire. I will give orders."

Rhonwen felt a stab of guilt, knowing that the condition of her eyes and cheeks had nothing to do with sickness, unless it be of love. She and Bryn drank hot soup and coffee and ate sandwiches, unable to do more than exchange glances beneath the eyes of a servant, but content to be together. Later Rhonwen relaxed before her fire in a tub of steaming, scented water carried to her room by a procession of maids.

That night, in spite of her weariness, she lay awake for a long time, her mind a tumult of joy and apprehension as she thought of her new-found love, then of the prospect of breaking her news to Cristin.

She knew she must waste no time, and as soon as breakfast the following day was over, she asked if she might speak privately with him. He glanced impatiently at his watch. "Will it take long? I have an appointment."

"I . . . I do not think so, but I must talk to you."

He looked sharply at her as her voice shook in spite of herself, and Bryn half rose in his chair. She gave him a small warning frown before she preceded Cristin to the library. The fire had not yet been lighted and she drew her shawl about her, but her shiver was more from trepidation than cold.

"Well, my dear?" said Cristin, making an obvious effort to remain patient.

She drew a deep breath. "I have something to say which may —which must—distress you, Cristin. I . . . I have to beg you to release me from our engagement. I cannot marry you."

She had begun strongly enough, but her voice faltered before the impact of his look, though he was controlled as he said, "Nonsense, Rhonwen! You have pre-wedding nerves, that is all. I believe this kind of thing happens to many young brides. You should forget your fears. When Frances rises, you must have a talk with her. She is sensible and will soon set you to rights."

He had actually made a move to leave when she cried, "No! It will not do! I cannot marry you. I will not!"

"Cannot? Will not? But I have your promise, and it is one to which I mean to hold you."

Rhonwen stared disbelievingly at him. "You cannot wish to wed me knowing that I have changed my mind."

"I refuse to be swayed by a young girl's whim." He smiled. "It is clear that your mother raised you without certain knowledge of matters pertaining to marriage. It is natural to feel nervous. I can only repeat my advice. Apply for help to Frances. When you comprehend the true meaning of wifely duty, you will feel quite differently, and I shall be gentle as I teach you."

Rhonwen closed her eyes and saw again the shepherd's hut in the flickering firelight and felt Bryn's arms about her. It was ironic that Cristin should assume her reluctance to be due to maidenly modesty.

She opened her eyes to see Cristin watching her. He said impatiently. "I really must leave you now or I shall be late."

She felt she could not endure another such interview. "No!" she gasped, "I must make you understand. I am not afraid or bashful! I have discovered I do not love you!"

Cristin sighed and looked again at his watch. "We are back to the same thing. Your doubts will all be resolved on December twenty-sixth. I can vouch for it."

Again he made as if to go, and Rhonwen cried desperately, "I love someone else." She had his full attention now as she continued. "I love him as I never cared for you. I did not know what true love was until . . . I am deeply sorry to have to hurt you."

"I do not understand. Were you not heart-free when you came to Wales?"

She nodded, and he said slowly. "You have had no opportunity to meet anyone else since you arrived here. No one except . . ." A murderous expression filled his face. "Bryn—and you —alone on the mountain—unable, so you say, to return from a shepherd's hut. Is it he?"

"Yes, oh yes, it is Bryn. I love him so much. Please let me go, Cristin. Truly, I could not help myself."

Some quality in her voice touched his deeper awareness. His face grew pale and his eyes were slits of rage. He grasped her wrist and said in tones of deadly quiet, "Could not help yourself! What exactly does that mean?"

He had turned into a monstrous stranger with cruel fingers that tightened, sending pain shooting through her bones. "Answer me! What could you not help?"

She could not find the words to lie. The truth must be written in her face as surely as he knew the answer to his question.

"Let me go. Please let me go."

"Not until you answer. You will tell me!"

"We loved—Bryn and I. We lay together! Don't look at me like that, Cristin. I am not wanton. I was taken over—we both were—by a power beyond ourselves."

He released her wrist, and she rubbed the sore flesh. "Some power beyond yourselves," he grated. "How amusing you must have found my concern for your virgin reserve. Lust is what took over. Lust and betrayal. My dear brother found you helpless and forced himself upon you. A man has killed for less."

Terror drove her to seize his hand. "Oh, no, please . . . please, Cristin. It was not his fault alone. We do love each other. What happened was wrong—I cannot deny it—but it was done out of love. I am also to blame."

Cristin seemed to grow calm as he stared down into her face with an indefinable expression in his eyes. "So, my brother has knowledge of your body. I have given you the respect I thought your innocence merited, but he took you like any common shepherd with his slut. But no man keeps what is mine. Bryn knows that, and you will learn it. You are mine—promised to me. Our betrothal is a fact known to our friends, as is our wedding date. All will proceed as arranged."

"You cannot mean that! Cristin, we will go away. You need never see us again."

"You must have bewitched him if he said that, but you will not go away. You will stay here, and Bryn may choose for himself. He can, if he so desires, watch our nuptials and remain to see you bear my children, but he will not have you."

His voice was quiet but his face was twisted with fury, and Rhonwen shrank back. "I love Bryn—I always shall."

"Then that must be your punishment."

She watched him walk from the room and sank onto a chair, feeling utter disbelief. She had braced herself to brave scorn, anger, rejection. Not for a minute had she supposed that he would insist upon marrying her.

The door opened and Bryn hurried in. "What happened? I expected him to come looking for me. I was waiting, but he galloped off like a devil out of hell. He took it badly! That is understandable, but he will recover."

"He says he will not release me. We are to be married."

"What! He wants you knowing you love me! I cannot believe it. He will not persist. We have hurt his pride badly, but he will let you go. Perhaps he could have forgiven you more readily if I had not been the one to supplant him. We must give him a little time."

"There is not much time," protested Rhonwen, "and you did not see his face or hear his words. He terrified me."

"Well, he does not frighten me. Don't worry, Rhonwen, I will speak to him, as I should have done in the first place."

She rubbed her aching wrist again, and Bryn drew back her cuff and frowned. Then he bent to kiss the bruise and she looked down at his dark head. He seemed so sure of himself, so convinced of Cristin's eventual capitulation.

He looked up into her troubled face, then rose and slid an arm about her waist. "Do you not trust me, my love?"

"You know I do! Have I not given enough proof? But Cristin seemed implacable—and I . . ." She stopped. 'I am afraid,' she had almost said, 'afraid of Cristin—afraid of the strange accidents I seem to be suffering lately.' She felt trapped in a situation with no logical meaning.

She leaned her head on Bryn's shoulder. "I have been such

a fool," she said miserably. "It is my fault for being too ready to think I was in love. I suppose I craved so much to be part of someone, or somewhere; but now I know that nothing but real love is worth a farthing."

"You are not to blame for your inexperience. Well, there is only one thing left to do. When Cristin returns I will tell him we are lovers. He will not persist when he knows."

Rhonwen swallowed hard. "I . . . I told him. I am sure he had guessed. He forced the truth from me."

Bryn held her away and stared at her. "You are sure he understood? And he insists on proceeding with the marriage!" He began to pace the library. "Does he truly love you, then? Or is he merely determined not to let you come to me? I have never known him constant in affection!"

"His love is not like yours, Bryn. He is cold and distant. He makes me fear him. Sometimes it seemed that he has some strange relentless purpose in his pursuit of me!"

She bit her knuckles. What had made her say that? For an instant she felt as if the pieces of a jigsaw puzzle lay jumbled in the hidden reaches of her mind.

Bryn came swiftly to her and held her trembling body close to his. "You will not marry Cristin, darling. Whatever happens, however he resists, I shall not allow him to part us."

He kissed her tenderly, and even in the midst of her doubt and torment she felt her senses stirring in her need for him.

A letter in the second post, confirming the date of Miss Reeves's arrival, gave Rhonwen pain as well as pleasure when she considered the likelihood of her former teacher becoming involved in problems when she should be looking forward to Christmas.

Cristin had gone to Harlech and Bryn was visiting the shepherd whose flock had lost the old ewe to tell him that he had found her dying and put a merciful end to her suffering.

'He must have come straight from killing the sheep to loving me,' thought Rhonwen, and her worry increased as she thought of the strength of purpose of both Cristin and Bryn.

Edwina was growing more withdrawn, leaving the orders for the seasonal festivities to be given by Frances, who said, "We shall curtail our pleasures in deference to your mourning, Rhonwen. Instead of the usual large gathering for the county we will hold a small dinner for close friends. The servants should not be disappointed—you will not wish them to forgo their party, will you?''

Rhonwen shook her head, then remembering that she had not yet purchased gifts, asked Edwina if she might have a carriage to take her shopping. She rode with the hood down, allowing the wintry breeze to flow around her, wishing that her tempestuous fears might be as easily cooled.

She recalled Bryn's words before he left the library—''I shall speak to Cristin—it has become imperative. I shall make it absolutely clear that you are mine, now and always.''

After using some of her precious sovereigns to buy presents, she decided to call on the Evans's.

Mary came running to greet her with a kiss. ''There's nice it is to see you,'' she exclaimed, then flushed. ''Oh, I shouldn't be so familiar now.''

Rhonwen hugged the little Welsh woman. ''Mary, pray do not talk such nonsense. You will always be my friend. I need you.''

Her voice cracked, and Mary peered into her face.

''You look well enough, love—but your eyes are sad.'' She glanced up at the Caradog coachman, then back at Rhonwen. ''Can you stay a while?''

''I would be delighted,'' Rhonwen assured her. The horse was unharnessed and led into a stable, and the coachman settled happily enough in a corner of the warm forge with a glass of hot negus, a warm pie and anticipation of a gossip.

In the kitchen Marged and the little ones greeted Rhonwen with pleasure, and she was intrigued to see the table covered by an assortment of homemade sweetmeats. A delicious aroma of hot toffee came from the saucepan Rose was stirring over the fire and pulling at the bubbling mixture, her face pink from heat. The small children were pasting pictures on boxes and cutting waxed paper wrappers. ''We always do these for the old folk hereabouts,'' said Mary.

''What a kind idea! Oh, do you think I might have a try? I have bought gifts, but these are so much nicer.''

Enveloped in a large apron, her hands busy with marzipan and melted chocolate, fondant cream and icing sugar, Rhonwen forgot her worries for a while. Perhaps she and Bryn would find contentment in a humble life, but the intrusive memory of Bryn's attachment to his home once more attacked her peace.

She glanced at Mary, who was usually conscious of other's moods, only to realise that she, too, was immersed in some dilemma of her own. She had resolved to try to help when the door flew open. Owen stood there, his huge frame filling the doorway. "It's good to see you back in our kitchen, Rhonwen. David, my son, you will have to give a hand in the forge."

David left the book to which he had been giving intermittent attention while watching the sweet-makers, rose obediently and followed his father. Soon afterwards Rhonwen went to the window as she heard the crackle of fire and smelled smoke. Owen and his son, assisted reluctantly by a sweating coachman, were lowering a white hot metal rim onto an enormous wheel, which spurted in small flames.

Mary joined her at the window. "Oh, thank the lord they've managed it. The farmer wants his wagon quickly. I was afraid they might fail without Tomos's strength."

Owen splashed cold water onto the metal rim, it hissed as it contracted and bit into the wood, encasing it with a powerful shield.

"Where is Tomos? I thought wheelmaking was one of his favourite tasks."

Mary went back to knead shortbread. "Well might you ask. I'm that worried about him!"

A tear splashed onto the floury board, and Rhonwen put her arm about Mary and led her into the parlour where she explained, "Tomos has been acting so strange for some days past. He went out for one of his rambles and came back as wild-eyed as if he'd seen a ghost, and not a word of sense could we get from him. Now he's off every day with his food into the hills. He comes back ravenously hungry, and when we question him, he just rolls his eyes and looks really soft in the head. He was always a zany, but now we're afraid he might be going daft enough to be locked away. It would kill him. He's as free as a bird here."

She dabbed at her eyes. "Owen tries to be patient, but the work's falling behind! Hugh can't help like a full-grown man, and David is in trouble for being weak and bookish, which is something my Owen has never said before since we are always hoping that he might end up a schoolmaster."

Rhonwen could offer little help. If Tomos really was becoming insane, he was far too strong to be allowed to roam at will. Mary gulped back her tears. "What am I thinking of? Christmas is almost upon us and I'll be upsetting the children."

Rhonwen was waved off with smiles and was driven home, the hood up against the damp evening air, four ribbon-bound boxes of sweets on the seat beside her.

She felt regret at leaving the homely atmosphere of the Evans's cottage but immediately became conscious of the fact that she had begun to regard Castell Craig with a sense of belonging and grew agitated afresh at the realisation that she and Bryn might be forced to leave.

She had time only to change for dinner. Cristin was a little late, and the meal was conducted in near silence as each member of the party appeared lost in thought. Cristin and Bryn spoke briefly of estate business, and Edwina was aloof. Frances clearly sensed tension, and her dark eyes were speculative as she looked from one brother to the other.

In the drawing room Edwina sat in unaccustomed inactivity, deep in sombre meditation. Frances was at the piano picking out tunes with one finger, while Rhonwen's nerves grew more and more taut at the knowledge of what Bryn must now be saying to Cristin in the dining room.

Chapter 14

WHEN FINALLY the men joined them, it was clear that both were deeply angry. Cristin walked straight to Rhonwen and lifted her hand to bestow a kiss, and she recognised as a deliberate act of possession. She knew that Bryn had failed to gain his brother's promise to release her.

"Pray, excuse me, my dear," he said. "There are matters that require my attention before we can leave on our wedding trip."

Rhonwen threw Bryn a look of entreaty and he held out his arm. "You have not yet seen the gallery, have you, Rhonwen?" Forestalling any attempt by Frances to accompany them he continued, "You will not wish to be bored, Fran, and Edwina should not be left alone."

His voice held such significance that in the corridor Rhonwen queried his meaning, and Bryn said, "Edwina always gets melancholy at Christmas. It gives some substance to the rumour of her dead lover, whom she is supposed to have met here in December."

His voice was harsh and his stride so urgent that Rhonwen had to stretch her legs to keep up. He led her up stairs and along passages lighted at intervals by oil lamps until he threw open a door and revealed a gallery that stretched away into shadow. He took a lamp from a bracket in the corridor and placed it on a carved chest before closing the gallery door and taking Rhonwen in his arms.

His lips were hungry as they drew a willing response from hers. "I've been aching to do that, my love," he murmured.

"Rhonwen, I cannot visualise life without you. Cristin refused to be moved by any argument I put forward. All he will say is that you belong to him. He says you are in honour bound to him and he *will* marry you."

His arms tightened around her. "Such a marriage would be a sacrilege! It is unthinkable. If he refuses to understand, we must go away."

He released her and began to pace up and down, and Rhonwen sank onto a ladder-backed wooden chair and watched him. "To desire my brother's betrothed will seem a heinous crime in the eyes of the world. Indeed, I would agree if he showed some distress, but his only reaction is anger. All he talks of are his rights—as if he owned you, Rhonwen. Do you think he loves you?"

Giving her no chance to reply he went on, "No, I know he does not! He is like a man possessed of a devil—he seems to hate me—and I wondered if he had not begun to hate you also."

Bryn stopped before her, and his face expressed the shock of his voiced thoughts. "That cannot be! Unless his love for you has turned to loathing because he knows you desire me."

Rhonwen could not bear to look at his tormented face and turned her head. The gallery contained pictures by the score, and she stared at Caradog countenances in gilded frames. "Why have you brought me here? It must be the room where the past most haunts the present—and the future."

"I had not considered it so. It is simply a place where one can walk and talk. In ancient days the ladies often spent the whole winter indoors, using this gallery for their exercise."

He pulled her to her feet and they walked the room, and Bryn sometimes lifted the lamp to illumine a particular face or explain a turbulent love story. Some of them had dared much for their passions, but he spoke of no one who considered a lover worthy the price of perpetual banishment from the home of their fathers.

In the alcove there were cabinets, and Bryn lifted the lids to display a collection of miniatures on crimson brocade. Many were exquisite in their small perfection, and in spite of her desolation Rhonwen was fascinated. She leaned forward. "Look, Bryn; there is a light oval shape on the brocade here.

Something has been removed. Who is missing?''

"I don't know, but there is a catalogue, which Idris has brought up to date." He opened the double doors of a carved cupboard, drew out a large book and turned the heavy linen pages with care. "Here it is! 'Miniature by Andrew Plimer, of Mari Caradog, painted in 1796, and presented to her parents, Caillin and Gwynne, on the occasion of her marriage to Stephen Wilmot of America.' ''

He replaced the book and closed the cabinet lid. "I daresay Idris has put the miniature safely in his room. He was probably in the middle of making a likeness of it when he returned to school. We had better say nothing, for he should not have removed it. He can show you when he returns. I think you will like Idris.''

He stopped and frowned, and Rhonwen said miserably, "You are thinking that we shall be gone from here when Idris returns. Oh, Bryn, I almost begin to wish I had not entered your life.''

Bryn had picked up the lamp, but now he slammed it down so that the flame flickered and made their shadows dance on the walls and ceiling. Then he drew her to him roughly and held her so close she could feel the rapid pounding of his heart. "Never say such things again. Do not even think it. I love you more than life itself.''

His kisses were impassioned, and her own fervour matched his. Yet as they retraced their steps, between the painted eyes of long-dead Caradogs, Rhonwen could not rid herself of the fear that if she was responsible for depriving Bryn of his home, he might end by blaming her. Was she doomed to provoke hostile reactions in those around her? Even her mother's love had seemed erratic.

She made a decision that she would not allow herself to ride upon the chance happenings of fate. She must make a positive move to clarify her position, and she would begin with Edwina.

She went to her room after leaving Bryn, and as soon as Susan brought her word that Edwina had retired, she asked her to lead her to the turret.

It took Edwina time to drag herself from her private world to comprehend what she was hearing, but when she did understand she did not express the disgust Rhonwen had feared.

"You say that you and Bryn have fallen in love! But how can you be so sure? You have just accepted a proposal of marriage from Cristin!"

"I know—I know," said Rhonwen unhappily. "I am entirely to blame. I should have given it more thought."

"Well, you cannot love both men as you should a prospective husband. Perhaps you do not care truly for either. One thing is certain—you must not marry without being sure. Wedded happiness is the most desirable state on earth. You must have no doubts."

Rhonwen was amazed at the vehemence of Edwina's tone. Surely only a woman who had contemplated marriage with an adored lover could be so convinced.

"Would you like me to speak to Cristin and Bryn?"

"I would be so grateful," said Rhonwen. "I know that Cristin has right on his side, but I cannot marry him. Bryn has come to the conclusion that we should leave Castell Craig for good, and I have to agree with him. At least, *I* must go somewhere where I can think in solitude."

"Have you forgotten Miss Reeves?"

Rhonwen was chagrined. "Oh, how could I be so selfish? She is arriving tomorrow and will need rest and tranquillity after the ordeal of Mr. Baker's long illness and death. Edwina, what am I to do?"

"Nothing at present. Both men are hotheaded and wilful, but they are not cruel. They will—they must—understand that you should not be harrassed."

Edwina put her arms around Rhonwen, who leaned against her, and for a moment there was complete sympathy between them.

Edwina wasted no time, and the next morning Rhonwen learned that Cristin was prepared to make the concession of setting back the wedding date to late January. "But I will make you mine then," he insisted. "You need not suppose because you have played upon the susceptible heart of a kindly woman that I shall release you. The new date will be sent to our friends."

Bryn and Rhonwen talked again in the gallery. "Cristin was angrier than I have ever seen him," said Bryn, "but we have given Edwina our word that we will not spoil Christmas with our quarrel. But afterwards, Rhonwen, it looks as though we shall have to slip away together."

Later that day Cristin insisted on accompanying Rhonwen to the tiny halt to meet Miss Reeves. She stepped onto the platform, and Rhonwen held out her arms as she ran to her. "Oh, Miss Reeves, how lovely it is to see you. But you look thin and so weary. You will recuperate in the mountain air. I was desolate at hearing of dear Mr. Baker. Was he in much pain?"

Miss Reeves hugged her. "His death was not easy, but he did not complain. He refused to give me permission to tell you and was very happy to learn of your splendid prospects." Her eyes slid to where Cristin was supervising the unloading of her luggage. She whispered, "Is he your betrothed?"

Rhonwen nodded helplessly as Cristin turned to face them, and Miss Reeves peered at him. "I have seen him somewhere before."

Cristin carried a portmanteau and a leather box along the platform. "Welcome to Wales, Miss Reeves."

"Thank you, sir. I was just saying to Rhonwen that your face seems familiar to me."

"Is that so? Well, I am in London often, though I do not think we have met. Let us waste no time. It will soon be dark."

He ushered them to the carriage, strapped on the luggage, and they drove back to Castell Craig, the two women bringing one another up to date with news.

Miss Reeves and Edwina liked each other on sight, and Bryn was in a mood to take to anyone who was fond of Rhonwen. Only Cristin remained aloof, and later Rhonwen was in the pretty guest room alloted to Miss Reeves, who said, "I *have* seen him before, Rhonwen, and I wonder why he denies it. He must know I caught sight of him when he visited your old lodging."

"You must be mistaken!"

"I know I am right. I was entering the front door as he left Mrs. Mason's rooms, and she was so wreathed in smiles and so oily of voice I knew she was very pleased with herself. I guessed that someone had given her money. I confess I looked with curiosity at her visitor, who most definitely was your Cristin Caradog."

"He did not want you to come!" exclaimed Rhonwen; then

she flushed. "Oh, dear, how inhospitable that is, but one wonders if he had a good reason. Yet how could he have known your name?"

"Because Mrs. Mason, in her gloating way, was so pleased to show off her well-set-up visitor that she greeted me loudly by name. He knew who I was, and he knew that I had had a clear view of him."

After dinner Rhonwen asked Cristin about her teacher's assertion, and he admitted, "Yes, all right, I did go to your lodging. And why not? By that time I wanted to marry you and I knew only what you had said about yourself. Was it so fearful a thing for me to investigate the girl I was going to make my wife?"

"Bryn loves me without reservation," burst out Rhonwen, indignation making her unwise.

Cristin's lip curled. "I wonder you are so brazen as to talk of love in connection with my brother in view of your infidelity. But I promised Edwina I would not discuss the matter at present, so be so good as to help me keep my word."

Rhonwen was forced to bite back her angry questions, and the evening passed in outward calm. At bedtime Miss Reeves congratulated Rhonwen on acquiring so handsome and rich a suitor. Yet there was no warmth in her voice, and Rhonwen knew that she did not care for Cristin. Well, it would make it easier later to tell her the truth.

As Christmas approached, the castle began to bustle with life. Outdoor servants brought in great bunches of holly and mistletoe, laurel and ivy, and the glossy green leaves and red and white berries glowed like jewels against the oak-panelled walls. A tall fir tree stood in a corner of the hall, and Frances directed footmen, who climbed ladders to hang baubles and candles on the perfumed branches.

Edwina moved about with studied calm, smiling and approving without reservation; yet always Rhonwen sensed that the true woman dwelt in a place where no one might enter.

Gaily wrapped gifts began to appear at the foot of the tree, and Rhonwen added hers to the pile. She had packets of lacy handkerchiefs and boxes of sweets for the ladies, and silk cravats for Cristin and Bryn. On Edwina's advice she had purchased tobacco and books, diaries and scarves for the servants' tree, which would be presided over by the housekeeper, who would dispense the presents in a protocol as strict as the one pertaining above stairs.

Miss Reeves was far too well bred to pursue the subject of Cristin's evasive behaviour, and now that Rhonwen saw her friend in a new setting, she began to appreciate how she must have suffered during her years of deprivation.

Rhonwen was in Miss Reeves's room helping her sort out the sheet music and almanacs she had brought as her gifts. "And I have a box of *Chocolat Menier* for Miss Watkins. In my experience lady companions receive few such luxuries. And for Miss Caradog there is this carved mother-of-pearl needle case."

Rhonwen picked up the slender case and ran her fingers over the delicate outlines. "She will love it. Pray, do not be put out by Edwina's air of abstraction. It seems that she lost her lover about this time of year."

Miss Reeves flushed and turned away to begin her wrapping, and Rhonwen wondered if she, too, had lost someone dear to her. The world was full of elderly spinsters, many who lived out their grey lives in the service of others. If she left Castell Craig, might not Cristin and Bryn decide that the price of marrying her was too high? Would she end her days seeking genteel employment, aching for the feel of Bryn's arms about her?

"What ails you, Rhonwen?" Miss Reeves voice was gentle. "You should look happy, but you don't. You seem almost— despairing."

"That is what Mary Evans said. Oh, Miss Reeves, I have got myself in such a tangle."

It was a relief to pour out her problems, and Miss Reeves agreed that a time spent away from the castle could do only good. "You should have written to tell me. I could have had you for Christmas. You must come to stay with me."

Rhonwen murmured her thanks, but as she descended the main stairway and her feet sinking into the deep pile carpet, her hands caressing the newel posts of the bannister rails, her eyes delighting in the silk wall hangings and priceless ornaments, she had to fight a sense of shame that she should so dread the idea of returning to the dingy lodging house in London. Castell Craig had woven a spell of enchantment about her.

On Christmas Eve a few friends gathered at a dinner party

and regarded Rhonwen with curiosity. The women were re-
served, though the men's expressions left her in no doubt that
in her gown of moonstone grey silk, worn at Cristin's insistence, his gift of pearls, her red-gold hair brushed to shining
perfection and coiled with white silk flowers, she was beautiful.

Cristin seemed as anxious to avoid her eyes as she his, but
Bryn's heart and soul were in his gaze and the look of love he
bestowed on her was so intense that she glanced quickly about
to see if anyone had noticed. Only Miss Reeves was watchful,
and Rhonwen saw a shadow cross her face.

Late on Christmas day the family made a concerted descent
into the kitchen quarters where they were stared at by young
maids and boys who spent the rest of the year scurrying about
like mice at the behest of almost everyone.

Edwina was led into a country dance by the solemn butler,
while Grace Bell, unfamiliar in royal blue satin with many pink
bows, was partnered by Cristin. Bryn manfully led the
housekeeper into the dance and a bashful footman escorted
Rhonwen. Family mingled with servants in this once-a-year
festive familiarity until, duty well performed, they returned
upstairs, leaving sounds of laughter and merriment that found
only pallid echoes above stairs.

Presents were unwrapped, and Rhonwen found herself the
owner of a cashmere scarf from Edwina and a magnificent,
fur-lined cloak from Cristin. Bryn gave her a pretty basket; and
when she opened it, she found beneath the packets of needles,
strands of silk, small silver scissors and thimble a tissue-covered
gift labelled with an instruction that it should be opened later.

She and Bryn found no opportunity to be alone, and when
the family retired, Rhonwen went to her room with a sense of
relief. Eagerly she opened her secret present and discovered,
to her surprise, a wooden spoon, its wide rectangular handle
carved in a delicate tracery of hearts and flowers.

Susan came in her pretty gown to ask if she needed help.
"You are not supposed to leave your party," said Rhonwen,
"but perhaps you could unhook my dress." She had requested
assistance only to be able to ask, "What does it mean when a
young man gives a girl a wooden spoon, Susan? Is it a Welsh
custom?"

Susan stifled a giggle. "Oh, has Mr. Cristin given you one,

miss? Why, they are love tokens. All the carving must be done by the giver. That's a lovely romantic thing to have done. There, miss, I expect you can manage now. In Wales we girls think that a wooden spoon from a lover is better than a gold one."

After Susan had gone, Rhonwen turned the spoon over and over in her hands before pressing it to her lips. Bryn had taken the trouble to carve the evidence of his love in a hardwood as durable as he vowed his love to be.

She slept badly, her old nightmare weaving its way in and out of her brain, and rose early, entering the breakfast parlour as the servants finished laying the table. A footman poured her a cup of coffee and she drank it, standing by the window, looking out into the winter gloom.

Cristin, Bryn, Miss Reeves and Miss Watkins arrived, and Edwina decided to join them though she seemed to have little appetite. The post was brought in and Edwina, after reading a letter eagerly, gave a cry of relief. "This is from Idris. He says he has been unwell, but he is improving now and wants to come home."

"What nonsense!" declared Cristin. "He is nothing but a namby-pamby creature! He must learn to face up to life's difficulties. Unwell, you say? Not actually ill?"

"No, but enclosed is a letter from Lord Barnwell, who is so very kind. Cristin, how can you have supposed that he would have objected to our dear boy refusing his invitation? He says all that is most generous, seeming fully to comprehend that Idris is pining for his home. He even goes so far as to wonder if Idris is a suitable boy for boarding school."

"What damned impudence!" Cristin held out his hand for the first page of the letter, and his frown grew deeper as he read aloud " '. . . a sensitive boy . . . artistic . . . his emotions strongly linked to his physical stamina.' . . . I can scarcely think that Lord Barnwell was not laughing as he penned these words."

Edwina protested. "No, indeed, he could not have been. Here he explains that he has a young brother who was not sent away to school and who has become a respected man of letters, though not robust. He most certainly does understand Idris."

"I will not have it! Idris must—shall—stay to see out his visit, and, furthermore, he will return straight to school afterwards!"

Edwina stared at Cristin. Her face was pale but held all the dignity and authority of the true chatelaine of Castell Craig. "You forget yourself, Cristin. *I* am the final arbiter, and I say that Idris's future will be for me to decide. Pray, pass me my letter."

Cristin handed back the sheet of paper and grated, "If Idris is unwell he will need to remain at Barnwell Towers for the present."

"Not so," denied Edwina calmly. "His lordship says here, 'The boy is much recovered from his indisposition and can come to no harm by returning to you in our family coach under the care of my secretary, who is a distant relative and most solicitous.' Oh, thank God, Idris will be arriving home tomorrow." She rose. "I shall go at once to direct that his bedroom be aired and made ready."

She left an awkward silence, which only Cristin broke as he tapped a spoon on the table until Rhonwen's nerves were stretched. Frances entered and looked around curiously. "What has happened? I have just passed Edwina, and she looks as joyful as you are dismal. She uttered something I did not catch about Idris."

Cristin explained and Bryn added, "Our cousin is coming home and it seems to cause Cristin much irritation."

Frances laughed carelessly, "I must say I think Idris is somewhat unmanly in his attitudes. However, I shall not allow this to spoil my day. Cristin, do please stop glowering. And Netta, take that dismal expression from your face."

She settled to enjoy a plate of kidneys and bacon, exhorting Cristin to display some good humour until he rose and flung himself out of the room.

When Rhonwen emerged he was waiting for her and made a polite request, which she felt she could not ignore, that she should accompany him to the library. His eyes were almost feverish in their glare, and she had to prevent herself from shrinking from his touch as he put a hand beneath her arm and hurried her along. Yet when they arrived he seemed in no haste to begin speaking. He walked to the window and called her to join him. "Look out there, Rhonwen. The Rhinogs! Do they look menacing to you?"

Without awaiting an answer he continued, "They are part of

my life, as is my home here. Why did you come to despoil my peace?"

His voice lost its harshness and became almost gentle as he asked, "Rhonwen, I must ask you once more. Will you give me your promise that you will raise no further objection to our marriage? I will treat you well. This fancy you have for Bryn will pass."

Rhonwen answered evenly, "I am sorry, Cristin. You have just cause for complaint, but my love for Bryn is not simply a fancy, and it will not pass. Our love will remain as steadfast as . . . as the Rhinogs."

Cristin stared again from the window. Then he sighed, "So be it," almost, it seemed, to himself.

"Rhonwen, you will be released; but first you must do something for me. I would like you to take a walk to a part of Castell Craig you have not yet seen. Will you oblige me in this?"

Her relief was so overwhelming she felt she could have complied in anything, and she agreed at once. He led the way through the hall, along a passage and opened a door leading to a flight of steps that, in their turn, led to another door. This one was of thick, studded oak, and Cristin lifted a lantern from a bracket and lit it, carefully replacing the glass dome. Then he unlocked the door with a large iron key he took from his pocket and pushed it open. A wave of cold air made her shiver. Cristin glanced at her. "I should have thought of cloaks. I shall not keep you long. Will you be all right?"

Rhonwen peered into the blackness beyond the door, then back at Cristin. His face held such a look of resignation that she felt guilt at the pain she must be causing him. The whole episode was beginning to assume a quality of such strain that she wanted to finish with it as soon as possible. "If we are not too long I should be able to manage."

Cristin closed the door behind them, and Rhonwen pulled her shawl closer about her shoulders as she followed him down a flight of steps between granite walls. They reached a large cellar filled with wooden racks containing many hundreds of bottles.

"Some of this wine was laid down long ago," explained Cristin. "It is precious and no servant ever comes here without the attendance of a senior male of our family." He touched an empty rack. "This awaits a supply of this year's brandy—a very fine year and a good yield."

"I see." Rhonwen pulled her shawl around her throat.

"You should not be too cold here, Rhonwen. The temperature is kept at an almost even level of fifty-five degrees Fahrenheit. And, of course, the atmosphere is dry."

"Cristin, this is all very interesting, but surely you have not brought me here to discuss wines."

"No, indeed. I simply thought you might find it of passing interest. We shall continue."

She followed him the length of the cellar until he placed the lamp on the floor to turn a large wheel that controlled another door, this time of steel. He completed a number of turns, then pulled until the door swung open and air from the inner cellar touched Rhonwen with icy fingers.

"The first of the flood doors, Rhonwen. We must be quick or the cold will affect the wines."

He stepped through and waited with such obvious impatience that she scrambled through the narrow aperture. He swung the door shut, turning a wheel on the other side. This time they were in what looked like a wide passageway, and the lamp began to flicker.

"Hurry," he urged. "The air here is close and bad. We should not linger."

"Please, Cristin, can we return. Surely I have seen enough."

"Oh, no, Rhonwen, you have not yet arrived at the place you must see. Come."

He walked swiftly along the passage, and she had no choice but to follow him until again he laid down the lamp to turn a wheel on a door. "The second and last of the steel flood doors. The air is purer on the other side. There must be minute crevices leading to the open air, though no one ever seems to have discovered them."

He closed the door and Rhonwen waited for him to manipulate the wheel, but he smiled. "No need for one this side, Rhonwen. You will soon see why."

They were on a ledge leading to some roughly hewn steps leading down, and Cristin lifted the lamp. "This is what I brought you to see."

She gazed about her as his lamp picked out great granite

masses above and to every side of them. Then she followed him down the steps and stared round, fascinated by the ancient formations and, far above her head, clusters of stalactites, each with its slowly changing drop of water.

Cristin began to walk along the stone-strewn floor of the cave, and Rhonwen went with him until once more he stopped. "We are below the lake here. That is why we built the flood doors. About ten years ago we had heavy snow throughout the winter, followed by torrential rain. The waters of the lake overflowed into the cave and almost reached the wine cellar. I supervised the replacement of the normal doors myself. We had no need to put a wheel on the last one, for when they are closed, no one remains in this cave."

He raised the lamp high above his head. "Look around you, Rhonwen. Here are the foundations of my home. Castell Craig rises from the living rock. The castle grows from the mountain and is one with it, as I am one with the home of my ancestors. No one is going to take it from me. I shall never allow them to do so, Rhonwen, do you understand?"

His voice frightened her. "No one wants to, Cristin. You had no need to bring me here to tell me so. I have understood from the beginning how much your home means to you. Now please take me back. I am cold—so cold—"

"Are you so? Probably it is the damp that penetrates your bones. I feel no cold, only a regret, a great sadness, that so much loveliness must perish in so lonely and desolate a spot. Beauty such as yours demands a more tender deathbed."

She stared at him, feeling the blood leave her face. "Why do you talk so horribly? Cristin, please, take me back."

"You do not comprehend yet, do you? You see, Rhonwen, you will not return. I do most truly regret the necessity for your demise, but I can do nothing but allow it to happen. I shall go back, but you must stay here forever."

She tried to tell herself that he was playing some cruel joke to revenge himself for the slight she had put upon him; but his expression, his voice terrified her. They held no attempt at domination, no hatred; only genuine regret that he was forced against his nature to perform some dreadful act.

It crossed her mind that he must be mad. Perhaps if she reasoned with him . . . "Cristin," she said, forcing her voice to gentleness, "I admit to being much at fault in accepting your offer and then betraying you with Bryn. It happened out of the love I bear for him . . ."

She stopped. That was hardly the way to placate him. "Cristin," she tried again, "I will swear to you here and now, that if you take me back, I will leave Castell Craig forever. I know Bryn will come, too. I can answer for him as well as for myself."

Still Cristin did not speak, and his face was impassive. "Cristin," she begged, "please—is it necessary to play such wicked games with me?"

"I play no games, my dear Rhonwen. This is only too real." He looked at his watch, "I have time—it is fair that you should know why you cannot be allowed to live. When first I saw you from the forge in Glyn Dedwydd I recognised the threat you were to my security. I knew your face."

"We had never met, I am sure!"

"No, indeed, but I knew your face. I have seen it many times looking at me from a miniature that was kept in the gallery. Fortunately only one other knows of it, and I had the presence of mind to remove it as soon as I returned that day."

"So you have it! Bryn and I noticed the mark it left. But it cannot have been a picture of me!"

"No, of course not. It was a likeness of Mari Caradog, who went to America. You are her image, feature for feature. Even your hair is exactly the same colour."

"How is it possible? You must be mistaken!"

"I assure you I am not, and from the moment I saw you, I have been diligent in making enquiries. Your Miss Reeves, damn her, was right when she said she saw me. I learned from Mrs. Mason that Beatrice Morgan arrived at her lodging house eighteen years ago carrying a baby only days old. I deduced that she had borne a child in the castle itself and that its father must have been Meredith Wilmot, Mari's grandson. It was easy to discover from the old housekeeping books that he had been a guest here at the relevant time."

"Meredith!" said Rhonwen. "That is the other name my mother moaned so often in her sleep. You knew who I was and you did not tell me. That was cruel."

"I tried to make you leave. Remember that. I tried to help you when I knew that you were the daughter of Meredith

Wilmot. I did not want Edwina to discover your identity. She would have wished to make over money to you—there could have been scandal."

"I do not want your money. If that is the only thing that is worrying you . . . !"

"You little fool! Do you think I would damn my immortal soul for the little you might have received or for the necessity to hide the bastard of a dead servant and her dead lover? My God, I have done all I could to avoid harming you—even offering you marriage. Do you honestly believe I would turn from a girl like Frances to ally myself with one reared in a London slum without good cause? Love! Breeding, wealth and power are what I have always cherished."

"Then why . . . ?"

"Remember the day you sprained your ankle and bathed it in the stream? I was affected by your deformity. Oh, how little you understood the extent of my horror. I have seen such feet before, when Edwina took us picnicking as children and dabbled her toes in the water. Four on each foot, just like yours, Rhonwen, and like her mother's Isobel Woodford and her mother's before her. It is an accident of inheritance handed down from mother to daughter through the years.

"Everything fell into place in my understanding. I had often pondered the tales of Cousin Edwina's lover who died at sea. Of her long, unexplained illness when she could not play with Bryn and me. Meredith Wilmot was drowned on his way back to America. I remember him a little. Edwina's sickness covered the time when you were born."

He gave a small bow and a smile twisted his thin lips. "Welcome to the very heart of Castell Craig, Rhonwen Caradog, daughter of Edwina Caradog and Meredith Wilmot."

Rhonwen stared at Cristin, trying to encompass the enormity of what he had told her, striving to grasp the meaning of the words that bounced among the granite crags in eerie echoes.

"I am a Caradog, Cristin?"

"Not just 'a' Caradog! You are the daughter of the woman who heads our family—and the heir to all that goes with her."

"It is not possible! It is incredible! Edwina my mother!" Rhonwen put her shaking hands to her face. "And that is the reason you asked me to marry you?"

"Naturally. And everything was going according to my plan. The truth would have emerged when Idris returned, but by then you would have been my wife and I should have been master of your estates. Then that stupid youth fell ill of homesickness. Idris—a boy you have never even met—signed your death warrant, Rhonwen, for he knows the pictures better than any of us, and he would have seen your resemblance to Mari at once. Questions would have been asked, and I did not care for the answers that would have been found."

Rhonwen stared at Cristin and said, "Are you telling me that Edwina gave birth to a child and that my mother—Beatrice— stole it from her—and that Edwina caused no enquiries to be made? Even the need for secrecy would not stop a mother from trying to get back her baby."

"You are right, of course." He looked again at his watch. "I must be quick, but I will finish what I have begun. The point was one upon which I pondered, and suddenly it seemed to be clear. I confirmed my idea when I dug up the so-called dog's grave."

"So it was you! That was horrible!"

"But necessary. There was no dog in that small mound, my dear Rhonwen. I found the skeleton of a baby. Time had not yet worked upon the bones, which were perfect. And I thought of Sophy's memory of Beatrice—so white and ill, she said."

"Again I consulted the housekeeping books. Meredith Wilmot arrived here in October, 1859, when Edwina was away visiting friends. Beatrice had been ill with influenza and did not accompany her mistress. She must have been easy prey for a bored philanderer. Then Edwina returned—beautiful, young, rich. Meredith forgot his unimportant maid and took another woman to himself in a union producing you, my dear, while the woman you have always called your mother concealed her pregnancy and the birth of her baby and tended her mistress through her own time of trial. How Beatrice must have suffered! It makes it easier to comprehend her behaviour later."

Rhonwen kept her wide eyes upon Cristin as he said, hurrying a little now. "Beatrice must have carried her child to term and delivered it herself. Perhaps it was born dead, or maybe it died because its mother had to leave it while she went to her mistress, who gave birth to a baby earlier than she should. A girl who lived. Beatrice's jealousy and anguish came to a head. She substituted her dead child for the live one and fled, carrying Edwina's child with her. Old Parry helped Edwina by burying the baby she believed to be hers and Meredith's in the grave in her special garden, while you, Rhonwen, grew up in London.

"Then an accident on the Thames sent you here to tear apart the whole fabric of my life. At least, it might have done, but I shall not allow it."

Rhonwen said dully, "I suppose you hoped I might die on the mountain when you set me near a precipice on an untrained mount and encouraged me to walk alone where you must have known the perils. And the bed curtains—the fire—you tried to murder me then."

Cristin sighed. "Your language is immoderate. I gave fate chances to remove you from my path. I pulled the curtains and pushed the candle near. You seemed to bear a charmed life—until now. This time I shall not fail. This time I must succeed. Your love for Bryn and your insistence on marrying him demands that I rid myself of you."

She hung on to the shreds of reason and tried to control her shaking limbs as she said, "If I do not return, everyone will ask where I am. Bryn will search for me. He will never give up."

Her voice broke and Cristin said, "You are well aware that no one will dream of looking down here. I am going to your room to pack your bag and remove it. I shall tell everyone that you came to me in great distress to confess that you could no longer bear the way you were disrupting our lives and have gone away and will get in touch with us when you are more settled in your mind."

"They will not believe you!"

"They will have no choice. When you do not write, Bryn may look for you—I daresay he will—but he will not find you. And no one will prove that I had a hand in your disappearance. I shall have plenty of time to dispose of any—evidence."

"Susan may catch you in my room," burst out Rhonwen desperately.

"Clutching at straws? Susan has accompanied the housekeeper to the Methodist church to decorate it with some of the castle flowers for tomorrow's services. They will be away quite a time. I was happy to grant my permission. I had to find a way to entice you here without our being seen. Idris left me no more time. Look around you. You came to Wales seeking your roots, and now you have found them."

Rhonwen sank onto a flat-topped boulder. "Cristin—please —you protest that you are not a violent man; how can you think of destroying me?"

His voice was almost toneless. "I shall not harm you, Rhonwen. That is, I shall not lay a hand on you; but you *will* die. Down here you will not long survive."

She fought the choking panic. "You can't leave me here alone. I shall perish of hunger—thirst—of terror, I think . . ." She looked about her. "Please, Cristin, show mercy. Don't abandon me here."

"But this is as much Castell Craig as the rooms we have left, my dear, and you will not die of thirst. Water is always somewhere about. When I am gone you must listen carefully for the trickles. But I do not think you will search long. Already your teeth are chattering. The cold will send you to sleep and you will know no pain. You will simply sleep your life away and be no more trouble to me."

As he spoke, Rhonwen's hands had been moving in the gloom as she searched for a weapon—anything that might help her to escape. Her heart was thudding so hard she could scarcely speak as she tried to gain time. "I suppose you sent me along that awful path by the river meadows for a reason also."

Cristin's brows lifted. "What a trivial matter to raise. I hoped I might discourage you from returning to Glyn Dedwydd, but I little knew your tenacity of purpose."

For the third time he consulted his watch. "I must leave you now."

Rhonwen's fingers closed round a piece of jagged rock. The lantern flickered and Cristin's shadow writhed over the great granite masses. For an instant his attention was diverted, and she sprang. He was catlike in his swift defence. As she raised the stone above his head, his hand went up to grasp her wrist and twist it sharply. Agony shot to her shoulder, and the primitive weapon fell harmlessly behind him.

"I should not have underestimated a girl reared in the gutter," he conceded. "Besides you are, after all, a Caradog and should not lack spirit. Let us hope it supports you in the hours ahead.''

Without warning he gave her arm an extra twist so that she cried out and fell to her knees. The next second he was racing for the cave entrance. She rose, giddy with pain, and staggered after him, calling his name, imploring him not to leave her.

She saw him swing open the heavy door. "Cristin!" she screamed. "No, please, no! At least leave me a light." She was at the foot of the stone steps when he stepped through the aperture, taking the lantern with him. She heard the thud of the closing door and the scrape of metal as he turned the wheel on the other side. After that there was silence and black dark.

Chapter 15

FOR MOMENTS she remained absolutely still, staring at the spot from which the light had disappeared, fighting down hysteria. If she gave way now she knew she would never regain control. Cristin had spoken of crevices. She looked about her, but there was no glimmer anywhere. In her heart she was not surprised. Cristin would not have risked her escape.

Was she to die then, alone, in so desolate a place? She was shaking violently from a mixture of cold damp and nervous anguish. She heard a faint rustling sound and realised that a part of her brain had been aware of it since the silence fell.

Rats! She almost screamed aloud her horror before she understood that the sound held form. It was a hoarse whisper that sighed its way over the crags of granite to reach her in a distorted, husky gabble.

Her battered mind flung the word "haunted" at her, and again she struggled to maintain calm. Listening hard and stepping very slowly, she followed the sounds. Terror tried to drag her back from the unknown, but her instinct to live, to search out any means to that end, drove her on.

She was within feet now of the sound and knew that in the darkness ahead someone shared her imprisonment.

Still the murmurs made no sense, and she edged forward again. "Where are you," she begged in a whisper. "Please say something I can understand."

Suddenly her ankle was gripped, and she tasted fear beyond her imagining. She wanted to kick with all her strength at whatever lay at her feet, this creature that moaned. But she forced herself to bend and touch the thing that held her. She felt flesh, cold but human, and she gave a sob of relief. Her ankle was released, and the hand guided hers to the unmistakable shape of a lamp. She groped around until she found matches and with trembling hands struck one and put it to the wick. Then slowly she looked down.

She stepped back with a cry of revulsion. "Dear God! Who —what are you?"

She stared at the human being who lay on a pile of sacks. Its face was a travesty of proper form, one eye closed by a disfigured lid and a mouth so contorted that speech seemed impossible. Wisps of white hair grew in patches from a scarred scalp, and the right arm appeared to have been broken and allowed to set without a surgeon's skill.

It was a woman, and, swallowing hard, Rhonwen knelt beside her. "How have you come here? Can we get out? Please —try to speak to me."

The woman's struggles became so agonised that Rhonwen forgot her revulsion and was swept by compassion. Perhaps it communicated itself, for the woman's efforts grew more controlled and, at last, she pronounced a recognisable word.

"Rhonwen!" She said her name and in a voice she knew. The woman on the sacks was Beatrice Morgan, her mother, whom she had last seen lying dead on the bank of the Thames almost four months before. Rhonwen tried to speak, gasped, staggered to her feet, then a sick wave became an engulfing sea and she fell into welcome unconsciousness.

Someone was patting her face and hands, calling her name. She kept her eyes closed until she realised that it was Tomos who was trying to bring her to her senses. When he saw that she was alive, his face broke into his foolish, sweet smile and she grabbed his enormous hands.

"Tomos! Oh, thank heaven you are here. I thought I was to die in this awful place. I have had a hallucination. Oh, no, you cannot understand that, can you? I thought I saw my mother— no, not my mother—Cristin said . . ."

She could not continue and Tomos scowled. "That one! Always you get hurt by him."

He helped her up and she said, "Tomos, I don't know how

you come to be here, or why, but please show me the way out."

Behind him the voice said a distorted word. So it had not been a figment of her imagination. She peered past him at the figure on the sacks.

"I brought blankets," said Tomos proudly. "She was cold, but I covered her. I have been looking after her."

So that was why he had been spending time in the mountains and taking away food. Rhonwen said, "Tomos, I thought I had gone mad. That cannot be Beatrice Morgan—yet she has her voice—or I thought she had."

Tomos's opaque eyes were uncomprehending. "Bettrys! I found Bettrys!"

Bettrys! Welsh for Beatrice! Rhonwen went to the woman and crouched beside her. "Are you indeed Beatrice Morgan? My . . . my mother. But that cannot be. I saw you dead. I saw your body—your brooch—I was not mistaken."

The shattered face worked again, and speech was brought painfully forth. "You must have seen Ida. I lent her my brooch. We quarrelled. I am Beatrice, but not your mother. I heard that wicked man. I stayed still. It was the only way to save you."

A tear trickled over her mouth. "I did you and Edwina dreadful wrong. All he said is true. I had a devil of jealousy in me."

Rhonwen's heart swelled in pity. "Whatever you did you have been punished a hundredfold."

"Tomos," whispered Beatrice, "did you get the brandy?"

The big man put a gentle arm around the frail body, lifted her and put a cup to her lips. Brandy ran into her mouth and some trickled down her chin. Tomos wiped away the dribbles gently with a corner of the blanket.

"We must get you out of here," said Rhonwen. "Tomos must help me take you somewhere warm where you can recover."

"No!" The word was unexpectedly strong. "No, Rhonwen, I have little time left. I used all my remaining strength to reach Wales. I must tell you what you do not know."

She motioned to Tomos and again he helped her drink. "You are Edwina and Meredith Wilmot's daughter and heiress to Castell Craig. But you must prove it beyond doubt. Did you bring the carved box?"

"I have it in my room."

"Good! The ring—the gold one—you have that, too? The design hinges out to form a key. It fits a lock hidden in the heart of the rose. Only Edwina and I know the secret. My confession is there. It will be enough, with the proof in your face—and your feet."

She coughed and blood flecked her lips.

"You must be taken from here!" cried Rhonwen.

"It will be too late. Already it is too late."

"Oh, this is terrible! I thought you had died. I would never have left London if I had known. Could you not have written to me?"

Beatrice raised her shaking hands. "I have no skill left here —I cannot control a pen—and I could not have written anyway. I was saved from the river by mudlarks, poor little waifs who swim like fish and scavenge for a living. They said they found me floating on a spar. They despise authority and told no one and I was out of my senses—and terribly injured—and my lungs became inflamed—I think the water has damaged them. Only the need to redress the evil I have caused kept me alive, and the mudlarks were kind in their rough way. They fed me and brought old clothes for me to wear. I suppose they salvaged them from the river, too. When I recalled who I was I went to Shoreditch. No one knew me—I wanted it that way—I could no longer run from my conscience, I was so ashamed. I spoke to some of Jacenta Lane's girls. One said you had gone to Wales. She said she had been to our rooms one evening. I was worried for you, Rhonwen."

Beatrice reached for Rhonwen's hand. "I have been praying to the God I abandoned that He watch over you. I thank Him now. He did not forsake us, for He sent me to this dark place in time to help you."

She looked imploringly at Rhonwen. "Forgive me, please, for my wickedness."

Rhonwen bent over Beatrice and forgot everything but the sorrow swamping her. "With all my heart," she said softly.

Beatrice sighed. "I sold my false wedding ring, but the money only bought a rail ticket to Barmouth. I wore a veil. A carrier gave me a ride to Dyffryn along the coast. He shared his food with me." She smiled grotesquely. "I knew him in the old days, but he did not recognise me. Nor did the good folk of Dyfrynn, but they are as ready as ever for a little talk."

Rhonwen gave a dry sob at the ironic amusement lying beneath Beatrice's tones. "They soon revealed all they knew of the beautiful girl from England who had found a lover at the castle. I took the hill path to Castell Craig. I needed to see you —I could not face anyone else, but I was weaker than I knew. The cold and walking brought a return of the lung fever. I collapsed—I would have perished on the mountain, but Tomos found me. Dear, foolish Tomos. Somehow he knew me. He brought me here and tended me. I was too ill to do anything when I arrived." Her voice was growing weak, and she sounded inexpressibly weary. "Go with him, Rhonwen. He will guard you. Find the small picture Cristin spoke of."

She closed her eyes and stirred uneasily, murmuring in Welsh. Then she dragged herself back to reality. "Go now! Cristin must not destroy my confession. Promise me that Edwina will read it—promise me—promise . . ."

"I swear it!" cried Rhonwen, "then I shall nurse you back to health."

The ghastly smile twisted Beatrice's face again. "Good Rhonwen. Oh, my dear Miss Edwina—I have wronged you . . ." She lapsed again into Welsh and Tomos touched Rhonwen's shoulder.

"We have to go. Bettrys says so."

"Cannot we take her with us?"

"Bettrys says we must go," he said stubbornly. "We must obey her."

He bent and put out the lamp and Rhonwen protested.

"Bettrys likes the dark. It is her friend, she says. Darkness and death are her friends."

Beatrice's voice came out of the blackness. "Don't be afraid, Rhonwen. Poor Tomos brought me here. I thought we should reach you through the wine cellar—I did not know of the storm doors. I have been trying to make him understand."

Tomos tugged at Rhonwen and she allowed him to lead her. She would never forget her feeling of unreality as she followed him through a fissure in the mountain. "He must have eyes like a cat", she thought, "and know the way of old, for he does not falter." He led her through places where the sides seemed to close in like a tomb, and twice they had to crouch in tunnels floored with mud. Only desperation could have forced her on. Only Tomos's great strength could have carried Beatrice on such a journey.

Rhonwen's greatest wish at that moment was to deliver Beatrice's letter so that she could be helped. She was sure that Edwina would not fail in christian charity.

At last they began to climb, and there was room for Tomos to reach back and haul her up a steep slope. Then he was pulling aside thick bracken and they were on the mountainside, dragging in breaths of icy air. Rhonwen opened her arms to the sky in thanksgiving before she said, "Guide me to Castell Craig. We must be fast."

She had been surprised to find it still light. It had seemed a lifetime since Cristin had taken her to the cavern. The wind cut through her soaked clothes and cold robbed her legs of power. Tomos shook his head, then removed his jacket and wrapped it round her before he picked her up and half-walked, half-ran down the track until they reached the gates of the castle. Here she told Tomos to put her down and, handing him his coat, she hurried as fast as her cramped limbs would allow and entered by a small side door. She longed for Bryn but there was no time to search for him, and she reached her room unchallenged. Cristin had begun his plan to eradicate all sign of her, and her personal possessions had been removed.

Where would he have taken them? To his own room, probably, since he had no fear of being disturbed. She raced along the corridor to his bedroom, passing a maid who gaped at her. What a sight she must look, covered in mud, her hair flowing behind her. She opened Cristin's door without ceremony. Her bag lay open on his bed, and he was seated at his writing desk.

"What the devil!" He whirled round and she saw that he had forced the lid of the box and was examining the contents. For a second he did not recognise her, then his eyes dilated. She began to cross the room towards him, and he grabbed the things he had removed, stuffed them back into the box and slammed the lid. Then he sprang to the fire roaring up the wide chimney and hurled the box into the centre of the flames.

Rhonwen, filled with the horror of what Cristin had done to her, tormented by the memory of Beatrice's terrible plight, leapt at Cristin with the ferocity of a tigress, clawing and tearing at him. Taken by surprise he staggered from the fireplace and, impervious to the flames, she reached into the fire and grabbed the box, beating at the smouldering wood with her muddy hands.

She was through the door and running, and she raced up a flight of stairs with Cristin close behind. Panic was infiltrating her being; all her senses were in its control. She could smell the stench of Thames water, taste the acrid fumes of an oil lamp held high to illuminate a row of covered bodies and a lamp in a dark cavern where Beatrice lay dying. Beatrice—she had sworn to take her precious confession to Edwina, but Cristin was too close.

Then something outside of will seemed to direct her and carry her feet over the ground as if she were flying. She was on a narrower stairway and she was living her nightmare. Danger was behind and around her. It lurked in the door ahead. Would it open? Would she find peace or terror? She turned the handle, the door opened and she fell into a room. Edwina's room.

She was clinging to the box as Cristin tugged at it. She felt his despairing rage as he engaged with her in a personal duel. "Thief!" he shouted. "We have been grossly deceived. She was trying to steal from us."

Edwina stared at Cristin's distorted features as he struck viciously at Rhonwen's scorched hands. She could fight no longer. Exhaustion and pain deprived her of resistance and she released her grip. He was leaving. Her promise could not be kept, and Beatrice would die with her guilt unassuaged.

"Edwina," she sobbed, "make him come back . . ."

Cristin turned to throw her a look of hatred, and at that moment Tomos's huge form appeared and blocked the doorway. He reached out and grabbed Cristin's shoulders.

"Always you hurt my pretty Rhonwen. Always she falls."

He began to shake Cristin so that his head snapped back and forth. His eyes bulged and his breath gasped in his throat. Edwina screamed and Rhonwen staggered after her. Both women dragged at Tomos's great arms in a futile effort to control him. The pain from Rhonwen's hands became too much to endure, as a voice from the passage outside spoke in a tone of command, which Tomos obeyed. Bryn at last!

Cristin had dropped the box and was clawing at his collar,

while a shocked Frances, who had been close behind Bryn, helped to support him.

Bryn put his arms around Rhonwen. "My dear love—what happened? One of the maids came running—she was almost incoherent—she said you were covered in mud and looked terrified. I could hear Cristin yelling . . ."

Rhonwen leaned against him. "Quickly, give Edwina her box."

Edwina herself was picking it up with a startled exclamation. Behind her Rhonwen saw Frances help Cristin from the room. He did not look back, and she said nothing.

Edwina came to the couch where Bryn had led Rhonwen to examine her hands. His expression was grim as he called to Grace to bring liniment and bandages.

Rhonwen's head was swimming, and her voice grew thick as she said carefully, "Edwina—look at your box—it is—a matter of life and death."

Edwina gave her an incredulous look and walked to her dressing table where she laid the box down. "Why did you not give me this before? It is the one your mother took from me."

"She's in no state to be answering questions," said Grace. "Look at her! Scratched, bruised, dirty and soaked! Mr. Bryn, I must ask you to wait in another room while I see to her."

Rhonwen tried to protest, but her voice came out as a croak. She was becoming increasingly anxious about Beatrice and felt sure that if only she could tell Bryn he would go to her aid without asking questions. But she was forced to lie and watch him walk away.

As Grace bathed and dressed her wounds, washed her and put on a clean white nightgown, Rhonwen was scarcely aware of discomfort. She was willing Edwina to hurry.

Edwina flipped open the gold locket. "Meredith's hair," she breathed. She studied the black curl, which Rhonwen realised must have been cut from Beatrice's dead baby. Then, with maddening slowness, she picked up the drawings, throwing Rhonwen a glance that told her she understood what had led her to Glyn Dedwydd.

At last she lifted the ring. She turned it over and over in her hands, as if reluctant to use it. She looked over at Rhonwen, who was accepting hot coffee from Grace. Then with a air of trepidation she inserted the key into the heart of the wooden rose and turned it. A small drawer slid out from the bottom of the box. Edwina took out two letters.

"This one is in his hand," she exclaimed. "It has never been opened. Rhonwen, how much has your mother told you of past events?"

"Beatrice says she is not . . ." stammered Rhonwen, then she stopped, remembering Grace was listening. She felt more than ever vulnerable. She had heard too much to comprehend at one time. How much was truth? The past hours began to assume the dimensions of a dream—or a nightmare—but the charred wood and her throbbing hands told her that they were real.

"Please read your letters," she begged.

Edwina broke a seal, and Rhonwen thought of the times her mother—no, Beatrice—had pored over the sealed letter, longing to know its contents, yet unable to bring herself to read it. She had stolen Edwina's child, but could not open her mail! It was almost funny! Rhonwen put her hand over her mouth to smother a strangled laugh, and Grace Bell looked up anxiously.

"Nearly finished, my pet," she comforted, "then it's bed for you. Perhaps for both of you," she finished as Edwina gave a cry.

"He did love me truly. He writes so wonderfully—he intended to return to marry me. All these years I have lived with nagging doubts because he did not keep his vow to write before his ship sailed. And he had written! Then his ship foundered in a storm. Oh, Meredith!"

Intent upon Edwina, Rhonwen had not given thought to the fact that Grace was removing her stockings until she heard the maid give a surprised gasp. Instinctively she made an attempt to pull her feet away, then remembered that pretence was at an end. Grace washed her feet as Edwina opened Beatrice's letter.

"This is from your mother, Rhonwen, and written many years ago." As she read, her face crumpled with grief. "But she says she was loved by him—my Meredith . . ."

"Please keep reading," said Rhonwen. "Grace, ask Mr. Bryn to come back. There is something I must tell him. I can wait no longer."

Grace threw a rug over her, and Bryn came to her swiftly. He knelt and held her face between his hands. "My darling, what has been going on? I can't make sense of Tomos. He babbles about a cavern and someone called Bettrys—is it your mother he speaks of? I thought she had died."

Before Rhonwen could answer, Edwina cried out and came to stare down at Rhonwen. "Grace, leave us," she said, faintly.

She waited for the maid to close the door behind her and said, "Rhonwen, Beatrice says something I find too incredible to believe. That you are my daughter—that she bore a child that died and that she gave me the dead baby and took mine away. She says she did it in a fit of dreadful jealousy because I had captured Meredith's love, and she was left with only a stillborn baby. She says she lived with her revenge because she was afraid to return. She repented—she always meant to tell you the truth—all through the years she meant to speak, but she was too ashamed . . ."

Edwina paced the room twice before she returned to stare down at Rhonwen again. "She could not have been so cruel to me! Not Beatrice! We were as sisters rather than mistress and maid. Could anything have made her commit so dreadful a sin?"

Bryn had been looking from one to the other. "Only two things seem certain to me at the moment. Rhonwen and I love each other—and somewhere a woman lies in desperate need of help. Rhonwen, where is she?"

"She is in the cave below the lake. Oh, Bryn, hurry to her. She is dreadfully ill, disfigured and hurt in body and spirit. She may die if aid does not reach her soon."

Bryn did not wait for further enlightenment but, to Rhonwen's relief, went out calling for Tomos.

Rhonwen told Edwina what had happened to her, and Edwina picked up Beatrice's letter to read it again. "I want to believe her," she murmured. "But the long, barren years have made a coward of me. I could not endure further doubt. I would far rather live out my life in quiet isolation."

Rhonwen felt cold disappointment. In her headlong race to Edwina she had not considered that Beatrice's confession might be doubted. The barriers Edwina had raised were not so easily breached. She leaned back and closed her eyes. It was like her nightmare again. She had reached the room, but found only sadness.

A knock at the door sent Edwina to answer it, and Grace handed her a package. "Susan gave me this, ma'am. She says that Mr. Cristin told her to bring it to you. Susan says that he has packed a bag and left with Miss Kendrick. He told her this was his parting gift."

Edwina tore off the tissue paper and looked down at what she held, then she read Cristin's note. Afterwards she was still for a long time before she seemed to gather her thoughts and walked resolutely to Rhonwen.

"Cristin has confirmed everything. He has also told me of his behaviour to you and the reason for your engagement. Even of his desecration of the grave I believed held my child. He has sent this for us to see. If I had ever looked properly at the miniatures, I could not have failed to connect you with the family."

She handed Rhonwen the painting. Except that the girl in the picture wore a low-cut gown richly encrusted with pearls and an amber necklace, she might have been Rhonwen's mirrored image. They shared the same smoky blue eyes in an oval face framed by red-gold curls. Mari Caradog! Grandmother to Meredith Wilmot—her father.

Edwina said slowly, as if she feared to voice the words. "In his note, Cristin tells me to—to examine your feet."

Again the power of motion seemed to have deserted Edwina as Rhonwen tugged the blanket aside; then slowly she slid to her knees to put her hands on Rhonwen's shoulders. "You are indeed my daughter—mine and Meredith's. After so many years the emptiness is over."

Sadly Bryn returned to tell them that Beatrice had not survived. "She seemed to be waiting only to learn whether or not her dear Miss Edwina had received her letter before she gave up. She told me her task was done and it was better to die. I am so sorry, Rhonwen."

He helped Edwina to rise to her feet and brought a chair for her. "Now, I have been patient, but it is high time I learned exactly what has been going on. Especially how you came to be in such distress, my dear love."

He listened in a silence he broke only when Rhonwen spoke of Cristin's last desperate action. "He left you to die alone in that awful way. Thank God for Tomos. He used to tell me of secret tunnels, but I thought it one of his games."

His fists clenched. "It is well for Cristin that he has gone!"

Seeing his dark rage Rhonwen agreed with him. There had been too much suffering, too much violence. And Beatrice was dead. She had said that darkness and death were her friends; she had not been alone—Bryn had been with her. She would not want anyone to grieve for her, but emotions were not so easily controlled. She had cheated Edwina of her daughter's childhood and Rhonwen of her rightful upbringing, but Rhonwen again wept for her. In the end Beatrice had suffered most.

When Rhonwen was stronger, she and Bryn returned the miniature of Mari Caradog to its place in the cabinet. Bryn stood looking at it for a while, then he turned. "Have you realised that Castell Craig and all that goes with it will one day be yours without the necessity of marrying me?"

Rhonwen looked into the half-teasing, half-serious dark eyes. "I would marry you if we had to share that shepherd's hut. You will not so easily elude me."

"I believe you, my darling. And I love you with all my being. We are fortunate. We have discovered true happiness."

"Cristin made some reparation," said Rhonwen. "He has lost everything he values."

"Not quite everything. He will marry Frances. He is very fond of her, and it will be the easiest way for him to take. And she loves him—she always has."

They closed the cabinet lid and walked the length of the gallery, their arms about each other. Before he opened the door, Bryn pulled Rhonwen close and, beneath the painted eyes of their forbears, his lips found hers in a kiss that sealed the promise of their future.